One Good Man

Ruth Rowling

ISBN 978-1-904101-03-1

Published by:
Infinity Junction
PO Box 64
Neston DO
CH64 0WB
United Kingdom

Website with on-line purchase facility at:
www.infinityjunction.com

Front cover design by Tine Poppe

Layout and typesetting by Infinity Junction
e-mail infin-info@infinityjunction.com

Foreword

I offered to write a foreword to 'One Good Man' as a way of giving tribute to what I believe is a well researched and exciting novel about the second World War. I also see it as my duty to offer to help people who are interested in history and trying to get an understanding of how it actually was during the 1940s in Norway. I am impressed by all the details which Ruth has picked up on and used in the story such that one is able to re-live the period. The atmosphere of fear, excitement and uncertainty in all areas of ones life is well recreated in this story. I admired the doctor and pitied his wife, and was glad to see that the heroine, after suffering the undeserved fate of a traitor, was finally protected by the Resistance.

This is, of course, only a story and I have to say that my own experience of the Gestapo here in Oslo was more brutal! However if one is to study history then one should seek out the many histories and biographies written from the period – some of which are listed in Ruth's acknowledgements. But if one is to re-visit the period with hindsight and try to understand it from other points of view then I would thoroughly recommend this novel.

I hope Ruth finds the success she deserves and write with my best wishes.

Gunnar Sønsteby

Oslo, 5 September 2006

Dedication:

Lege
Christian Grüner Sundt
10-4-1913 † 24-8-1972

Acknowledgements:

It is difficult to know where to begin and I am truly grateful to many
people for their information, their experiences and their advice. I have
listened to many stories, followed countless leads on the internet and read
much. I am especially thankful for the following:

Gunnar Sønsteby	Rapport fra 'Nr. 24'
Bjørg Fodstad	Brystkaramellene: Fra XU til Grini
Olav Riste and Berit Nøkleby	Norway 1940-45: The Resistance Movement
Jerzy Pindera	Liebe Mutti
Michael Burleigh	The Third Reich
Christabel Bielenberg	The Past is Myself
Corrie ten Boom	The Hiding Place
Thomas Nielsen	Inside Fortress Norway
Line Esborg	Krigshverdag
E. Ancher Hanssen	'Så vi vant vår rett': En Bildehistorikk
Schubert/Müller	Die schöne Müllerin

I would like to thank my publishers, especially Neil Gee who encouraged
me with a first quick and positive response to my manuscript. Roger
O'Brien who had the courage to ruthlessly expose the flaws in my first
manuscript and who has encouraged my writing for – well he knows how
long. Jan, Jean and Stan who avidly read work in progress. Arnfinn
Moland who checked historical accuracy. And finally Gunnar Sønsteby,
for his inspiring personal account of the war years, his suggested
amendments to the text and his enthusiasm.

Author's note:

While there is a wealth of detail in the story which is taken from historical
fact, what I have written is fiction. Any apparent similarities to actual
people are accidental and unintentional. There are also details in the novel
where historical fact gives way to literary unity, most notably the
simplification of Gestapo operations, which I have focussed in Victoria
Terrasse instead of confusing my reader with a constant change of
location.

R. E Rowling, Oslo, 29 August 2006

9th May, 1945
Prologue

Her final scream woke her. She was drenched in sweat and the tears were dry in her eyes, her pain dumb and impotent.

Astrid took in the faded wallpaper of her mother's spare room. The gloom of early dawn exacerbated her torn emotions as she focussed on the fragments of her days, oppressing her with thoughts of the long awaited peace, her missing husband and her traitor sister. She stared at the white ceiling, at its elaborate plaster work from the last century and allowed her anger to blot out the pain of the other emotions which threatened to engulf her. Her anger bore with it a certain grim satisfaction, although she wished she could ignore the persistent image of her sister which haunted her. Mia's sudden and shocking appearance at the apartment that afternoon played and re-played itself out in Astrid's thoughts.

'Talk to me, Astrid, you have to talk to me,' Mia had said as she pulled her hat off to reveal short tufts of crudely cut hair. There was dried blood from a cut down one side where the barber had enjoyed his brutality. 'Astrid!'

'Put your hat on,' Astrid had said, 'and go. Don't let mother see you like that!'

'Astrid! Please, you have to listen.' But the voice had been demanding, not pleading.

'Why should I listen to you? Find somewhere else to hole up. Why should mother and I help you?' And she had banged the door shut in Mia's face.

'I hate her! I hate her!' Astrid whispered to herself quietly in the dark.

It wasn't enough to hate the Germans.

She got up from the bed and crept softly to the bedroom which she and Mia had shared as children. She went in quietly and sat on the bed watching her sleeping child, where he slept with one arm flung over his pillow and his mouth open so that she could hear his steady breathing.

What had it all been for? What had any of them hoped to

achieve? Couldn't she and Petter have been enough? Been enough for Christian.

***

Mia stood looking at the closed door for some time. After a little while she recollected her sore head and quickly put the hat back on. She ought to feel angry.

She looked at the door again and tried to feel angry about Astrid. This was her home, not Astrid's. Astrid should go back to the little flat above the surgery, or was she going to stay with their mother for ever? Mia pressed her hands against her eyes to stop the tears, a prayer in her thought, couldn't Christian miraculously and wonderfully come back? They didn't yet know the death tallies from the concentration camps in Germany, but Mia suspected, even understood, that people weren't meant to come back, at least not people like Christian, who had been traitors to the Third Reich.

Mia turned from the door and started walking mechanically down the street away from the town and away from the celebrations. She would go to Frank's old lodgings.

Frank had promised her that nothing, not even Friedrich, would come between them. It had been a promise for the future, to give them something to believe in during the three, long years since 1942. But the future wasn't going to obliterate the past, Mia realised sadly. The sadness caught in her throat, Friedrich had gone, at least he had been arrested by the re-instated Norwegian Authorities. Poor Friedrich had been betrayed by his own ideals and trapped by the failure of the Third Reich, but she would not devastate him with the proof of her own duplicity. Frank would know that she had refused to testify against Friedrich and Frank would begin to understand that she cared about Friedrich. She paused on that last thought, her feet, as it were, rooted to the pavement, as a faint strain of music echoed in her mind

Mia took the back streets, weaving her way to Frank's flat. He hadn't lived there since he had had to go undercover, which had also been in 1942. How strange to suddenly go back there now, but if there was to be a future she had to spend some time re-visiting the past. Her thoughts returned to Astrid, was there any future which could cure Astrid's cancer of hatred? And in the void of Astrid's hatred Mia's thoughts turned with a familiar ache to Christian. If only Christian could come back to them all! If Christian came back perhaps Astrid would understand, perhaps Astrid would be able to forgive.

'I should have saved him! I could have saved Christian,' she repeated to herself. Perhaps it had been possible and she should have taken her chance, she had had enough contacts to find somewhere to hide. It was one of the many impossible decisions the war had demanded of her but self-preservation had taught her how to live without the comfort of guilt.

She reached Frank's flat, found the key in its old hiding place and let herself in. Frank was out. She took off her coat and turning caught her reflection in a mirror which hung in the dingy entrance. She moved up close to it and carefully tugged off the beret which covered her bruised head. She saw the blood, which had run down the left side of her head, and the tufts of hair sticking out at awkward angles. But this, she questioned a long absent deity, had she deserved this particular piece of mindless brutality?

***

Frank was walking back to their temporary headquarters in Victoria Terrasse, the unfamiliar uniform scratching at the collar. He glanced at his watch, his thoughts willing Mia to be there with the others. He had had to take a place as a guard in the convoy at the last minute after further directives from London to step up security since the Brigadier's arrival in Oslo. They had also been busy trying to go through the German records, which they had saved from burning hours before the official surrender in Norway.

He hadn't seen Mia for a few days. He had expected to see her somewhere amongst the celebrating gangs, but there were a lot of people about. He arrived at the headquarters where a few people were milling around as usual, but not Mia. He went into the office he shared with a couple of other officers of the homefront forces and looked distastefully at the desks, which were laden with paperwork. He sat down feeling suddenly tired, until his thoughts were disturbed by a familiar voice in the hallway, and Tom walked in.

'Have you seen this?' Tom asked, and slammed a report down on the desk in front of Frank. It was a neatly typed document with a handwritten covering letter pinned to the top. He looked more closely at the writing, it was Mia's. He cast a questioning look up at Tom, then read the letter.

'I present this report on the understanding that it will only be used as an archive document to verify facts and that it will not itself be used as evidence against the prisoner, that it will not be presented to the prisoner or presented in any future court hearing. If these wishes are over looked I will not verify any of the enclosed information in person or allow myself to be presented as a witness against the prisoner.'

Frank pushed the letter back towards Tom.

'Dammit, what's she playing at!' Tom exclaimed. 'She can't possibly want to protect the bastard, she knows what he's done more than any of us.'

Frank had a feeling of things spinning out of control. He shook himself. 'I'll talk to her,' he said to Tom.

'Talk to her,' repeated Tom. 'I want to nail that bastard.'

'Believe me, so do I,' Frank added.

Tom paused and scrutinised Frank through hardened eyes. 'She'll come round,' he said, and added bitterly, 'half of us are doing nothing but celebrate and the other half are spread all over Europe. God it's hot in these bloody uniforms, come and have a beer.'

They walked back out of the building and round the corner to a bar which had miraculously managed to furnish the populace with a seemingly endless supply of beer. A couple of girls on the opposite corner smiled across at them shyly, as a pleasing reminder that the homefront forces were the heroes of the hour. Tom put his arm on Frank's shoulder and followed him into the bar. He grinned back at the two girls.

'Bloody women,' he said to Frank happily.

Frank smiled, distractedly, thinking about Mia, but his thoughts were full of unease and doubt. Why was it so difficult to find her anywhere? Was it possible that she was avoiding him?

Several hours later he finally left Tom and went home. He didn't put a light on in the hall and so missed the signs that Mia had left of her presence. He went straight to the bedroom. He switched on the light and saw Mia lying on the bed fully clothed and fast asleep, an ugly stain of dried blood spread across the white pillow where she had turned in her sleep. He stared at the vision of her savaged head, his thoughts momentarily confused by his fierce desire to blame the Germans, but he knew that this wasn't the Germans, this particular outrage had been committed by his fellow Norwegians. He sat down gently beside her, not wanting to wake her. Compassion emasculated him, and drowned all other thoughts and feelings.

The letter concerning the prisoner was forgotten.

***

The prisoner was sitting in one of his own cells. The one, small, barred window was high up in the wall, where it was too high to see out of, and the heavy door, with its closed grill, was double locked. He had been given a table and chair as well as a narrow bed. On the table was pencil and paper tempting him to take time to reflect and write a statement, but the paper remained blank and he had said nothing to the so called officers of the homefront in their new and ill-fitting uniforms.

He had put on full SS regalia when he was arrested as a final act of defiance, although now it felt to him like an absurd and impotent gesture. He had discarded the tunic, a black, but empty symbol of regal power lying like an angry stain on the thin grey blanket that covered the bed.

Friedrich paced the narrow cell. Pausing by the table his fingers automatically tapped out a rhythm on the plain, wooden surface; a refrain from Schubert; a heavy chord from Beethoven.

The Fuhrer dead! Russians in Berlin! What had it all been for, what had any of them hoped to achieve? Doubt tormented him, he paced back across the cell and, defeated and exhausted, he collapsed onto the bed. There would be no reprieve, no future.

Only death.

September 1935
One

Christian followed the flow of people out of the church. He turned casually to one side and took a cigarette from the crumpled packet in his jacket pocket and lighting his cigarette he quietly enjoyed the scene of people streaming out of the dark interior into the sunshine. He drew on his cigarette, a smile on his face. He nudged his glasses up slightly off his nose. They had thin metal rims, but the round lenses were heavy.

'Hello, doctor,' someone greeted him.

He raised his trilby and nodded a greeting in return.

'Nice service,' the voice continued.

He ran fingers through his hair, which was light and curling, then straightened his hat and drew on his cigarette again. He looked at the woman and remembered that it was Mrs Berg, a patient who had come to him with bunions a few months ago. The smile never left his lips and played around the rest of his features. The features weren't good, the nose was too long, the mouth a little short and the eyes too owl-like behind the glasses. He was a tall man and had to look down as Mrs Berg came nearer.

'Have you got family being confirmed then?' She asked him.

'Yes, yes,' he answered.

Another patient joined them, but luckily she walked on with Mrs Berg and he could continue to watch the scene with lazy enjoyment. Within the darkness of the church he thought he could make out the robust form of his future mother-in-law. She was slim and neat, like her younger daughter. Her younger daughter, Maria, or Mia as the family called her, was being confirmed, her eldest daughter, Astrid, was his fiancée. He dropped the cigarette butt and ground it into the pavement. It was likely that Astrid would come out now unless she was waiting for Maria. The fond smile twitched at his lips, Astrid. Perhaps she was a little too tall, perhaps even awkward, but she was charmingly naïve and had a serious intelligence which he valued and respected. When he had first met her he hadn't really noticed that one of his students was a woman, she was as tall as the men and tended to hide behind the group. He first singled her out in the maternity ward. She had rubbed her hands and apologised to the patient that her hands were cold before feeling the baby in the woman's womb. She had then looked up at him for confirmation of her diagnosis and they had shared the pleasure of telling the patient that the baby had turned in the eleventh hour and that she wouldn't have a breach birth. It had been a short distance from shared pleasure to coffee in the hospital canteen, a new film and, later, his bed, in their future home above a small surgery they would run together.

'Daydreaming old chap?' A familiar voice broke his reverie. Tom studied him for a moment and followed his gaze into the church. 'Ah ha, so it is true. Thought you would have had more sense.'

'I take it you're not here with a fiancée,' Christian replied wryly.

'God, no! My cousin.' Tom reached into the pocket of his double breasted jacket and pulled out a packet of Tiedemann cigarettes. He passed one to Christian and then offered him a light. They both stood looking into the church.

'So it is the Gram girl?'

'Do you know the family?' Christian asked politely.

'My Aunt knows the mother, widowed isn't she?'

Christian nodded, but there was something in Tom's tone calculated to disturbed him.

'If I were you I would have waited for the younger sister, she's going to be…' both men saw that Astrid was coming out towards them. The words dried up and Tom drew on his cigarette.

Christian watched her come out towards the open door. An anxiety pulled at her mouth, she blinked in the bright sunshine and then saw him. The smile broke out instantaneously and spread through her whole being as she came to join him.

'Cigarette?' He asked. She shook her head. Mia hadn't come out yet. She cast an anxious glance back towards the church then turned back to Christian.

'Have you met Tom?' He asked. 'Tom Grobæk.'

'No, at least not properly. I've seen you in the hospital.' She turned to Tom smiling and held out her hand. The gesture was awkward, but Tom noted that Christian merely found this charming. 'Are you Siri's cousin?' She asked.

'It's a small world isn't it!' Tom nodded ironically.

Astrid turned to Christian. 'I said we'd go on ahead and check that everything's okay at home.' She smiled apologetically at Tom.

'We'll catch up in the morning,' Tom called to Christian and Christian raised his hat in acknowledgement.

Astrid had put her hand through his arm and was already pulling him away from the church. When he had proposed she had done the same, not said anything, just put her hand in his. She had given herself to him without condition and without regret and he loved her in return with a gentle protective love and the responsibility was a joy, not a burden. He put a hand over hers now and slowed her eager pace down the street.

***

Mia was fifteen. It annoyed her that she was still so slight and that she looked younger than her years, which meant that she was still treated like the baby. Her confirmation dress was the same one that Astrid had worn ten years ago for her confirmation. Their mother had had to cut it up to make it small enough and it didn't hang properly from the shoulders. Astrid hadn't had to have a made-over confirmation dress, but their father had still been alive when Astrid was confirmed. She was also irritated by the long school girl plait which hung down her back, the rich golden colour was no consolation. One day she was going to have it all cut off. What she really wanted was a fringe and a neat bob, something modern.

Now the service was over she was impatient to go, but the priest wanted to talk with them for one last time before they joined their family parties. Siri was standing next to her and fidgeting with a loose scarf which was draped around her neck. Siri was well formed and could easily pass as eighteen.

Mia pressed her foot over Siri's. 'Stop fidgeting or he'll never begin,' she hissed into Siri's ear. 'I want to get out of here.'

'I can't help it. My cousin Tom was in the congregation. Did you notice?'

The priest coughed in irritation and Mia pressed Siri's foot again, harder. Siri grimaced and stopped fidgeting. The priest began droning on about their commitment to the Church and Mia allowed her thoughts to wander. She had noticed Siri's cousin. She felt that it was wrong for girls of fifteen to notice men of about thirty, but he was a good looking man with an air of risk about him. Mia had also been watching her own future brother-in-law as she had made various furtive glances round at the congregation during the service. She admired Astrid's wisdom in choosing such a man, or perhaps Christian had chosen Astrid? She rather suspected that Astrid would have said yes to the first man who came along whatever he'd been like. Well, luckily for them it had been Christian. She liked Christian, she made him laugh.

One of Mia's other irritations was that because Astrid was clever everyone assumed she was also wise. Astrid had followed in their father's footsteps and become a doctor. It had been tough being a woman in medical school, but she was not the only woman doctor and Mia privately thought it had been tougher being the one at the end of all the scrimping and saving so that Astrid could study. Astrid had needed anatomy books, and Mia had squeezed into last year's boots. Astrid had needed equipment, and Mia had worn her mother's old coat to school. Astrid had worked hard and when she finished next year she would be married and have a medical practice all set up and running for her to step straight into, and she would remain oblivious of their sacrifices. Mia shook the irritation from her thoughts, now Christian could look after Astrid and maybe next year Mia would have a new coat.

'Come on dopey, he's finished, we can go now.' Siri was pulling at Mia's sleeve. She took Mia's arm as they walked out into the sunshine. 'I think everyone's gone,' she continued, 'let's walk home together.'

The two girls lived in the same square off a street which ran towards Frogner from Majorstuen. Mia's family lived in the comfortable purpose built apartment from the last century which her parents had bought nearly thirty years ago. Siri's family lived in a house newly built with English brick on the site of an old barn.

'Are you having a big party?' Siri asked as they walked arm in arm down the street.

Mia shook her head. 'My father's mother, two aunts and an uncle.'

'And Astrid's fiancé,' added Siri. 'He was at medical school with my cousin Tom you know.'

'I know,' answered Mia.

'Tom's so handsome, he looks like Tyrone Power,' Siri continued dreamily.

'No he doesn't,' Mia responded shortly.

'Don't get cross Mia. I've persuaded Mummy to let me go to the new matinee next Saturday. Will you come?'

Mia made a noncommittal noise. If she got money for her confirmation she might not want to spend it on the flicks, she might save it so that she could have her hair cut.

'What's he like?' Siri's question startled her. 'Christian, what's he like?'

Siri didn't really need an answer to this. She just wanted to open up the subject. What she really wanted to know was if Astrid kissed him, to which Mia's answer would have to be, she supposed so. Kisses covered a multitude of mysteries for Siri and Mia.

'Mummy says she's never seen Astrid looking so well,' Siri continued.

Mia and Siri had long lamented over Astrid's lack of beauty.

'She's happy,' answered Mia simply.

They had now reached Mia's apartment. Mia pushed open the heavy door which lead to the communal stairwell. Mia's apartment was on the first floor. She peered back round the door to wave at Siri.

'Do you think we'll get our first taste of sherry?' Siri was asking Mia.

Mia wrinkled up her nose. 'Taste it for me,' she called after

Siri. She pushed the heavy door closed behind her and leant on it for one long moment before facing the aunts, the grandmother and the one token uncle.

***

Astrid was looking out of the window. 'There she is at last,' she exclaimed. She had caught sight of Mia and Siri dawdling down the street. 'What can they have been doing?'

Christian joined her at the window. He couldn't help noticing that Tom was right, Mia was going to be very attractive. He was irritated that Tom had pointed this out as he had enjoyed the easy role he had played with her as Astrid's young sister. It was uncomfortable to have to deal with her as a woman as well.

There were a lot of women in Astrid's tight family circle. Damn Tom for pointing that out too! The reference to the widowed mother-in-law had not gone unnoticed by Christian and he could hear the aunts murmuring in the background.

'I remember Astrid's confirmation, she was such a pretty thing too, and Petter had organised such a nice party for everyone.' The reference to Astrid's father encouraged the grandmother to pull a large handkerchief out of her handbag and proceed to sniff into it. Astrid rushed over and put an arm around the old women. The grandmother patted Astrid affectionately on the knee.

'You're so like him, my dear,' she sniffed.

The mother was bustling round paying little attention to them all and Christian sensed he was watching a familiar scene. Something caused him to look towards the door and he noticed that Mia had slipped in unnoticed. She caught his eye and raised her eyebrows in a silent question, then put a finger to her lips and slipped out again. The gesture reassured him that she was still a child, and he couldn't help smiling.

Astrid came back to the window and looked out anxiously. 'Hasn't she come in yet?' She sounded cross.

Christian put a hand to his mouth and cleared his throat carefully, but Mia made her own grand entrance carrying a silver tray laden with small sherry glasses, the sweet, brown liquid dully gleaming against the newly polished silver.

'Grandma!' She announced, offering her grandmother a glass of sherry. She noted the milky eyes, still wet with tears. 'I think this is meant to be a party,' she added ironically.

The aunts and uncle took glasses and Mia turned to Astrid and Christian who were still standing. Astrid looked round at Christian self consciously as she took a glass. The action annoyed Mia and she held the tray out to Christian defiantly.

'No thank you,' he said.

Mia continued holding out the tray.

'Mia!' Astrid's tone was chastising but Mia didn't understand why.

'I don't drink,' explained Christian.

'Shall I get you something else?' Astrid asked.

But Mia wasn't satisfied, she wanted to know why, although she now understood Astrid's little gesture as she took her glass.

'It's not a very edifying story,' Christian smiled at Mia. Mia looked meaningfully at the glass still on the tray between them, her expression was eloquent and it was clear to him that she was contemplating taking the glass herself. He glanced over her head at the brooding relatives.

'Maybe it would be edifying for me,' Mia responded, looking straight at him.

He laughed out loud and Mia had to smile. 'I drank too much aquavit one night in my youth and haven't really had a taste for alcohol since.'

Mia wondered whether to believe him, but she had lost her desire to drink the sherry.

Astrid was bristling with impatience beside her. 'I think we should help mother,' she said to Mia. She turned to Christian, 'Will you excuse us, darling?'

She headed for the kitchen indicating that Mia should follow.

Mia leant towards Christian. 'I know Aunt Sophie looks fierce but at least she's sensible – you probably know her from the hospital.'

'Yes I do.'

'So you know what a bully she is?'

'Go and help your mother,' Christian pushed her away

laughing again. 'Are you always such a bad influence?' He added as she turned to go.

***

Astrid Maria Gram had been fussing with the table in the dining room, not to fuss, but to avoid entertaining her relatives. She had hoped that Petter's mother wouldn't come. The old woman was over ninety and Astrid Maria strongly suspected that she was incontinent. She was closest to her sister Sophie, but Sophie had been agitating her recently, telling her she needed to get out more, even that she should take up nursing again. Astrid Maria knew she was right but wanted to make her own decision about what she did. As for her other sister, Elisabeth and her husband, Gunnar, she had never been close to them. They ran a busy iron mongers in Bogstadveien, which they had inherited from Gunnar's father. Elisabeth was ten years older than Astrid Maria. She wished that her brother, Per, would come to town sometimes, but he ran the family farm in Hønefoss and never travelled.

When her two daughters joined her she had returned to the kitchen and was busy organising plates of boiled cod and vegetables. Mia's eyes danced towards her mother's and she performed a subtle mime of her grandmother sipping sherry and dabbing at her milky eyes.

'Mia! That's not kind! Help me with this food!' Her mother scolded.

Astrid Maria found Mia's perceptiveness disconcerting at times and wondered how, at fifteen, she had managed to become so cynical. She was hoping that Christian would be a steadying influence over Mia, and felt eternally grateful that Astrid had managed to attract someone with so much natural charm and calm intelligence.

Astrid Maria turned to Astrid and asked her to organise their guests into the dining room so that she could keep Mia in the kitchen and out of trouble. She was dreading the confirmation speeches and the comments, if any, Mia might make.

November, 1939
Two

Two aunts and the uncle followed Astrid's request to go into the dining room. Astrid Maria had prepared boiled cod and the cold air was making them feel hungry. It was cold in the apartment and Astrid Maria had only just lit the fire in the dining room.

Mia was sitting by the fire in the sitting room holding the baby. Petter Christian Krogvold was two months old and Mia adored him. Astrid had been up all night with him and was relieved to be doing something as normal as sit down to lunch. She left Mia with the baby and helped the aunts find seats. She glanced gratefully at Christian who was helping Aunt Sophie into her chair.

'Isn't Petter sleeping?' He asked Astrid.

She nodded.

'Then I'll tell Mia to put him in his pram.'

Astrid felt half her mind leap to stop him, a lunch without Petter and Mia would be so quiet. She dwelt on the word 'quiet' in her mind with longing, but Christian had already crossed the hall and was standing in the doorway of the sitting room.

Mia, now with her hair in a thick, rich golden bob which bounced off her shoulders when she talked, had grown more beautiful. She was bent over the baby, singing softly. Christian watched them with the joy of seeing a painting of familiar objects suddenly brought into harmony by the skill of the painter. The painter had certainly spent some effort on Mia. In the perfect oval of her face the nose was finely drawn and the lips a healthy, natural red. The lower lip was slightly exaggerated, perhaps too full for beauty, but the painter had chosen his imperfection well. The grey green eyes were both a challenge and an allurement, and this same benevolent creator had made her slim without being short, and tall without being large boned or clumsy.

Mia sensed Christian's presence and glanced up.

'He's so beautiful,' she whispered smiling at Christian.

'Put him down and come and eat!' He responded softly.

Mia sighed gently. She rose carefully and moved across to

the pram, which had been carried up the stairs and placed by the window. She tucked the baby in carefully before turning again to Christian.

'The world seems so confused and frightened and Petter so simple. Should we be frightened?' She asked Christian as she joined him by the door.

'You mean of war?' He asked.

His voice carried across the hall into the dining room and they met Astrid's worn look as they entered the room.

'Not the war again, can't we talk about something else for once, just for Petter's christening?'

'Is there anything else to talk about?' Mia challenged as she took her seat.

Christian watched Astrid sink into her chair. He looked carefully at Mia.

'Yes I think there are lots of other things we can talk about, at least for an hour or so.' Mia picked up the irony in his tone and was satisfied.

'Mia?' Aunt Sophie's question was a command. 'Your mother tells me you've started at the University? I thought you were working for 'The Post'?

Mia studied her Aunt for a moment before replying. 'I just worked there during the summer holiday. I can work other holidays too, to help pay my way.'

Astrid Maria distracted the others by handing round plates of food. Astrid heard Petter stirring in the other room and held her breath until he was silent again. Aunt Elisabeth pulled her cardigan around her shoulders to indicate that she was cold. Christian raised a questioning eyebrow at Astrid before getting up to close the door.

'So you're not going to be a journalist?' There was a sneer in Aunt Sophie's voice, but it was more a habit after long years of bullying hospital wards than from any malicious intent.

Mia resisted the temptation to sneer back and shrugged her shoulders noncommittally. 'I don't know yet. I did do two pieces for 'The Post' but mostly I was just copy-typing and taking the telephone.'

'What does one need with the University?' Aunt Sophie asked the others. Gunnar was struggling with a bone and Elisabeth had a mouth full of food. Astrid thought guiltily of her own years of studying and kept quiet.

'One needs the opportunity to become more than a...' Mia's eye had a dangerous glint.

'I am only grateful that Mia can have the same opportunities as Astrid had,' Astrid Maria said loudly. Astrid cast a grateful glance in her Mother's direction.

'I can understand the need to do medicine, but what is it you are studying Maria?'

'German, and some English.'

'Humph! German and English! And what good do you think that'll do you?' Aunt Sophie was used to having things her own way.

'If there is a war?' Mia's tone was high and the irritation was apparent.

'I thought we agreed not to talk about the war,' Christian cut in quietly.

***

Astrid was nursing the baby in the comfort of an armchair by the fire. He sucked at her greedily, dribbles of milk escaping from his eager mouth as he stopped to take breath or, momentarily distracted from the main business of life, to smile at her. Her mother was clearing up in the kitchen. Mia should have been helping but she was huddled in the dining room with Christian talking about the war in Europe. It seemed ridiculous to Astrid. Why should a war in Europe affect them? Yes, last time there had been blockades and some shortages, but that was all, and such things hadn't affected Astrid in childhood. Norway had clearly stated its neutrality and why should Germany or England bother with them? Mia was always looking for trouble and excitement. Why didn't she go to England, or Germany for that matter, if she wanted excitement?

Astrid was twenty nine, happily married, a successful family doctor, and was now blessed with a first child. All this talk of war was a discomforting current disturbing the even flow of her life. She looked down fondly at little Petter. He had stopped feeding now and was snoozing in the warmth and comfort of her encircling arms. She wished her Grandmother had lived long enough to meet him, she would have been thrilled to think that another Petter had come into the world, but her Grandmother had died more than three years ago now and was missed by no one except herself, fleetingly, at such moments as the present.

***

Astrid Maria hung the last pan above the oven, wiped her hands dry on the kitchen cloth and took off her apron. She glanced at her watch to check the time, it was four o'clock. She had promised to go to the Red Cross centre in Majorstuen for a couple of hours that evening, in fact she had increased her hours at the Red Cross station in recent weeks. The politicians didn't fool her, the war was coming to Norway whether they liked it or not.

9th April, 1940
Three

There was no one left in the waiting room. Astrid hovered uncertainly between the consulting room and the door which lead straight off the waiting room onto the street. There was more than half an hour before morning surgery usually closed and there would normally be a queue of people still waiting to see the doctor. People had been asking her questions all morning. Did she have any news? What was happening? Was it true that German soldiers had landed at Fornebu? Where was Dr Krogvold? Usually Astrid happily accepted the omniscience with which most patients endowed their doctors, but today it was disconcerting, even worse she felt she knew less than most of the patients. Christian had left with a backpack and skis before seven that morning with a hurried request that she fill the jerry cans with petrol if she was able. She had been deep in a heavy morning sleep and he had gone before she could question him. Not knowing what else to do she had followed her morning routine, changed and fed Petter, cleared the kitchen and then agonised over what to do about morning surgery, which Christian usually did, as she hadn't yet got back into any regular pattern of work.

She didn't want to know what was happening and somehow she felt that if she carried on as normal everything else would normalise as well. She had taken Petter to her mother's. Her mother had agreed to look after him and she had come back and opened the surgery. There had been no sign of Mia and Astrid had avoided conversation with her mother.

Now she would have to close the surgery and collect Petter. She found the jerry cans and decided to walk on, after collecting her son, and get some petrol from a garage they used in Skøyen. The jerry cans would fit on the tray under the pram. She took an extra blanket for Petter, wrapped herself up carefully and reluctantly went out into the street. She put her head down and walked quickly to her mother's, glancing around as she hurried along didn't help her confusion, some offices and shops seemed open as normal and others were closed. On the main street she noticed a couple of cars laden with people and belongings and one family was heading for the station with large cases, but most people seemed like herself, confused and uncertain about what was happening. She dreaded her mother being better informed.

Nervous about any ensuing interrogation from her mother, she hesitantly let herself into the apartment with the key she still kept. Her mother indicated that Petter was sleeping and insisted that Astrid had a cup of coffee and some bread and cheese.

'Did Mia ring?' Astrid Maria finally asked as they sat down with their coffee.

Astrid shook her head avoiding eye contact with her mother.

'I told her to ring you from the office and give us any news.' Astrid Maria did not have a telephone, but Astrid and Christian had one in the surgery.

'No one rang.' Astrid looked at her mother fearfully.

'She rushed off to 'The Post' this morning to get news and fill in if people didn't turn up for work. I'll go down to the Red Cross now, they'll know what's going on, besides which, they'll probably need help. They've been bombing the stations, ' she added, after a somewhat dramatic pause.

'Who? Who's been bombing the stations?' Astrid's voice was scarcely more than a whisper.

'The Germans!' Her mother exclaimed indignantly. 'What did Christian say? He must have said something?'

Astrid shook her head dumbly. 'He just said that I should fill the jerry cans with petrol.'

'Hush! More planes! Can you hear them?' Astrid Maria rushed to the window and craned her neck to see out. 'Look, there, German bombers! Five or six of them.'

Astrid had followed her to the window and just caught a glimpse of the heavy bombers droning over the city. 'They couldn't be ours?'

'They're not ours!' Astrid Maria turned back to her coffee. Astrid stayed at the window. She couldn't eat the bread.

'Christian didn't say anything?' Astrid Maria asked again.

'He left before seven. He took his skis and a rucksack. He just said to fill the jerry cans.'

An unhappy silence filled the room.

'Should I join you at the Red Cross?' Astrid asked.

'No, dear,' Astrid Maria put her hand out towards where Astrid still stood at the window. 'No, you stay with Petter.' She was trying to decide what to do with Astrid and Petter and she was anxious to get to the Red Cross. 'We'll wait and see if we hear anything from Christian, then maybe I'll try and put you and Petter on a bus to Hønefoss in the morning.'

Astrid shook her head miserably.

'In the meantime stay by the telephone in case he tries to ring.'

'I should get petrol. Perhaps I should take the car somewhere?'

'No, not on your own.'

Astrid felt like a child again, powerless and helpless, unable to think for herself she could only follow her mother's suggestions without questioning. Her fear for Petter and Christian was overwhelming. 'What can Christian be doing?' She finally managed to ask her mother.

'There are probably some patrols in the woods. He may be trying to join them.'

'Patrols? You mean soldiers? He's fighting Germans? Why should he be fighting Germans? He's not a soldier, he's a doctor!'

'Exactly! Maybe they need doctors.'

'But they have soldiers who are doctors!'

Astrid Maria glanced up at her daughter, but said no more. They both heard Petter stirring in the sitting room.

'I'll just feed him before I go.'

'Do you mind if I leave you to it?'

Astrid shook her head miserably. She held the warm child closely and fed him slowly on a little stewed apple and oatmeal left over from the morning.

Dumbly following the only advice she'd been given by her husband, she wrapped up the child and began to walk towards Skøyen. The atmosphere in the streets had changed and uncertainty was breeding panic. A couple of people asked her where she was going as if they too were looking for direction. A few patients approached her.

'Has the Doctor any news?' They asked, but she could only shake her head in reply.

Other people had made up their minds to leave and there was a steady stream of laden cars and people heading for trains and buses. There were rumours that westbound trains were still leaving town.

As she walked on towards Skøyen she passed the offices of 'The Post'. She could go in and try and find Mia, but the large red brick building looked too daunting and unapproachable. Also Mia was not on the regular staff and it might be difficult to find her, if she was there at all.

Astrid turned a corner and cut through a side street to reach Drammensveien, but something strange seemed to be happening. People had stopped moving and were standing still, as if transfixed. She paused next to one of the groups and realised that people had stopped to listen. There was a low, persistent thudding noise. And before the small, knotted groups had identified the sound a large contingent of German soldiers, in full battle dress, came marching past them.

The soldiers had landed at Fornebu in large transport planes and were heading for the centre of the city where their fellow Germans were already taking control of parliament, justice buildings, the central police station and communications networks.

***

Mia had been typing since eight o'clock that morning. The newspaper offices were inundated with new reports and revised reports as journalists tried to find and verify information. Her mother had asked her to telephone Astrid with latest updates. She had finally managed to get through just after lunch, but no one had taken the telephone, also the information was changing so much all the time that she didn't think it was worth trying again.

The editor wanted to get a late afternoon edition out by five and reporters were pouring in with endless 'latest' bulletins. Mia was keeping a look out for a young reporter called Frank Olsen. She knew him by sight, but today was the first time she'd done any work for him. To Mia's critical eye his reports were much more lucid, astute and better observed than the others she'd typed that day. She was hoping he would come in with a last edition item and was determined to catch his eye before anyone else got the work of typing it up. As far as she could see, it would contain the most reliable information she could hope to obtain that day.

But by three thirty there was still no sign of Frank Olsen and her back was aching with sitting at the typewriter all day. She wandered into another office, which received most of the telephone calls. She was hoping to pick up more news, but the office was short staffed and at least two telephones were ringing that no one seemed able to take. Some unknown voice shouted at her.

'Pick up the bloody 'phone, can't you!'

Mia pounced on a telephone but it went dead as she picked it up. She looked around trying to locate the other telephone, which was still ringing. She ran round a couple of desks and grabbed the receiver.

'Post,' she gasped down the receiver.

'About bloody time. What are you guys doing in there?'

'I just came through from another department, to help,' she added to make herself sound more official in the face of the angry voice at the other end of the line.

'I need to file a report. I take it you do shorthand as you've been put on calls?'

Mia took a deep breath and rummaged around on the desktop to find pencil and paper. 'Yes,' she lied.

'Okay?' Mia settled the receiver firmly between her cheek and shoulder and waited.

'Okay, Frank Olsen reporting from,' he paused and she heard him shouting into the room where he was. 'Where the hell am I?' The name had electrified her and she tensed every nerve to take down his words. 'Reporting from the I.N.C. Shipping offices, Karl Johan. Germany invades Denmark and Norway...'

Mia gasped down the line, 'Denmark as well!'

There was an irritated pause at the other end of the line. 'German soldiers, in well-planned attacks invaded main cities in both Denmark and Norway today. Warships were sited from several coastal stations, including the Oslo Fjord late last night. Air sirens were heard in the early hours of this morning and German soldiers landed on Norwegian soil mere hours later. Strategic positions here in Oslo are already in German hands, including Akershus, which was abandoned by Norwegian military this morning. There are few reports of resistance although the standing army has been mobilised. We have reports of a German ship sunk in the Oslo Fjord but can find no further details of this rumour at present.

The Nazi flag is flying here in Karl Johan and there is little sign that anyone is going to tear it down.' The last words were spat out through gritted teeth and the voice paused. Mia, grateful for the break, scribbled down the last words, hoping she could read the shortened longhand she had improvised.

'If anyone asks, I'm going AWOL. There must be some pockets of resistance somewhere worth finding.' There was another pause.

'I'll get this typed up and try and make the deadline.'

'For what it's worth,' the voice was now dispirited. 'I'll try and find my way out of here, but the street is riddled with German soldiers.' There was another pause and he seemed reluctant to let the line go. 'They were too well informed,' he said darkly. Mia could think of nothing to reply and found herself holding a dead line. Frank, she presumed, was now making a run for it.

She took the notes back to her typewriter and rattled off the paragraph. Could it all be over that quickly? From being a free country to an occupied one within twenty fours hours? There had been other reports of Allied aircraft making a counter attack on the coast, of an army gathering somewhere north of Oslo, of successful resistance over several key communication points, but Mia had set her mind on hearing some truth from Frank Olsen and now she felt that she had heard it. A few raw sentences which, when summed up, meant capitulation.

She handed over the piece to the editor and decided to leave the building. There might be more to find out on the streets, but somehow she doubted it. If people were gathering in the woods to resist she could try and find them, like Frank himself, but she guessed that that would only lead to more uncertainty.

She paused at the desk just before she left the Newspaper building. 'I'll check in again tomorrow,' she told the receptionist. 'You can tell the editor that Mia Gram will come again tomorrow.' The receptionist was grappling with a switchboard jammed with calls and only nodded vaguely at Mia. Mia didn't really expect her to do anything. What she had done was commit herself to a line of action, as running away, even to fight, didn't suit her.

The streets were chaotic. Cars and vans jammed with people and possessions were queuing to get out of town, people were dragging children and suitcases in all directions. There seemed no sense or purpose in any of it. She was tempted to go to Karl Johan and see for herself, but her reason talked her out of it, it smacked too much of voyeurism. The one person she knew who would talk sense was Christian, so she turned her steps homeward sure of finding him there or at the surgery.

***

Christian had at last reached the headquarters of military operations deep into Nordmarka, although in his own mind the phrase already seemed filled with irony. He had picked up some students, including some of his own from the hospital, earlier in the day and they had followed the few leads they had had from a couple of patrols and finally found themselves at a small hut in the middle of nowhere, standing in as a military headquarters for action against the Germans.

He was not surprised when a familiar voice greeted him from the woodstove inside the hut. Tom and he had discussed such an eventuality many times during the last few months.

'What took you so long?' Was Tom's greeting from the stove.

'I've brought reinforcements with me,' said Christian

indicating the students crowding in the doorway behind him.

'And when did they last carry a gun in deeply wooded terrain?'

Tom was obviously itching with frustration. The others dumped their packs and joined him by the stove.

'I don't suppose you have any news?' He asked.

'I heard the air-raid sirens in the night and left at first light.'

'Pretty much what I did too. I see you're well armed,' Tom continued ironically, looking pointedly at Christian's rucksack stuffed with medical supplies. 'Luckily we do have guns, there's a few stacked with the wood outside and ammunition in the privy.'

'I didn't come to carry a gun.'

Tom glanced at the set face of his friend and shifted irritably on his stool.

'I brought medical kit,' continued Christian.

'I'm listed as medical staff, you didn't have to come at all.'

'I know.'

'Well if you're sure? I'm not hanging around patching blisters if you're prepared to. I'll show this lot the ropes and we'll check out the action. There's another outpost about half an hour north east of here, there might be more to do there, there's certainly nothing doing here. There's lots of tracks so it's easy to find, even in the dark.'

'I take it that's an instruction?'

Tom shrugged. He went off with the students. Christian filled the stove with wood and shut off the air intakes so that it would be ready to fire up if anyone came later. He didn't mind the extra half hour out in the growing dusk, what he didn't want was time on his own. He had made a choice in the early hours of the morning and he would make the same choice again whatever the outcome, but it wouldn't have been Astrid's choice and if he had talked to her she would only have tried to persuade him not to leave her. He had calculated that Mia and Astrid Maria would make whatever decisions needed to be made for Astrid. What he hoped was that they had all managed to get out of Oslo and go to their relations in Hønefoss. If Astrid had managed to get more petrol they would have been able to drive there.

None-the-less making a decision, however right it felt, didn't alleviate the guilt from not taking other decisions. He had chosen a path towards freedom and more grandiose responsibilities towards his country rather than the responsibilities consequent upon having originally chosen a wife and child. Christian's conscience was troubled, and his motives, although disinterested, not entirely confident of scrutiny during the dark hours of a lonely night.

In the long, slow dusk of early spring the woods were eerily silent. The only noise which troubled Christian's thoughts was the rasping of his skis as they slid along the tracks now icing over in the evening chill. When he found the out-post there was no more time to wrestle with his conscience. The small hut was over run with people, and two soldiers had minor gun shot wounds, which needed immediate attention.

***

There was no one at home. Mia checked around for messages, but found nothing. The kitchen still bore the evidence of a hurried lunch, two plates and a bowl of some unidentifiable mush. Mia guessed rightly that Astrid and Petter must have eaten with their mother, but there wasn't anything unusual in that. Seeing the remnants of bread and cheese reminded her that she hadn't eaten anything all day, and before going on to the surgery to see if she could find Christian, she made herself a sandwich. She stood at the kitchen window munching on the rather dry bread. Her mind was racing with the implications of the day's events, the excitement, fear and confusion.

Weary with not being able to draw any of her thoughts together she went back out into the street and headed towards the surgery. It must have been about five o'clock when she hammered on the surgery door.

The banging broke into Astrid's dazed reverie. She had managed to feed Petter but was unable to eat anything herself. She had been sitting listening out for the telephone ever since she got back home that afternoon. The site of the German soldiers had paralysed her mind and filled her with fears for Christian's safety. She had long forgotten the quest to fill the jerry cans and they were still empty. His sure death at the hands of the Germans put all other thoughts out of her head. She sat listening for the telephone relentlessly. She had also put the radio on, but it just played endless music. The banging at the door jolted her so much that she startled Petter, who had been dozing peacefully on her knee. He set up a low whimper and put an arm to her neck.

She went down the stairs to the waiting room to open the door but didn't put any lights on. It could be a patient? It could be Germans? But it could also be Christian. Her heart was thumping so much it hurt. She tried peering through the waiting room window but the person was out of sight. When, finally, she opened the door a few inches and looked out, Mia's hand was raised to knock yet again.

'Astrid? Thank goodness you're home!'

'Mia!'

'Well let me in!'

Astrid opened the door and locked it again behind Mia. 'You're not with Mother?'

'No I haven't seen her. Have you?'

'No, not since lunchtime.'

'Did she say where she was going?' Astrid's evident paralysis brought out a hint of irritation in Mia's tone.

'She was going to the Red Cross centre. I expect she's still there.'

'Of course. Is Christian at home?'

Astrid looked at Mia dumbly, the fear showing in her eyes. She shook her head and for a moment Mia thought Astrid was going to swoon. She quickly took Petter and rocked him in her own arms. He was reluctant to leave Astrid and stretched his arms back towards his mother pathetically, 'Mamamama.'

'It's okay, darling,' Mia said quickly, 'Mummy's just going to make us some coffee. Let's play with your bricks.' Mia led the way upstairs into the little sitting room, took some toys out of a cupboard and sat down on the floor with the child.

'It's cold in here,' she said to Astrid.

Astrid had followed her hesitantly. The radio was still bashing out music and Mia turned it down. 'I'll get the fire going,' she said to Astrid. 'Make some coffee,' she added gently, 'I've hardly had anything all day.'

Astrid made two cups of coffee and when she came back into the sitting room an air of normality had returned. Mia had switched the light on, the fire was blazing and Petter was happily scattering bricks over the rug. For a moment Astrid blocked the nightmare out and smiled at them both, until Mia broke the spell.

'Is Christian out on call?'

Astrid put the coffee down on a side table. 'He's,' she cleared her throat, 'he's fighting Germans,' and she burst into tears.

Relieved at the outburst Mia put out her hand towards her sister and waited for her to calm down again. In the meantime she continued to distract Petter. Astrid recovered herself sufficiently to sit down.

'Tell me?' Mia asked.

'He left this morning, really early, before I was properly awake. He had skis and a backpack and that's all I know. I've heard nothing since.' She bit her lips. 'Mother says he's probably joined patrols in the woods, fighting Germans.'

'That wasn't very helpful of her,' said Mia dryly. 'Astrid, you know how Christian feels about fighting, he's not likely to be joining patrols to fight, even against the Germans. Couldn't he have gone for some other reason? Perhaps he's gone to help? Perhaps he thought he should be there in case there were casualties?'

'Do you think so?'

'It seems much more likely.'

'So he's not likely to be in the midst of any fighting?'

'No,' Mia responded firmly, hiding her own misgivings. Frank and Christian fighting in the woods? How ridiculous it sounded.

The music stopped playing on the radio and the crackling suggested that there might be some kind of announcement. Mia got up from the floor quickly and turned up the volume, both sisters held their breath and listened.

'The chief of police in Oslo, on the instructions of the German commander, advises the people of Oslo not to evacuate the city. In addition he advises that everyone return home and resume their work as usual. All citizens should remain calm and be assured that there is no need for undue concern.'[1]

'What does it mean?' Astrid's voice was no more than a whisper.

'It means they've given in,' Mia announced aggressively.

***

'I'm putting you two girls on a bus and sending you to Hønefoss.' They were eating breakfast in the tiny kitchen of the surgery flat. It was only just past seven o'clock the next morning.

'But the radio announced...' Astrid tried to say.

'Never mind what the radio said. Christian probably thinks you're all safely tucked up in bed at the farm in Hønefoss and that's where you're going to be this evening. The radio!' Astrid Maria spat out derisively. 'You know the German's took over the radio network yesterday evening!'

Mia was biding her time, waiting for Astrid to agree to leave with Petter.

'I suppose that's what Christian meant yesterday, but it said there was no need to leave Oslo. I should keep the surgery open.'

There was wisdom in that last remark, but Astrid Maria didn't think her eldest daughter would cope with the strain, on her own, without Christian, and Astrid Maria didn't want to spend every hour holding her daughter's hand. 'It may just be for a few days,' she said in a more conciliatory tone. 'Just give time for everyone to settle down and then Christian will come and get you.'

Mia could see that Astrid had accepted her mother's plan. 'I'll help you onto the bus but I won't go with you,' she cast a wary glance at her mother, 'I promised I would fill in at 'The Post'.'

---

[1] This announcement was actually made by Norwegian Radio at 15.30, but the radio network was taken over by the Germans at 17.30.

Astrid Maria merely raised an eyebrow. She wasn't going to fight both her daughters, and Mia was more than capable of looking after herself. They could pick up the bus to Hønefoss, assuming it was running regular hours, quite near 'The Post's' offices.

The bus was late, and, scarcely containing their relief at getting rid of Astrid, Astrid Maria and Mia bundled mother and child onto the bus. Astrid Maria turned back the way they had come and wheeled the empty pram home. Mia went on to the newspaper offices and as she signed on for a second day at 'The Post' she couldn't entirely suppress a feeling of excitement, change had its own allurements.

***

At about five o'clock the same morning Christian was roused from an uneasy sleep in the crowded hut by a noisy new arrival. The man had congealed blood showing through his hat and was badly out of breath.

'They've taken your positions further down the valley. You should send re-enforcements or re-group further into the woods.' The man was dressed in civilian clothes and despite his air of authority the others, now all rousing from sleep, were reluctant just to take him at his word.

Christian stepped forward. 'Let me look at that blow to your head.'

'It's just a low branch I hit earlier before it got light. I've been out in that bloody wilderness all night trying to find someone. I heard some gunfire a short while ago and went to have a look.' Christian was carefully taking off the woollen hat. The man winced, but didn't cry out.

Christian quietly cleaned the wound while the man got his breath back.

'I reckon your lot will be here in less than half an hour and it would save time if you were all ready to move quickly. Ouch, what the hell are you doing to me?'

'Iodine.'

'So you are a doctor then? How did you get out here?'

'The same way as you I expect. Christian Krogvold.'

Christian washed his hands in a bowl he had for the purpose and extended his arm to shake hands with the newcomer.

'Frank Olsen.'

Christian wondered if Tom had been part of any action. There seemed to be patrols all over the place failing both to make contact with each other or the enemy. For Tom's sake he hoped he had met up with some Germans, it would be much better if he managed to vent his frustration on the enemy rather than agitating his comrades. It was strange how it was suddenly legitimate to shoot Germans, strange how easily one slipped into the language of war.

His reflections were rudely interrupted by the return of the scouts with half a dozen soldiers, who were obviously injured. Christian immediately set to work.

'The rest went round another way to draw the German's off. You've got enough time to see to this lot then we'd better get out of here.'

For the first time they all started to feel hunted.

One of the injured soldiers was fighting back tears. 'One of the guys back there. Bullet in the neck…' the tears finally won. Christian, feeling jolted himself, wondered when there had last been open combat on Norwegian soil. How many generations ago? Three? Four?

Busy with his patients Christian became aware of a familiar voice in the background.

'They mean business, there must be hundreds of them. We don't have a snowflake's…'

'I thought you had orders to draw the enemy off another way,' the cold voice of an officer broke through.

'And leave Krogvold with this lot to deal with, and make an escape. You forget, I'm the medical officer around here.' And Tom set to work. He didn't stop to remove a dark woollen hat which was pulled low over his eyes, or clean his face, smeared with sweat and grime. He was scarcely recognisable.

Frank, under cover of the commotion, had slipped off. He wanted to make his own assessments.

***

'Brighten that stove up, and throw us a light while you're at it.' Tom lit a cigarette and leant back on a wooden chair until it rested against the log wall. They were in yet another hut, way north and, for what it was worth, well behind their own lines, although the notion of 'their own lines' merely filled them all with a sardonic humour. Tom had worked with Christian all day, maybe his one skirmish with gun in hand had been enough. There were, in any case, enough wounded for the two of them to deal with, as the fighting had intensified. They were grimly aware that the Germans would want to nip any resistance quickly in the bud and they certainly wouldn't want pockets of guerrilla style resistance left roaming in the woods relatively close to Oslo. The only thing that had kept the Norwegians going at all was their skis, as Tom had bitterly pointed out to them more than once.

Christian was now patching people up in the hope that they could get themselves home and avoid further trouble. He wasn't sure, yet, whether Tom had given up or not. Checking the temperature of the worst patient, he didn't notice the commotion outside until the door burst open.

'What the…' Tom's voice drowned the other exclamations.

'The Captain's dead. An hour or so back down the track from here. We're disbanding.'

'Not surrendering?' said Tom nastily.

'Orders are to return home. Go in twos or threes. And be careful.'

'It's all over?' Christian wasn't sure who said this, but no one replied and it became a statement, not a question.

April, 1940
Four

Astrid Maria had just taken the opportunity of stocking up with more tinned foods. Mia was sitting at the kitchen table drinking coffee and flipping through the pages of the day's 'Post'. She ignored her mother, who was standing on a wobbly stool and pushing tins onto the top shelf of the kitchen cupboard, as far as Mia was concerned the kitchen was already ridiculously over-loaded with tinned foodstuffs.

'I don't like tinned sardines,' she said caustically into the newspaper.

Astrid Maria ignored her, grunting in her efforts to stack the over-flowing shelves.

'Where did you get that stuff from?'

'Here and there.'

'You must've spent a fortune!'

'It'll be more useful than money in the bank.' Astrid Maria stepped down from the stool and joined Mia at the table. 'Any news?' she nodded her head towards the newspaper.

'Not in here.' Mia shut the paper and pushed it across the table to her mother. 'There's been a subtle shift in management over the last few days.'

'Already?' Astrid Maria raised an eyebrow.

Mia nodded.

'And what will you do?'

'I'm planning on staying.'

Astrid Maria raised the other eyebrow and took a little, sharp intake of breath. Mia met her disapproval then changed the subject.

'Are you doing the nightshift?'

'Yes.' There was a slight pause before Astrid Maria continued. 'I wish you'd go over to the surgery, in case anyone is trying to ring.'

'You mean Astrid?'

Astrid Maria didn't respond.

'And what do I tell Astrid? That we still haven't seen or heard anything from Christian? Sorry, mother.' Met with further silence Mia finished her coffee and took the cup and saucer over to the kitchen sink. 'I'll go over to Siri's and see if they've heard anything from her cousin, you know, Tom, that friend of Christian's?'

'I know who Tom is,' Astrid Maria responded crossly. 'Make sure you take a key...' but Mia had already shut the kitchen door behind her.

Siri was sewing the buttons on a new blouse she had just made for the summer, she was sitting in their kitchen where the light was better. Her parents were huddled over a radio in the study. Mia fingered the light cotton print of the blouse, she could sense that Siri didn't want to talk about the war. Siri broke the cotton off the last button and held the blouse against her.

'Looks a bit tight,' Mia said, a slight irritation creeping into her voice. She wanted information from Siri, not let's pretend nothing has happened.

'It's the fashion.'

'Fashion?' Mia looked at her sharply.

Siri ignored her. 'I got a job,' she waited until she had caught Mia's attention, 'with the police, filing and typing.'

Mia was confounded. 'With the police?'

'Yes.'

'You know what that means don't you?'

'Yes, it means I've got a job. Daddy says it means I won't have to do war work.'

'But you know who you'll be working for Siri?'

'They're Norwegians.'

'It doesn't make any difference.'

'Well what about your job then?' Siri, unusually, turned on Mia. 'Won't you be working for *them*?'

'Yes, but I'll be...' Mia suddenly let the anger in her fizzle out. 'That's great Siri, and the blouse is lovely, let's not you and I quarrel too.' Siri put a gentle hand on her friend's arm. 'We still haven't heard from Christian.' Mia willed Siri to volunteer some information.

'Oh? Tom was here last night.'

'He was!'

'He was very cross and Daddy told him to get back to the hospital where at least he could do some good.'

'Did he say anything about Christian?'

'Christian? No, why should he?'

Siri folded the blouse neatly and tidied away her sewing things. 'I promised Mum I'd take the grocery order to Petersen's. Do you want to come?'

'No, no thank you, I should get back.'

Mia put her coat on and Siri walked to the door with her. It had got suddenly dark outside and the first heavy drops of spring rain were splashing onto the icy slush still lining the gutters. Mia breathed in the air and lifted her face up to the rain, she didn't want anything to have happened to Christian, she needed him to talk to. Remembering that she'd forgotten her door key, she rang the bell hard a couple of times and waited for her mother to answer. She rang again. 'She can't have gone already!' She exclaimed to the rain, she would have to go to the Red Cross centre, but at least it was something to do.

There weren't many people about even though it wasn't late. Mia felt strangely vulnerable and conspicuous as her footsteps tapped out on the wet pavement. A closed car went by spraying slush and water up from the road. New officials or Germans? She wondered.

The Red Cross centre was packed, temporary beds had been set up and people with makeshift uniforms were rushing backwards and forwards with bowls and bandages. The smell of disinfectant and antiseptic stuck in Mia's throat. She hurried to a room just to the left of the door, which seemed to be the official centre of comings and goings. In this small room stood Astrid Maria apparently in charge of operations. Mia was startled, if she'd imagined her mother doing anything it was sitting by bedsides telling people that it didn't hurt that much now and couldn't they please go home.

Astrid Maria saw her daughter and after discharging another roll of bandages came out to meet her. She held the door key up and handed it to Mia without saying anything, she then jerked her head backwards indicating the beds lined up in the room beyond her. Mia followed her silent instruction and gasped. 'Christian!' She exclaimed too loudly.

Christian was kneeling by one of the beds dressing a wound and instructing a nurse. The patient was a young man, deathly pale and in obvious pain.

'Get him out of here as quickly as you can, take him home and get him cleaned up,' Astrid Maria hissed to her daughter.

Mia was still staring. 'Shouldn't he be in hospital?'

'Christian, you fool, get Christian out of here.'

Completely confused, but knowing better than to ask more of her mother, Mia made her way swiftly over to Christian, she put her hand lightly on his arm. He looked round tense and nervous.

'Mia!' He looked terrible. He turned away from the patient and stood up. He seemed so tall in the crowded room. 'Mia.' She was so beautiful and unscathed.

'Come, Mother says I have to get you home and cleaned up.'

He sighed wearily, the brief smile leaving his eyes. 'I'll just get my things.'

'Shouldn't that boy be in hospital?' Mia asked risking a backwards glance as they escaped into the fresh dampness of the evening air.

'With gunshot wounds.' Christian asked rhetorically. 'No he's better taking his chance in there. Astrid Maria will look after him and get him back home as soon as possible, then at least I can visit him.'

They walked quickly up the now dark streets towards the apartment. Christian remained absorbed by his own thoughts and Mia struggled to keep up with him, his skis kept knocking into the awning over shop windows as he strode along.

Mia let them into the apartment silently and they hurried up the communal stairs relieved to finally close the door behind them. Mia took his things from him and led him into the kitchen.

'Is Astrid here?' He asked.

'No she's in Hønefoss, with Uncle Per.'

Christian looked relieved. 'Look, I presume you've got the surgery keys? I'll just take them and get over there.'

'But no one's been there for a couple of weeks, there'll be no hot water and no food. Stay here tonight and go over in the morning.' Mia's voice was coaxing, tempting.

Christian relaxed his shoulders a little. 'Okay.'

'Go and wash and I'll find some food.' Christian nodded his assent and went to the bathroom.

'There's an old bathrobe behind the door,' Mia called after him.

Mia prepared food quickly her mind racing. She desperately wanted him to tell her what had happened, but wasn't sure she could bring herself to ask him if he didn't say anything. It was sometime before he emerged, clean but still with two weeks growth of beard. Mia sat him down and watched him expectantly as he ate.

'It's not much fun Mia,' he said, glancing up at her. 'I've been a doctor for over ten years now and seen nothing as wonton and destructive as a gunshot wound.'

'But was there much fighting? We rather thought that there wasn't.'

'There doesn't need to be much. Look to be honest Mia I don't really know what happened, there were a few skirmishes, but not much more, our lieutenant was killed and the recruits disbanded and were sent home. I followed with the wounded, which is why I've taken longer.'

'But where were you?'

'Oh, I'm not sure I even know that, somewhere in Nordmarka.'

Mia bit her lips, there must be more to tell, things must have happened.

Christian pushed his empty plate away and put his head in his hands. He needed sleep. 'Is Astrid okay?' He asked quietly.

'Oh, yes I should think so. We put her and Petter on a bus straight away.'

'What do you mean you think so?' Christian's arms fell down onto the table.

'Well she's bound to be, we haven't heard from her.'

'You haven't heard from her?' The tension shot back into Christian's voice. 'What do you mean you haven't heard from her? You put her on a bus in the middle of an invasion and made no attempts to check that she'd arrived safely?'

'Well you…' Mia stopped.

'I thought she'd be with you.'

'She'll be fine.'

'I hope so, dear God, I hope so.' He could feel his own guilt re-emerging. 'She'll be frightened.' He looked directly at Mia and Mia just nodded. 'You should have tried to contact her.'

Mia looked down. 'I didn't want to talk to her and tell her that we hadn't heard anything from you,' she said softly.

'I don't suppose Per has a telephone?' Christian asked. Mia shook her head. 'Then I'll go first thing tomorrow.' The poor boy with the festering wound would have to wait.

***

Petter had just managed to pull himself up on Astrid's chair. He was stamping a sturdy little foot, banging Astrid on the thigh with his fist and gurgling in his triumph, 'Mamamama.' Astrid was sitting in her Aunt's kitchen peeling potatoes, they were from the previous harvest and getting soft and rubbery. Astrid picked off the sprouts and cored out the grey pockmarks. It was about two o'clock in the afternoon, perhaps later, the old kitchen clock was slow and she had forgotten to set her own watch when they had listened to the radio the previous evening. Listening to the radio! She moved in irritation and Petter fell back down onto his bottom. He looked at her for a moment with disapproval then found his rattle and began to bang the floor again happily and resume his gurgling chant.

Astrid dropped the last of the potatoes into a bowl of water and stooped down to pick up the child.

'Come on old man we'd better get going if we're going to try ringing today.' She had come to hate the daily ritual she had made of telephoning home. She had to walk into the town and borrow a telephone in the grocery store, no one ever answered and the shopkeeper just shook his head and muttered whenever she appeared. Sometimes her Aunt or cousin came for the walk, but it was raining today and anyway they were all busy in the sheds with early lambs.

With the help of her aunt Astrid had rigged up a shawl which

Petter sat in and Astrid tied to her back. She could have borrowed a pram but the roads were still full of melting snow and ice, besides which Petter loved sitting up on her back, he peered over her shoulder and pulled her hair.

Armed with mackintoshes and souwesters they set off down the farm track. Petter snuggled into Astrid's neck to hide from the biting raindrops, which stung into Astrid's face. It was quiet in the town. Astrid stepped quickly into the shop and walked straight into a German soldier, another one was at the counter being served by the shopkeeper himself. Unable to control the rise of panic in her throat Astrid backed out of the shop, turned into the rain and carried on up the high street. Confused that her instincts hadn't lead her back to the farm she headed on towards the town square from where she could take another route home. What was it that they had heard on the radio, something about German troops spreading out over the now occupied territories? If only she'd paid more attention. Collecting her scattered wits she noticed that more soldiers were occupying the far side of the Square outside the police station. A bus was just pulling in, it was from Oslo, and as if to give her random flight some purpose she went to watch the passengers alight.

A tall, bearded, but strangely familiar figured jumped down first. Astrid stared at him mesmerised.

'Christian?' She whispered, not daring to believe that it was actually him. The man looked around as if to get his bearings, and then catching sight of the wet bundled figure of mother and child he came running over to them. Astrid was in his arms before she could take another breath. 'Christian,' she repeated still not daring to believe the reality of his presence. Christian was saying something about Mia ringing her and telling her that he was coming.

'She must have got through to someone then,' he was saying, but his hands were cupped round her face and he was kissing her and she didn't take in a word he was saying.

'Come let's get out of this rain.' Christian took Petter off Astrid's back and snuggled the child under his own coat, and, with his other arm around Astrid, they hurried back down the street the way she had come only moments ago.

'Are you staying with Uncle Per?'

Astrid nodded.

Christian smiled into her hair as he leant his face against the side of her head, his thoughts were full of gratitude and relief at finding her safe and unharmed.

***

Spring sunshine was streaming into the valley. Astrid's Aunt was minding the baby and Astrid and Christian had walked up through the melting ice and snow to a hilltop overlooking the town and farmsteads. For a while they sat catching their breath and sipping the hot thermos coffee they had brought with them. They could hear the river roaring down the hillside in full, Spring flood. Astrid leant her head against Christian's shoulder; married life contained few enough such moments.

'I'm sure Uncle Per meant it about staying in the cottage and working with old Dr Mohr, Petter would have cousins to play with.' Christian's eyes were screwed up against the sun and the smile, which habitually played about his lips, was missing. 'I don't mean for ever, just for now, here where...' her voice trailed off, Hønefoss was no less occupied by Germans than Oslo.

'Astrid, I came here to bring you and Petter back home.'

She moved her head from his shoulder and turned her face from him. Christian was still looking into the sun.

'We have to go home, Astrid.'

'Have to?' She turned to him sharply.

He glanced at her, unable to hide a strange guilt from her. 'I mean I want you to come home with me.'

Or stay here on my own? But the words stuck in her throat.

'We need to be together, Astrid, I need you with me, I missed you.' He turned fully towards her and gently cupped his hands around her face.

She flung herself against the rough tweed of his jacket. 'Don't leave me again, promise you won't leave me again,' she said.

He didn't say anything. He looked back into the sun, sadness pulling at the corners of his eyes. It wasn't a promise he could make.

Five

'So Mia, what exactly is this job of yours?' Mia was sitting on the rug building towers with Petter. Christian was still leaning on the door post just come in from a hospital visit. Astrid was in the kitchen thinning out coffee and setting a tray with cups and saucers.

'I translate.' She looked up from the building blocks, her eyes dancing with mischief, 'German rhetoric into dull, Norwegian prose.'

'Doesn't sound, er, very glamorous.'

Mia laughed. 'Or subversive?' she challenged Christian.

His eyes shot a glance back into the kitchen where Astrid was still preparing the coffee. 'Or subversive,' he replied lowering his voice.

'Have you read any of the articles?' Mia asked. Christian shook his head. 'No, nobody does and those that should either can't read the original German or my Norwegian version so I can just about write whatever I like.'

'And you do?'

'I do.' The laughter died on her lips. 'But there must be something more one can do apart from making cheap jokes out of petty translations.'

Christian turned back to the kitchen and took a tray from Astrid, who had come up behind him. Mia resumed her brick building with Petter.

'I hope things aren't going to get short,' Astrid remarked following Christian into the living room, 'Mother says everything is going to get rationed. She has a huge store of tinned food and sugar.'

'Sugar?' Mia and Christian echoed, puzzled.

'To make preserves,' Astrid responded practically.

'Mother's just getting weirder these days,' said Mia dismissively, 'you must have noticed. I think it's late menopause myself.'

'Mia!' Astrid interjected, unable to keep the shock out of her voice.

'I think the doctor can handle it,' said Mia dryly, flashing an arch look out of her grey-green eyes at Christian.

Astrid said nothing. She silently poured out coffee and gave Petter a crust to chew on, he was teething and sleepless nights were a much greater reality to her just now than rationing. Christian offered cigarettes around and Mia cleared her throat pointedly. He took a cup from Astrid and sat by the empty grate.

Mia drew on her cigarette and took some coffee, she sat down on the other chair by the empty grate. Astrid sat at the small table by the door and Petter chewed on his crust grinning stupidly at his mother. Astrid smiled at him distractedly. Mia stole a glance from Christian to Astrid and drew on her cigarette again.

'Aunt Sophie's been stirring things up at the hospital,' she said breaking the silence, 'flouting all the new rules.'

Christian smiled. 'Yes, she's quite popular with Tom these days.'

'Is she now? She didn't use to be!'

'Everyone's terrified of her.'

Mia laughed. 'It's a good job mother never went back to the hospital they would have been a redoubtable duo.' She paused. 'As it is I think the two of them might be up to something.'

Christian cast an urgent and warning glance at Mia, it wasn't the sort of comment one let slip idly. He bent down and scooped his son up onto his knee.

'Let's have a look at those teeth then.' He put the cigarette well out of the child's reach and gently examined Petter's mouth. 'Ah ha, I think it's come through,' he smiled at Astrid, 'you might get some sleep tonight.'

Astrid was surprised and pleased. 'I didn't think you'd noticed. Actually I'd better take him up now.'

'I'll take him.'

'No it's alright thanks,' she looked from Christian to Mia, 'I'll take him.' She took the child, glad to leave Christian and Mia to their innuendoes and double talk.

Christian stood up and kissed both mother and child on the cheek. 'Don't forget the blackout curtain,' he said casually. He didn't want over vigilant police disturbing them. Astrid bit her lips and glanced at him quickly before going through the door.

The apartment and surgery occupied a double frontage of a narrow street at the back of the main shopping streets around Bogstadveien, about a ten minutes walk from the more luxurious apartments near to Frogner, where Astrid Maria and Mia lived. The surgery and waiting room occupied the ground floor and the apartment the next two levels. Astrid now went up the narrow staircase to the top of the building. Although the first sharp winds of autumn had already begun blowing off the Oslo Fjord it was still only early September, two weeks before Petter's first birthday.

Astrid gently put her lips to the child's face, relishing his innocent smell. Petter's hands clutched around her neck, the small fingers pulling at her hair. She tried to stifle her irritation with Christian and Mia; the covert glances, the conversations which turned when she appeared, the silent code that they had adopted to protect her from the war. War, they talked about war, but there was no war. There were soldiers, there was fear, there was talk of shortages, but as far as she could see they were occupied by an apparently benevolent force. There were no arrests, no mass-slaughter, her child hadn't been taken from her and sent to a Nazi training camp for infants - for such were the rumours. Christian and Astrid ran the surgery and the same patients drifted through day after day. All the things she had feared hadn't happened, and yet, Christian and Mia whispered, her mother vanished off to the Red Cross centre with pursed lips and Tom, Christian's best friend, whom Astrid found difficult at the best of times, constantly disturbed them with his cynicism and frustration.

Petter pulled harder at her hair and kicked her stomach, laughing, trying to get her attention.

They were going to spoil everything.

Petter pinched her face, hard. She put him down on the spare bed in his room and undressed him while he kicked and gurgled up at her. She slid him onto a plastic mat and changed his nappy. The last of the late summer sun slanted through the window. She put clean pyjamas on the child and sat on the bed next to him, pulling him into her arms. For a time they lay there together quietly, the sun making a stripe across the bed where they sat. Down at street level Astrid heard a faint knocking on the surgery door, then Mia's quick light footsteps running down the stairs to answer it. She strained listening. Footsteps came back up the stairs and she recognised Tom's voice. The irritation returned and she got up, tucked Petter into his cot and pulled the blackout curtain closed in one quick, angry motion. Petter turned once in his cot, already fast asleep.

Astrid paused at the top of the stairs, reluctant to return to the reality which Christian and Mia were creating. She went into her and Christian's bedroom. The same slant of low sunlight also made a line across their bed. She turned to the small dressing table and sat down on the stool by it, the anxious reflection in the mirror looking out at her was rather drab and worn. The hair, never the true blond of Mia's, was light brown and the curl, set in happier times six months previously, had fallen out. Astrid picked up the brush and brushed the hair away from her face, re-set the hair grips and pursing her lips into the mirror she refreshed her lipstick. Her face had become thinner with age, it was long and awkward like the rest of her body, her nose a little too big and her eyes a little too close together. She sighed at the mirror and applied some powder and felt that at thirty she could see her middle aged self taking root. She stood up, straightened her skirt out over her hips and pulled her cardigan down over the waist band. As a last thought she turned back to the dressing table and opening one of the little drawers took out her pearls. She sat back down on the stool to fasten them, then pulling closed the heavy blackout curtains she finally went down to join the company.

Tom had occupied the chair on the other side of the fireplace and was leaning forward in some eager conversation with Christian, cigarette in one hand and a cynical smile on his lips. He ignored Astrid's entrance.

Astrid tried to follow the conversation. Christian cut through Tom's eager diatribe. 'I'm a doctor Tom, I've told you before

I'll stitch people up but...' The sentence remained unfinished.

'Stitch people up!' Tom scoffed ironically.

Astrid moved over to Christian and sat on the arm of his chair. He put his arm around her waist and she let out her breath steadily, relaxing against him.

Mia laughed softly. She was sitting at the small table by the door. 'You two are hopeless. I don't know what you're arguing about, there isn't any undercover activity to get involved with anyway.'

Tom turned his frustration to Mia now. 'That's what you know about it,' he said, derision edging his voice. He leant forward again drawing them all into a tighter circle. 'There's a group who're trying to make radio contact with London. You know that the King has established an official government in London and not sanctioned the new government here?' The last question he directed at Mia.

She nodded. 'I had heard,' she said vaguely.

'And that the Germans are trying to countenance their occupation by encouraging Quisling, or at least his joke of a Party, to front a supposed Norwegian Government?'

Mia nodded again.

'Well, people don't like it, things are happening,' Tom continued enigmatically, then he turned his derision back to Christian.

Christian's arm was still around Astrid's waist and the warmth was creeping through her body. He's not getting involved, she thought, and the warmth wrapped itself around her heart. She scarcely heard Mia's voice, so low it was hardly more than a whisper.

'I don't want to be left behind.'

The awkward pause which followed made the room feel cold.

'Shall I switch a lamp on?' Mia asked.

'No!' Christian's voice was sharp, then he relaxed and smiled his old familiar smile. 'No, we'd only have to close the blackout curtains. It's gloomy enough,' he added quietly, as if talking to himself.

'I should go and check that Mother isn't staying out late

again,' said Mia standing up.

Astrid slid off the arm of the chair and the men stood up crowding the small space around the fireplace. Mia stepped forward and gave Astrid a brief kiss on the cheek before running quietly down the stairs. She took her coat from the coat-stand in the waiting room and let herself out through the surgery door. As she pushed the door closed she felt resistance from the other side and Tom slipped through and joined her on the pavement.

Back in the little sitting room above, Astrid turned and put her arms around Christian, he held her to him, but he knew what she was thinking and it troubled him.

'Christian?' She questioned, looking up at him, a smile softening her tired features. He returned the smile but his eyes remained serious and sad.

'Astrid.' He moved back from her and held both her arms against her sides. 'It's going to happen, sooner or later it's going to happen.' She looked down. 'I'm not going to blow up bridges or set booby traps for German soldiers,' he paused, 'but people are going to get hurt and when the telephone rings and someone asks for help I'm not going to say no,' he paused again. 'I'm not going to say no, however risky it is.' But the last sentence dried in his throat, and all Astrid heard was 'however'.

They moved gently apart and Astrid took the dirty cups into the kitchen.

Tom closed the surgery door behind him. He gave Mia an appraising look.

'I'll walk you home,' he said. It wasn't a request.

Mia nodded in acceptance and they turned and walked along together in the direction of Frogner. It was a quiet, residential area, there was no traffic and very few pedestrians in the gathering dusk. Most of the traffic, anyway, was either military or commercial and it tended to keep to the larger streets. They walked past a long row of sheds and garages where Christian kept his car and then took an abrupt left turn, neither of them said anything. Mia stole surreptitious glances at Tom as he strode along beside her. He was tall with an athletic build and burnt with a frustrated energy. His hair was a dull blond, which he kept short and swept away from his face with Brylcreem, and he wore his hat pushed back from his forehead. His features, though handsome, had hardened over the years and exuded more cynicism than charm, but there was an animal hunger about him which excited Mia. She wondered why he'd never married as he'd never been short of eligible girlfriends.

They made another sharp turn, this time to the right. Tom seemed deep in his own thoughts and Mia didn't feel like distracting him from them. It was scarcely ten minutes before they reached Mia's apartment house. Mia thanked him for seeing her home and reaching into her pocket to find the door key turned to enter the building. Tom was still standing on the pavement unmoving, but something made her turn back to him, the door key now clutched in her fingers ready to place in the lock. He made one swift step towards her and gripping one elbow with his hand pulled her against him. His face came down towards hers and for one heady moment she thought he was going to kiss her. His eyes were on a level with her own and he held them fiercely.

'Sixteen Thomas Heftys Street, tomorrow evening at eight o'clock, and refer to your contact as Helge, not Tom.' His voice was low and constricted. Sensing that she needed no further instruction he turned abruptly from her and walked quickly back down the street the way they had come. Mia memorised the message and let herself into the apartment building. She ran up the stairs, her heart racing, she was going to get a piece of the action after all.

***

The Red Cross centre was teaming with people. Astrid Maria was running a training course and had ten girls a little younger than Mia tied up in bandages, another ten were trying to unravel them. Astrid Maria smiled grimly at their attempts and went to check the few genuine patients who were hidden at the back of the crowded room. A familiar voice caught her attention before she reached the first patient.

'What on earth are you doing!' The voice boomed over the tangled trainees and Astrid Maria recognised her sister's dominant tones. The filial ties between them had strengthened with the occupation and the years had also brought them closer in looks, although Sophie was rather shorter and broader than her younger sister, who retained an echo of the slender beauty which Mia had inherited from her.

Sophie came nearer and repeated her question. 'What on earth is going on?'

'I'm recruiting,' Astrid Maria answered calmly.

'It's not your job to recruit is it?' Sophie demanded.

'I'm not waiting for instructions,' was Astrid Maria's terse response.

'Is there anywhere less busy?' Sophie asked, lowering her voice.

Astrid Maria guided her into the small supply room. The door was wedged open with a box of bandages and wouldn't close. Sophie eyed it distastefully.

'I've got a couple of boys who are being too closely scrutinised for my liking,' said Sophie, getting straight to the point.

'Patients?'

Sophie nodded.

'How bad?'

'Moveable.'

'I'll send the van over. When does the duty roster change?'

'Six.'

'I'll send them over just before six then.'

Sophie nodded again. 'Damn these new officials,' she said.

The exclamation seemed somewhat off the point. Astrid Maria looked closely at her older sister for a few moments and hazarding a guess at some new source of irritation she paused before asking bluntly. 'Shouldn't you have retired this year?'

'Retire!' Well she'd certainly hit a raw spot, Sophie's considerable scorn came lashing out at her. 'I'm not moving. Not now.'

'But Sophie…'

'I changed my employment card and lost a few years.' She sounded distinctly smug.

Astrid Maria looked at her sister and after a moment of undisguised frustration they both exchanged the same grim smile.

'You'd better get back to those girls,' Sophie barked as she turned to march back through the chaos.

'Sophie?' Astrid Maria stopped her sister in the doorway. 'How?'

'There isn't much in that hospital I can't get access to,' was Sophie's parting shot as she braced her shoulders with more than a hint of self-satisfaction before sweeping a path to the exit door.

'I can well believe it,' and Astrid Maria gave in to a rare chuckle.

October

Mia sharpened her pencil, her eyes straying to the window. The late summer had turned suddenly into a dark and dismal autumn and people were huddling for shelter by the tram stop just below her window. She sighed quietly and went back to the dense German text she was translating, more dogma, it was endless, the months since the invasion were endless, all this waiting for something to happen was endless. She'd been to three meetings with the rather hazy group that Tom was involved with, she'd sat in some back room and typed up pages of illicit news from London, which was then circulated secretly, but it didn't feel very dangerous or exciting. She still amused herself by making a nonsense of the German doggerel in her translations, as she had quite rightly supposed nobody checked and if anyone read it, it just looked like incompetence on the part of 'The Post'. The first amusement had, however, worn off and it gave her little satisfaction now. She had tried to resign and resume her studies, but it had proved rather difficult, in fact she'd been rather shaken by the obstacles put in her way, and although not actually forbidden to leave it was clear that there was no real choice. One of the secretaries, a friend of Frank Olsen's she'd talked to a few times, had left and the girl was now marked as a 'suspicious character' and the office had been warned against keeping in touch with her.

Mia doodled idly on the side of her notes and continued to look down at the tram stop. The town tram had just gone so there were less people waiting now. Mia watched the few huddled figures still left until she noticed one of the editors watching her and she went back to her notes. After a few industrious minutes she glanced back up again. The editor, one of the old members of the team who had survived the change of regime, was himself looking out of the window. Mia followed his gaze. He seemed to be, like her, looking at the huddled figures by the tram stop. The editor stood up. Mia put her head down to her work again, but he had stood up to get a better view out of the window. Mia followed his gaze again just as one of the huddled figures glanced up at 'The Post' offices. It was only for a moment, but it was long enough for Mia to recognise him. The editor also seemed to be trying to put a name to his face. Mia bent down to her work again, Frank Olsen, she was sure it was Frank. Mia pushed her papers together and stood up. The action distracted the editor and he turned round to look at her, she put her hand to her stomach and affected a pained expression.

'I think I have to go home,' she said. She made herself sound embarrassed.

The hint of women's problems had the desired effect on the editor, who coughed and muttered something about deadlines. Mia took his embarrassment as assent, thanked him and rushed out to the cloakroom, she flung her coat on, put her bag over her shoulder and ran down the stairs. The tram going out of town was just coming down Frognerveien. She ran over the road and joined the queue at the stop just as the tram pulled up. It was Frank Olsen. He was standing a little back from the few people now eager to board the tram. Mia fell back with Frank for a moment, then without looking up at him she said quickly. 'Get the tram, Mr Stenberg has recognised you.' But the tram conductor, thinking they were waiting for another tram was already shutting the doors. Mia rushed forwards and hammered on the closing doors and reluctantly the conductor stopped the tram and opened the doors again. Mia stepped on and Frank slipped in behind her and sat at the back.

'Well make up your mind,' said the conductor, ruffled. Not wanting to follow Frank Mia went to the front compartment of the tram and then understood why the Conductor was bristling with anxiety; the compartment was full of German soldiers, and worse still, as the Tram lurched forward Mia found herself thrown against one of them, where he sat.

'Can't you watch what you're doing,' he growled in German. Mia glanced down at him and noticed the stripe on his shoulder.

'I'm sorry,' Mia replied in her now fluent German. Then, as a quick after-thought, she added, *'Lieutenant.'* He was probably only a sergeant but the mistake had the desired effect. He smiled and moved up on his seat indicating that she should sit down next to him. This was not the moment to hesitate so Mia thanked him and sat down.

'You speak German?' He continued.

'Yes,' she answered, hoping he wasn't now going to engage her in small talk. He looked as though he might like to but luckily couldn't think of anything to say. Mia had planned to keep an eye on Frank and see where he got off but she had already drawn enough attention to herself, so instead she went the three stops which took her closest to home, said something polite to the soldier, and got off the tram. As she turned towards home someone came up beside her walking in the same direction. She sensed it was Frank before she turned to look at him.

They walked on in an uneasy tandem until Mia turned into a quieter street near home. Frank now pulled ahead of Mia and turned sharply to face her.

'How do you know who I am?' He demanded.

Determined not to feel intimidated Mia carried on walking, which meant that Frank had to turn and walk with her. She returned his gaze for some moments before responding. Frank Olsen, she studied him closely for the first time. He was lightly built, about medium height, with brown hair smoothed under a cap. His face was thin with fine features that had a lopsided look giving him at once both an intellectual and youthful air. He was a few years older than her, mid twenties or possibly older. He was wearing rough tweeds with a brown jumper under the jacket and he looked more like a manual worker than a journalist. Mia could think of many questions that she would like to ask him!

She raised her head defiantly. 'And why do you look like you're dressed in some kind of disguise?' She asked.

He took a step closer towards her. 'I don't want to play games,' he replied.

'Can we talk?' Mia asked, her tone more conciliatory.

Frank hesitated. He didn't like this unknown girl, moreover an unknown girl who worked with the newly made over 'Post' and fraternised with Germans, knowing who he was. She was, however, very attractive.

'There's a café down the next street,' she looked at him with an invitation and a question in her eyes.

'Okay,' Frank complied, and they walked on in silence.

The front tables were busy with afternoon shoppers, but it was easy to slip to the back and sit a little distance away from the other people. Frank ordered two coffees and they both got out cigarettes. Frank lit them. Mia put her elbow on the table and leant forwards towards him.

'I've typed a few articles for you,' she said.

'And?'

'I've seen you around the office, that is before the invasion.'

'But I haven't seen you before,' said Frank bluntly.

'Obviously not,' said Mia archly.

'You're not one of the regular girls,' Frank said impatiently.

'There aren't many of those left,' Mia replied dryly.

The waitress dumped two cups of coffee on the table. Frank caught her before she left them and paid the bill. Mia sipped at the steaming liquid; there was more than a hint of chicory in the brew.

Mia sighed imperceptibly into the hot, watery steam and put the cup down.

'I remember you because I liked the stuff you used to write, and,' she hesitated, 'those of us left behind spend more time wondering what has happened to those of you who have left than you spend thinking about us.' While feeling the truth of her last statement Frank still had the feeling that his question wasn't satisfactorily answered.

'But you weren't on the staff, I'd have remembered you.'

It was almost a compliment! Mia smiled. 'I filled in, during holidays. I went in the day of the invasion for want of anything better to do.' She looked him straight in the eye. 'I typed the last report you filed.' A vague recognition stirred in Frank's memory and he looked as though he was about to speak but no words formed. 'You filed that report then you vanished. I've wondered since what happened, what you did?' Mia took a last draw on her cigarette then stubbed it out. Frank's cigarette was still between his fingers, unsmoked with a long ashen stump hanging from it. Mia pushed the ashtray over to him and he automatically dropped the ash.

Frank pulled his cap off and leant forward, his head resting on his hands. There was a mark on his forehead where the cap had been. He had an overwhelming desire to talk to this girl, the last few months had been lonely. 'I still don't understand. Do you work for 'The Post' or not?' He asked.

'Yes,' was Mia's simple answer. 'I carried on after April the ninth, it seemed a good way of getting information and I didn't know what else to do. I wanted to do something.' Frank could sympathise with that. 'I started doing a bit of translation.' Frank looked questioning. 'From German into Norwegian. I'm a language student and my German's pretty good. I suppose I just found myself signed up without really thinking about it. I tried to leave and go back to my studies, but it's not easy to move around these days.' She looked at Frank wondering what secrets, if any, he harboured. There were lots of other things she could tell him, about Tom and the secret newspaper, her mother's mysterious comings and goings at the Red Cross, Christian's time in Nordmarka, but one didn't just talk to anyone, one had to be careful, and even meeting as they had done, she felt, was something that Tom and Christian wouldn't approve of.

Frank swilled the coffee round in his cup and swallowed it

quickly. He stood up ready to make an abrupt exit when Mia put out her arm to detain him.

'Sixteen Thomas Heftys Street, tonight at eight o'clock,' she said softly.

She had no remit to invite people to these meetings. She had been forbidden to mention them, even to Christian and she knew that Tom would be furious, but there was something about Frank Olsen, some quiet resilience behind the boyish charm and the intellect that attracted Mia.

When he'd gone she realised she hadn't asked him why he'd been waiting outside 'The Post' offices that afternoon, and neither did she know why he was wearing a flat cap and working tweeds.

***

Frank was well aware that Mia's parting invitation was probably a breach of protocol. It could, of course, be a trap, but he didn't think so. He'd heard rumours of some command centre not so very far from the offices of 'The Post' and it was a group that he'd long wanted to make contact with. If it was the one he hoped it might be it was also rumoured that they had contact with the legitimate Norwegian government-in-exile in London, but there were many groups working in the dark, as Frank knew only too well. He'd spent the last month helping evacuate people out of Oslo and into Sweden; families at risk of being taken as hostages because their husbands or fathers had escaped with the King or fought in rearguard actions. Frank worked as a driver for a delivery company and it had proved an effective disguise so far, but it was time for a move. The authorities would either be onto him, or the company, sooner or later, and Frank did not intend to be there when it happened.

Sixteen Thomas Heftys Street, Frank had made an early inspection, was a house in a long, Victorian terrace now converted into apartments. There were no clues as to which apartment any meeting might be held in. Frank also checked for any back entrances, but the gardens just backed onto those of the parallel street. Luckily the evening was just as grey and overcast as the day had been and Frank found a shop entrance just a little further down the street, which afforded him some cover. At about half past seven a tall figure with a long coat and hat pulled over his face let himself into number sixteen. After that, at regular intervals, about half a dozen people came to the house, Frank watched them carefully noting the momentary pause as they stopped to ring a bell and wait for someone from the inside to let them in. Making up his mind to follow on the heels of the next person to arrive Frank caught the quick step of a woman coming up the street behind him. It was the same girl he'd met earlier that day. He fell in beside her, she smiled as if pleased to see him and they walked up to number sixteen together. She pointed out the correct bell to him in silence. They heard the intercom crackle but no one spoke into it.

'Groceries,' Mia said quietly into the speaker and the door buzzed open. 'Basement,' she said once they were safely inside. She paused. 'There'll be a bit of a tussle about you.'

Frank could have sworn she was smiling in the gloomy vestibule.

Tom, however, was not smiling when he caught sight of Frank hovering in the doorway behind Mia. He pulled Frank into the light of the room and scrutinised him closely.

'I've seen you before?' Tom questioned, his eyes burning into Frank's.

Irritated with himself Frank felt himself stepping backwards in the wake of the man's aggression.

'Frank, meet Helge,' Mia said, her voice thick with irony and suppressed humour.

'I think I'd remember if we'd met before,' said Frank, recovering.

Tom indicated a low basement room where Frank could see other people quietly chatting.

'Go in there, but no more introductions please!'

Surprised that she didn't follow him, Frank turned to see Mia following 'Helge' into another room at the back of the building. Mia caught his eye before she went off with 'Helge' and raised her eyebrows meaningfully.

Once out of sight of the others Tom took Mia's arm and

forcibly sat her on a chair placed by a table with a typewriter on it.

'I've met that man before, he was snooping around in Nordmarka after the invasion. If he recognises me then you're both going with the next courier to Sweden. And I've told you before, type up the newspapers, but keep out of sight. Jesus, Mia, this is not a game!'

Astrid Maria tugged aggressively at a large skein of red wool and then continued with her furious knitting. Mia looked at the oily sardines soaking into the bread on her plate disconsolately and made a half hearted attempt to eat some more. Astrid Maria had lit the old wood burning stove and the kitchen was warm despite the freezing December fog outside. A scattering of snow and ice had spread over the streets clashing with the warmer air from the fjord, and bringing with it the last of the autumn fogs before the deep freeze of winter finally settled over the city.

Mia chewed on the coarse bread; Astrid Maria had been baking as well as knitting.

'Mother, what are you doing with all that wool,' Mia said, breaking into the monotony of the click of her mother's knitting needles.

'Christmas presents,' was the response.

'Christmas presents?'

'I'm making woollen hats for us all,' said Astrid Maria patiently.

Mia burst out laughing. 'Nisse[2] hats for everyone! Mum you're hopeless. Where on earth did you get all the wool?'

'Sophie has supplies.'

'But we've never had Nisse hats at Christmas,' Mia protested, 'is this some kind of solidarity statement dreamt up by the pair of you?'

'You'd be surprised, I think Nisse hats will make quite a comeback this year. People don't have to go to secret meetings to resist you know.' Astrid Maria tugged at the wool and proceeded with another furious bout of knitting.

'How many have you got to make?' Mia was still laughing.

Astrid Maria grunted, but there was a trace of a smile as she paused from her knitting and fumbled in the wool bag at her side. She fished out a large, red, woollen hat and threw it over to Mia.

---

[2] Nisses are little gnome like creatures which are part of a traditional Norwegian Christmas, they wear red hats and the main Nisse is the Julenisse who is the equivalent of Father Christmas.

Mia put it on and they were both laughing.

'It's horrendously itchy,' said Mia, 'where on earth did Sophie get this wool from?'

'You can give it back to me now, it's supposed to be a Christmas present,' said Astrid Maria returning to her knitting.

'I hope you've made one for Aunt Elisabeth and Uncle Gunnar,' Mia said mischievously.

Astrid Maria just smiled a grim, satisfied smile. Mia chuckled again and returned to the serious business of the rough bread.

'If Sophie gives them one each too they'll end up with a whole heap of red hats, enough to sell in the shop.' Mia had to stop eating as she dissolved into laughter again. 'Aunt Elisabeth will be so...'

'That's enough, Mia!' Cut in Astrid Maria.

Aunt Elisabeth and Uncle Gunnar were rather out of favour with Sophie and Astrid Maria. 'Selling out' and 'pandering to those people' had been Sophie's dismissal of them last time Mia had listened to a conversation between the two sisters.

'I hope you're making tassels for them,' Mia put in after another pause.

Astrid Maria's grunt was interrupted by the sound of the doorbell from the hallway. Mia pushed her plate away and rushed out to answer it. Although they had welcomed the advance of the electric bell they hadn't wasted money on an intercom system and Mia had to run down to the street level door to see who it was. Siri was standing on the doorstep, stamping her feet to keep warm and holding a large bag. Mia let her in.

'It's so cold out there,' said Siri as she pushed in past Mia.

'Mother's lit the stove in the kitchen, come on up,' and the two girls ran up the stairs to get back into the warmth. 'Do you want some of mother's coffee mix?' Mia asked as they went into the kitchen. It's not that good but at least it's warm.'

'Yes please,' Siri answered politely.

'You'll be glad of my coffee mix, as you call it, by the time you've finished,' Astrid Maria said threateningly, tugging on the red wool.

'Hello Mrs Gram.' The bright colour of the wool caught Siri's attention. 'Oh,' she started, 'what are you…'

'Don't ask,' broke in Mia and she raised her eyebrows as if to indicate another of her mother's mad obsessions. She filled the coffee pot and put it on the old stove. It felt cosy in the small kitchen with the fog swirling outside, the logs crackling in the stove and the click of Astrid Maria's busy knitting needles.

Siri put her bag down on the table and Mia cleared the remains of her supper away.

'Mother said there's another broadcast this evening if you want to go over,' Siri said, turning to Astrid Maria again.

'Oh, what time?' Astrid Maria stopped her knitting.

'Um, I'm not sure but quite soon I should think, they usually broadcast at seven.'

Astrid Maria pursed her lips. 'Girls!' She muttered. 'I'll go over then,' she said. She packed her knitting into the wool bag and stood up, stretching out her back and loosening her shoulders. She picked up the knitting and went to the door. 'You can shut the air vent on that stove when the water's boiled,' was her parting shot to Mia before leaving the girls.

'But really what is your mother doing with all that wool?' Asked Siri pulling a chair closer to the stove and warming her hands.

'She's making Christmas presents.'

Siri looked up at Mia expectantly.

'I told you not to ask,' Mia smiled as she organised the coffee.

'Oh, I brought some material to show you.' Siri said, eager to share her provender. 'I got two ends of roles from Lundberg's.' She stood over the table and pulled the material out of the bag. 'I thought this green was really nice. The other's just cream silk but I thought a skirt and a blouse. What do you think?' Siri fingered the cloth lovingly. She loved making clothes. Her figure had remained much fuller than Mia's and she easily put on weight, but she still had a brown eyed innocence and the round face, with light brown curls which surrounded it, held a charm, which would not diminish with age.

'It's nice,' said Mia, 'you were lucky to get it.'

'I thought I'd make something up for you too if you like,' Siri continued.

'That's immensely sweet of you.'

'There's only enough for one thing for me out of both lengths, but I thought I might be able to squeeze something out of it for you too, you're so much slimmer than me,' she added. This was no accolade, Siri was quite happy with her adult fullness.

Mia made the coffee and closed the vents on the stove. 'I'll help with the hems but don't ask me to do any fancy stuff.'

'It's a deal,' said Siri happily. She put the cloth away, took her coffee and went to sit back down by the stove. Mia pulled a chair up to join her and the two girls were quiet for a time, sipping their coffee.

'You know there are rumours flying around,' began Siri enigmatically.

Mia looked at her friend, calmly waiting. She was acutely aware that Siri worked for the police and was careful to make sure her conversation didn't stray far from clothes and Siri's boyfriends.

'You know, rumours about you and Tom.'

Mia looked up abruptly and felt the colour rising in her cheeks. Siri was quick on the up-take when it came to men.

'So it's true, you've been having secret assignations with Tom!' Finished Siri, triumphantly.

Mia felt the panic rising in her throat. She waited a little. 'Who says?' She questioned.

'Oh you know, everyone,' answered Siri vaguely. 'I daren't ask Tom, he's so fierce these days.'

It sounded more like Siri was fishing for information. Mia calmed down a little. 'Yes, I suppose I do see him sometimes. He's often with Christian,' Mia added by way of an explanation.

'But why wouldn't you tell me?'

'Well you know, there isn't much to tell.'

'Oh Mia, I don't mind, I went off him years ago, but you never seemed that keen on him, I always felt you thought that

Christian was more attractive,' Siri continued, warming to her theme.

Mia felt trapped. If she denied the implications then people might look for other reasons for them meeting secretly. It had been bad enough introducing Frank to the group, but to draw attention to Tom and herself could be disastrous.

She sipped her coffee. 'It's nothing serious,' she said lightly.

'Well you watch yourself, he's had more women than you've had hot dinners, that's what my mother says.' Mia could hear the mother's warning tone in Siri's words.

'I'll be all right,' Mia answered, calm now. She smiled at Siri to reassure her although she hardly knew whether to laugh or cry with annoyance. People were so meddling.

'Actually I've got a new date myself, on Saturday night,' Siri said smugly.

'Oh?'

'He's a new recruit at our station.'

Mia looked sharply at her friend. 'New recruit? Where does he come from?'

'Stabæk.'

'I mean what do you know about him?'

'What do you mean, what do I know about him? I've only just met him! But he's really nice.'

Mia rolled her eyes to the ceiling, for nice substitute good looking, she thought, as if she, Mia, needed protecting from men. Mrs Grobæk should look more carefully after her own daughter.

'I mean, Siri, if he's a new recruit what do you know about him?' Mia paused wondering how she could spell it out. Siri looked unrepentant and Mia waded on reluctantly. 'I mean how do you know he's not a Nazi?'

'A Nazi?' Siri sounded shocked. 'Of course he's not a Nazi, he's Norwegian,' she finished indignantly.

January, 1941

Petter was ridiculously attached to the large red hat his grandmother had given him for Christmas, even though it was too big and made him itch all the time and Astrid had had to spend Christmas morning lining it with an old handkerchief. They were on their way up the hill to ski, to celebrate the new year which had dawned with fresh snow and sunny skies. Astrid was organising the sledge and harness that they pulled Petter along with and Christian was waxing their skis. He too was wearing the red Nisse hat from Astrid Maria. Astrid's hat was already hidden at the bottom of the glove drawer. There wasn't much room in the kitchen for waxing skis and Christian's glasses kept steaming up. Astrid was piling up blankets to wrap Petter in as it could be more than minus ten centigrade on the ski tracks in the woods. It would be cold for Petter, but the sun was too tempting and Astrid was looking forward to getting out.

The telephone started ringing downstairs in the surgery. Christian was noisily rubbing the hard wax into their skis and Astrid could hear Petter's happy gurgles as he tottered around the kitchen with lumps of ski wax gripped in his hot little hands. 'Pappa, Pappa, Pappa.' Neither of them could hear the telephone, which continued to ring with annoying persistence. Astrid sighed, put down the blankets she was arranging, and ran down the stairs to the surgery.

'Krogvold,' she said into the receiver.

'Dr Krogvold?'

'Yes, speaking.'

There was a pause. 'Dr Christian Krogvold?'

'Oh no, that's my husband.'

'Can I talk to him?'

'Who is it speaking? He's actually rather busy just now.' Another pause. 'Can I take a message?'

'I need to speak to him urgently,' the anonymous voice continued.

'He's out, he's busy, he can't talk to you today, for a moment the lies came flooding to Astrid's lips. 'I'll just get him,' she said, defeated. She knew what it was, it was one of the mysterious call-outs that Christian took now and again, call-outs that didn't go in the book, call-outs without names or addresses. She called Christian to the telephone and went back upstairs not looking at him as he ran past her to take the call. She went back into the sitting room and sat amongst the debris of harness and blankets. Petter came toddling in from the kitchen to find her, his red hat was at a rakish angle and his fingers were sticky with green wax. 'Mamma, mamma,' he cooed happily, 'ski, ski, ski.' He tumbled on top of his mother, sticking waxy hands to her jumper. 'Ski, ski, ski.' Astrid buried her face in the blankets to try and stop the tears.

***

Frank pulled his cap down and wound his scarf another loop around his neck in an attempt to cover his ears. It was bitterly cold. He had moved from his delivery job and taken on casual work for a coal merchant. It was dirty work, but they weren't too fussy about paper work and by the time he'd pulled overalls over his clothes he felt suitably anonymous. He'd had strict instructions from Helge that if he wanted to join the organisation he had to lie low for a while and keep his nose clean.

'If you take risks and then come here we all take that risk,' Helge had warned him.

'I don't take risks,' had been Frank's simple response.

There had been a few stand offs, like the teachers refusing to sign up with the Nazis, but there'd been no recriminations and the Germans seemed happy to stand back and let the new Nazi Norwegian Government take control. But Helge had made it clear to them all that it wouldn't last long. The Quisling Government was not taking control and the backlash, when it came, would be bitter. 'The Germans won't take kindly to failure,' Helge had instructed them. 'You've heard of the Gestapo? Well when they get up and running here secret meetings will be no game.'

Frank had grudgingly come to admire, even like, Helge. He liked his steely determination to resist occupation whatever the cost. Mia said that Helge had too much burning resentment to keep quiet enough, but Frank didn't agree. Helge's stringent, even obsessive security was unheard of in the other organisations Frank had brushed against during the last year. Frank, though not usually a team player, had accepted Helge's leadership of the group and for the first time had felt that organised resistance to the occupation could be a reality.

Frank was on his way to sixteen Thomas Heftys Street now. It was early for the meeting but he knew that Mia would already be there, typing a newssheet. He persuaded himself that it would be cheaper to warm himself at sixteen Thomas Heftys Street than burn the gas fire in his own flat. The other reason, the real one, that he might get a few minutes on his own with Mia, he didn't admit to himself.

There were no streetlamps, as the Germans were still fearful of Allied attacks on their positions in Norway. Frank slipped along in the gloom checking carefully for other shadows in the evening before turning into the porch of number sixteen.

As Frank had expected, Mia was working on her own. The gas fire was lit and the basement room was warm.

'Any news?' He asked, taking off his outdoor clothes.

Mia paused in her typing and sniffed the air. 'You smell of coal,' she said.

Frank sniffed the arm of his jacket. 'I can't smell anything,' he responded.

Mia laughed.

Frank pulled a face and moved next to her so that he could read the typescript over Mia's shoulder.

'Not really,' Mia answered in response to Frank's question about news. 'The British still claim to be making significant gains against the Italians in North Africa.'

'Oh?' Said Frank, reading over her shoulder.

'I can't see that advances in North Africa help us very much,' said Mia, pausing in her typing and turning her head to look at Frank.

'No it certainly feels like that,' agreed Frank. 'It's probably the only good news they've got to send us.'

Mia held his gaze for a long moment then returned to her typing. Frank hovered behind her, his hand resting on the back of her stool. Mia smiled as she typed. At the next paragraph she turned to him again.

'Why don't you make yourself useful and make us some

coffee,' she smiled up at him.

'Coffee?' He questioned hopefully.

'Well, okay, not actually coffee in the good old-fashioned sense. I stole a jar of my mother's mix, don't ask what's in it, I haven't dared, but it's hot.'

Frank laughed. He went through into a sort of annex attached to the main room that functioned as a basic kitchen.

'I presume you know what to do with that primus,' Mia called out to him over the hammering of the typewriter keys.

'I reckon I'll manage,' Frank called back as he experimentally fiddled with knobs.

***

Christian was sitting on a train heading eastwards out of the city. The last stop on the line would take him right into Østmarka. He watched his skis rattling against the side of the train as the city slipped passed them. The train was quite empty and his ski poles and rucksack leant against the seat next to him. It was already one o'clock and Christian hoped he would get to the outlying farm with enough daylight left to light his journey home.

It was the second call-out he'd had already in January. Luckily he'd taken the telephone call himself this time while Astrid and Petter were out shopping, and relieved not to have to face the recriminations in Astrid's gestures he had been glad to leave a note. None-the-less he would like to be back before it got too late and she started to worry.

The train pulled into the last station and Christian stretched up, eager to be on his way. If the instructions were correct he should be able to follow the ski track up from the station for about half an hour then take a turning to the left signed to Solsæter. The farm was about eight or ten kilometres away, which was not a long distance with ski conditions as good as they were today. Pulling Astrid Maria's red hat over his ears he set off. The air felt good and the sun, albeit weakly, was shining in the steely sky. Getting into the familiar rhythm of shifting weight from one ski to the other Christian felt the irrepressible joy of being out in the woods. The tracks were empty and the only sign of life were a set of prints from an elk which had crossed the ski tracks.

After about twenty five minutes the expected sign came into view and Christian turned off the main ski track and found himself following a steady gradient down into a wooded valley. After a few minutes he saw the chimneys of a small settlement and soon found himself in a pretty clearing in the woods with a frozen stream to one side. A farm track lead out of the valley back in the direction Christian had come, leading towards the town. A battered truck with an improvised snow plough tied to its bumpers was parked in the yard. Christian swung to a neat stop and bent down to undo the ski bindings. Sensing that he was being watched he looked up to see an old man standing in the doorway of the nearest building, a low, single storey, timber built dwelling. The wooden panelling on the outside of the cottage was painted a deep red and the windows were framed with white paint, which was flaking. The main farm house on the other side of the open yard was also timber clad, but was painted white. A thick pall of wood smoke hung in the still afternoon air.

Christian knocked the loose snow off his skis and leant them against the wall of the cottage. The old man was still standing in the open doorway. As Christian walked towards him with his usual, easy stride the man jerked his head backwards and rolled his eyes to indicate the inside of the cottage. Christian understood the gesture and, stamping his boots free of snow on the cleared threshold, he followed the man into the dwelling. It took a few moments for Christian's eyes to adjust to the dark interior. The old man indicated a chair where he placed his coat and hat. He took off his glasses, giving his eyes time to adjust and absentmindedly cleaned them on a handkerchief. When he put them on again he was able to focus on the simple interior. The cottage was just one room with a wood burning stove in the centre of the back wall. A table and two chairs were positioned under a window and an easy chair was placed by the stove. A simple step ladder led up to an open loft, which had two beds built against the side walls of the cottage. Under the loft, extending from the first half of the open room, was a more formal sitting area. It was a pretty space with windows on two sides, one looking into the farm yard and the other looking down the valley.

The old man jerked his head again.

'Couldn't get him up there,' he indicated the loft, 'he's over there on the sofa.'

Christian could now make out a prone figure lying on the sofa, covered with a rough blanket.

'Kid's gone off to see'f he can get more help,' the man continued. 'Pretty glad to see you show up I must say. Ole Brattland,' he concluded, introducing himself and stretching a worn hand out to Christian. Christian winced inwardly. Why did people always insist on telling him their name?

He shook the proffered hand. 'Krogvold,' he introduced himself reluctantly. 'Do you know what the problem is?'

'Reckon he's broken his leg.'

Christian drew a sharp breath, this was not going to be easy. He went over to the patient. The man looked up at him and smiled weakly, he was perhaps thirty years old and underneath the blanket he was wearing a parachute jumpsuit. At least he wasn't English, thought Christian, which made it a good deal easier to absorb him into the system. He'd obviously come with a parachute drop and presumably people from the reception party had managed to get him here.

'My name's Christian, I'm a doctor,' began Christian. The man acknowledged that he'd understood. He began pulling off the blanket and talking at the same time to distract his patient from the pain. 'Pretty bad luck, old man, but we'll soon get you right again.' He turned to his rucksack and fished out a knife. 'I'll have to cut the trouser leg off,' he continued, cutting at the cloth as he spoke. The right leg seemed at a skewed angle but there was no sign of blood and with luck it was a clean break. The pain was obviously great and tears sprang from the man's eyes. Christian glanced at him as he worked the cloth from the injured leg. 'I'll just assess the damage then see if I can give you something for the pain.' The man nodded again. Christian now started on the sock, the boots had been taken off earlier. 'Looks like a clean break above the ankle bone, I should be able to set it here and now and tie it with a splint. The problem for you is that it will take several weeks before you can walk without a couple of sticks.' Christian was fishing in his rucksack again. He found a bottle of morphine and administered a small amount to his grateful patient.

The old man had been watching the whole procedure intently. 'Looks like you know what you're doing,' he commented.

Christian turned from the patient, giving the morphine a few minutes to work before seeing if he could set the leg. He sat back on his haunches and looked up at the old man. 'I'll need a splint and some rags, an old sheet or something would be perfect.' The old man waited expectantly. 'A broom handle would do for a splint if you've nothing else.'

'Right, I'll see what I can find.'

Checking that the patient was drifting with the morphine Christian set to work on the leg, with a quick, but brutal movement he set the leg back at its correct angle, applied iodine and proceeded to bandage the whole limb from the heel to above the knee. The old man returned with a thin shaft of wood and a piece of cloth of indeterminate description, but it did the job and soon the poor patient was strapped up and fairly immobilized. He wasn't running very far if the Germans caught up with him, thought Christian grimly.

The sound of footsteps in the yard drew their attention from the patient, and within moments a young man, hardly twenty years old, put his head round the door.

'You got here then,' he said.

Christian presumed the young man was addressing him and acquiesced.

The youth hovered in the doorway looking anxious. 'We can't move him until tomorrow,' he said.

'He can't be moved anyway, at least not for a few days,' responded Christian.

'The lad can stay here, of course,' broke in the old man stoutly.

The youth continued to hover, his arms swinging helplessly, obviously not knowing how to proceed and needing guidance.

Christian sighed. 'You'll need to bring him food until you move him and you'll need to find him some clothes. I presume your organisation can then move him to a safe house?'

'Yes, I think so,' answered the youth.

'We'll be fine,' said the old man, keen not to lose his part of the action. The winters could be long so far from town.

There was very little daylight left and Christian was keen to get going. He refused the offer of a cup of coffee, dressed up again in jacket, hat and scarf, and went outside to strap his skis on. He was just giving last minute instructions on the handling of the patient when a shout assailed them from across the yard and a younger version of the old man came striding towards them.

'What the...' he began as he approached, jabbing his finger at them he continued aggressively, 'I don't know what's going on here, but we want none of it, you understand? None of it!'

The old man stepped out into the yard and faced his son. 'He's in my house and that's where he'll stay until I decide he can go.'

'It's not just you though is it? It's all of us. They'll find out and it won't be just you will it? It'll be Lise and me, and the boys.'

'Who's going to find out?' Challenged the old man.

'Well these people already know,' he said, jabbing a red, work-coarsened finger at Christian and the youth. 'And who else besides? I tell you we're having nothing to do with it.'

'Well it's a bit late for that now,' said the old man calmly. 'There's a Norwegian lying on my sofa with a broken leg, risking his life for us he is.'

The son realised he was trapped and the impotent anger bubbled up into his face. 'You'll all know more about this,' he shouted as he stamped back across the yard.

'Nice man,' said the youth.

Christian tightened the bindings on his skis. 'Just get him moved as soon as you can, possibly even as early as in three days, if the farmer doesn't calm down. And make sure you get food up here for him because if the winter stores start going down faster you'll get even more trouble.'

Christian turned to the old man and shook his hand. 'Thank you,' he said.

'I'm just happy to be of help,' the old man replied. 'Leif is just concerned for the young ones,' he apologised for his son.

The air was heavy with the pall of wood smoke and anger. Christian turned back towards the track he had skied down earlier. If he was lucky with the trains he might get home before Petter went to bed. He hoped Tom or Mia wouldn't come by that night, he needed some time on his own with Astrid.

August, 1941
Seven

St Pauli landingsbrücken, Hamburg's waterway station, was a mass of military activity. The dark hull of a U-boat was being surfaced for repairs and a heavily armed cargo ship had just docked. Anti-aircraft guns were primed and in position and a smell of fear and adrenalin had replaced the once familiar, pervading aroma of coffee and exotic spices.

Friedrich Hirsch sighed. He was glad that he'd persuaded his mother to stay at home. Home had been a modern villa by the Alster Lake but, being a careful man, Friedrich's father had let the house out to a senior Party official and moved his family into an apartment above the family business. The family business was a bookshop behind the Alsterarkaden, but, like everything else, book sales had reduced during the depression, neither had the war improved their fortunes and he was glad that his son had an established, and successful career with the Gestapo.

It was hot in the black tunic of the SS. Friedrich's mother had proudly sown another insignia onto the arm, but Friedrich was looking forward to throwing off the close-fitting jacket in the privacy of his berth on a ship bound for Norway.

Friedrich was also looking forward to taking up his new promotion in Oslo. He had spent an effective year in Denmark running a low key Gestapo operation in Odense. Co-operation and infiltration had been the objectives and Danish self-rule, with minimal interference from German occupying forces, had led to political stability and economic growth. Friedrich's ambition was to make the same stability possible in Norway. He was newly appointed as second-in-command of Gestapo operations in Oslo, where he expected to successfully weed out traitors and protect the happy majority of loyal citizens.

He pushed back a brown curl from his forehead and tried to weave a path through the crowds of soldiers and dock workers to the harbour master's offices. When his papers were stamped he could board the boat bound for Oslo and check that his things were safely stowed. There had been some attempts to ship his piano, but officials in Oslo had promised that a Beckstein Grand would be installed in his rooms prior to his arrival.

His eyes were also brown, a passionate brown, with a hint of steely grey, which he had learned to use to good effect during interrogations. The fine features and the beautifully chiselled mouth bore traces of his Hanseatic ancestry and were suggestive of the exotic trade with which his forebears had once dominated Northern Europe.

There was a queue at customs and Friedrich paced uneasily amongst the motley crowd all trying to get papers signed. He pulled at his tunic impatiently. At last someone recognised the insignia glowing on his sleeve and he was hurried into a private office and attended to with due deference.

With relief Friedrich made his escape to his private berth on board ship. Thankfully his things were in order. He cast off the restrictive tunic and then opened his trunk where he found a slim volume of Goethe, which was carefully placed on top. Friedrich was soon lost in poetry and happy thoughts of benign German dominance in a cynical and rotten Europe.

The mechanical jolt of the ship leaving dock roused him from a sleepy reverie. He noted, with some annoyance, that the Goethe had fallen onto the cabin floor and the binding had come loose at the spine.

***

The August sun beat down on the hillside above the farm in Hønefoss. Petter sat on a rock in the middle of a small stream, which bubbled down the hillside. The sharp cold of the water delighted him and he splashed his sturdy legs in and out of the water with unrelenting energy, calling up to his grandmother ceaselessly.

'Bestemor, Bestemor, look, look.'

In his sticky, summer fingers was a long necklace of blueberries threaded onto a reed. Astrid Maria stretched out her back, stiff from her determined blueberry plucking and clapped her hands at Petter, encouraging him from her position on the other side of the stream.

'Haven't you eaten those blueberries yet?' She called down to him.

Petter continued splashing. 'Bestemor, Bestemor, look, look.' His chuckles rang out over the hazy, summer heat.

Astrid Maria bent back to her blueberry picking, swotting a midge, which kept buzzing around her eyes, with blue-stained fingers.

Further up the hill Astrid and Christian dangled their feet in the same gurgling stream. Two half filled buckets of blueberries lay propped at dangerous angles on the bank above them with their boots and socks abandoned beside them. Christian had his arms around Astrid and kept threatening to push her into the water. His laughter joined Petter's in the hazy heat.

'Don't, don't,' cried Astrid laughing herself, 'I've got nothing to change into.'

'That's all right, I don't mind,' Christian's lips brushed her hair, 'I've seen you naked before.'

Astrid turned round in his arms, her eyes shining and her skin tanned and healthy with the summer. She put her fingers up into the thick curls of his hair and kissed him, a long, luxurious summer kiss. Christian held her tightly to him.

'I love you,' he whispered into the gurgling of the stream. Astrid took one of his hands as it encircled her and put the palm to her lips.

'I can't believe Mia didn't want to stay longer,' Astrid said, nestling into Christian's arms. 'It's so perfect here. It's so wonderful to get away.' She turned her face back to Christian. He was smiling at her.

'It is. It is wonderful,' he agreed with her

***

Mia pulled Frank up the final steep ascent. They had abandoned their bicycles way down in the valley below them. The summer dust of Oslo seemed a world away. They fell down together on the springy open turf above the trees scattered over the hillside below them. Frank was intoxicated with Mia. This gorgeous creature laughing into his face now, laughing at Helge and the group, laughing in the face of her Nazi employers.

Recovering his breath he turned to Mia. She was stretched out luxuriantly on the grass beside him. Her light cotton dress had fallen above her knees and lay provocatively over the sinuous shape of her slender body. Frank pulled her to him and held her tightly. For a while they lay quietly in each other's arms, soaking in the sun, listening to the drone of a bee.

'I love you,' Frank whispered into the summer air, 'I love you.'

Mia pulled herself away from him and stood up. For a moment she looked down at him, her expression strangely sad and serious.

'Don't,' she said, 'don't fall in love with me.' She then turned away quickly and started laughing again. 'Making love is bad enough, but being in love! Now that really would break all Helge's rules,' she said lightly. 'Come on, I'll race you down.' Mia started running down the hill, picking her way over loose stones and running round trees.

Frank followed in a daze. He hadn't meant to tell her he loved her, in fact he had decided he wasn't going to fall for her, but he had. The confusion was tight in his chest as he ran down the hill trying to keep up with her. If this was going to be serious there were lots of things they ought to do. He paused for a moment to catch his breath and watched the flash of Mia's dress as she seemed to dance down the slope. Serious? Frank was serious. As he watched her his mind cleared. Yes, he was serious, serious enough to propose marriage. Perhaps he could persuade her to leave the group, get a safer job, even go to Sweden for the duration, but even before he resumed his chase down the hill the heaviness in his heart told him that Mia wouldn't agree to any of these things, and any such conditions attached to a proposal of marriage would lead to a refusal.

When he finally caught her she was sitting on a rock by the abandoned bicycles.

'Slow Coach,' she said putting out her hand to him. He took the hand and sat down next to her. 'I think perhaps we shouldn't tell anyone,' she continued, 'about us.'

'Mia,' he paused, wondering how he could put words to his thoughts. 'Mia we can't, at least we shouldn't.' He paused again. 'Mia,' but the words wouldn't form. 'Mia do you love me?' He said suddenly, unintentionally. She put her hand gently on his cheek and kissed him. 'Mia we have to tell other people, we can't carry on like this. Helge's right about the group, it could compromise everyone.'

'I don't see how,' Mia replied unhelpfully.

Frank looked at her. 'Because I'll do things, make decisions which may be right for us but not for the group, because in a dangerous situation I may compromise everything to save you.'

'I understand the reasoning, but you'd do that anyway. I know we're not meant to but wouldn't any of us take risks to help the others if we had to?'

There was no answer to that.

'But if Helge finds out?'

Mia shrugged. 'He won't,' she said, her tone strangely flat, as if indifferent. 'We're pretty good at secret assignations you and I,' she added, laughing again. She stood up and straightened out her skirt. 'Come, I'm going home.' She pulled her bicycle up and they both set off back down the dirt track towards the city.

Mia loved her bicycle. She had bought it with what she thought of as her ill gotten gains from the newspaper. She loved the freedom it gave her to go wherever she liked. She peddled along building up speed, happily aware of Frank beside her. She was excited by the effect she had on Frank, attracted by his cool intelligence she was delighted by the boyish passion she had aroused in him. Mia couldn't remember when she'd last had so much fun.

September, 1941
Eight

Mia turned down yet another narrow lane. She turned impatiently to Christian, who was happily striding along at his usual easy pace.

'Aren't we going rather a long way round?' he asked.

Mia eyed the new recruit sharply. They were on their way to one of Tom's meetings. The venue had moved to an old warehouse in the warren of old streets to the north of the city centre. The new recruit had agreed rather reluctantly to come along because Tom claimed it was much safer to be attached to a proper group, rather than to be on call to any fly-by-night set-up with lax security. Christian still wasn't convinced.

Mia lead the way down a narrow alley pressed between the backyards of two parallel streets.

'There must be a more direct route,' Christian repeated.

'Always take a route which can't easily be followed,' Mia answered.

'And why the hurry?' Christian glanced at his watch, it was still only a quarter past seven.

'Rule number two, get there early and keep a look out before going into any meeting. You must always make sure you're not being watched.'

'Tom's rules or yours?'

Mia hesitated a moment. 'Mine,' she said. They were actually Frank's.

Christian was impressed. 'I'm in good hands then,' he said, smiling.

She suspected a touch of irony in that last remark, but she smiled back. Christian's smile was always irresistible.

Round the next corner they turned into a wider street. It was a largely residential area with a few dingy offices and one or too old industrial buildings on the farther side of the road. Mia continued her resolute pace and suddenly swung into a café tucked amongst a modest row of shops and opposite one of the old industrial buildings.

'Now what?' Asked Christian as he followed her.

'We sit in the window and you buy me a cup of coffee. Then we watch and wait.'

A waitress with a greasy apron came and took their order. There was no milk in cafés after the milk rationing in July, at least not in the cheap sort, although cafés where the German officers went had all sorts of things Mia had heard, even coffee. The coffee here was even worse than her mother's concoction.

'Don't look around,' Mia said under her breath and stretching out a warning hand to Christian's arm, 'you're so obvious. Look at me and I'll look around.'

There was another couple sitting at the back of the room and a man sitting by the door. Looking idly towards the window Mia caught sight of a huddled figure going towards the side entrance of the warehouse, over-dressed, she thought irritably, it was only September. Over the next ten minutes several more people slipped in through the same door, there were too many and too soon, she felt; Frank was a thorough teacher.

She took a cigarette out of her bag and leant over towards Christian. 'Light me a cigarette,' she said.

Christian took his own crumpled packet out of his pocket with a box of matches. He lit the match and moved carefully to light Mia's cigarette. Mia, he noticed was not looking at him, but over his shoulder towards the door. From the corner of her eye Mia had noticed the man by the door turn his head and some instinct told her that it was a watchful move, not an idle one. She turned a casual smile towards Christian, but the adrenaline was pumping round her heart. She glanced out of the window and noticed two more figures head into the warehouse. The man by the door stood up, looked about him and slipped out of the door. Mia, smiling and chatting to Christian, watched him like a hawk. Once out on the street he turned his collar up, looked around as if checking something, and then started walking quickly, too quickly, down the street towards the city centre.

'They've rumbled us.' Mia's heart was pounding. 'Stay here and order me another cup of coffee. I'm going to the privy,' she added. 'Don't move.' Christian watched bemused as she slipped out of the café. His first instinct was to follow her and he rose from his chair, still watching her through the window. She had now run over the road and gone into the warehouse opposite, she certainly hadn't gone to the privy. Suppressing the instinct to follow he sat back down at the table and called the waitress over.

'Two more coffees,' he ordered.

'Girl coming back then,' the waitress leered at him.

'Yes, she just went out to get some, er, fresh air,' Christian responded lamely.

Mia was back before the coffee.

'Shouldn't we get the hell out of here?' Christian asked.

'Maybe, but they could be filling the surrounding streets with patrols already. I think we'll sit tight.'

The waitress interrupted them with the coffee. This time she leered at Mia. Mia leant over the table and smiled wickedly at Christian. 'We have such a good alibi,' she smiled archly.

'I always said you were incorrigible,' Christian couldn't help noticing that Mia was enjoying herself. 'Have another cigarette,' he offered.

Mia dug into the crumpled packet.

'What about the others?' Christian asked suddenly.

'That's their problem, but at least they've been warned. There's a cellar at the back with an old entrance leading onto a back lane, and beyond that a main road where there's lots of traffic and a tram route. They should be able to lose themselves fairly easily.'

'Couldn't we have done that?' Christian asked, alarmed.

'Maybe,' Mia repeated inadequately. 'You never quite know,' she added evasively.

Christian drew on his cigarette and eyed her through the smoke. She wanted to see what happened, he thought, and she was using him as her cover.

Mia caught the thought. 'It's always helpful if someone can see what happens. We learn more for next time.'

At that moment police vehicles came storming down the street.

Mia leant over to Christian. 'And we might not have had time for an heroic escape,' she said.

The waitress went to the entrance and stood in the doorway open mouthed. The couple at the back of the café came forward anxiously and stood by Mia and Christian. The proprietor emerged from the dingy kitchen and stood by the waitress in the doorway.

Half a dozen police vehicles were now lining the street outside. Engines were running and a couple of them had lights flashing. Police officers were streaming out and taking up positions around the warehouse opposite the café, and within a couple of minutes they had the building surrounded.

'Wow,' said Mia.

'What is it? What's going on?' Asked the woman who had come from the back of the room. Her voice was shaking and the man, presumably her husband, was holding her arm protectively.

They all turned to the proprietor expectantly.

'Looks like a raid,' the proprietor answered gruffly his eyes fixed on the scene out in the street. Police officers were now breaking down the door at the side of the building and various instructions were being shouted around the building and across the street. The officers were armed.

'Norwegians,' murmured Christian.

'Well organised Norwegians,' said Mia.

The proprietor gave them a quick look.

'But why here?' Continued the woman. 'Why here? What do you mean a raid?'

No one answered her. They all watched with baited breath, waiting for the arrests, waiting for the poor huddled figures to come out of the building, their fellow countrymen dragging and forcing them into the waiting vehicles. A silent audience had gathered on the pavement outside.

They waited.

Police officers came out of the building again and some started forcing another door. There were still no arrests as far as they could see. Mia could feel Christian's eyes on her, but she kept her own resolutely on the scene being played out on the other side of the road.

More officers came out of the building.

'Check the surrounding area.' The barked order reverberated in the gathering dusk. The audience shifted uneasily as four officers bounded across the street towards them. Two questioned the people on the pavement and another two burst into the café pushing the waitress and the proprietor back into the room. The poor frightened woman clutched at her husband. Mia put her hands across the table and looked Christian steadily in the eye. He stubbed out his forgotten cigarette and put his hands over hers.

'Anyone else been in here?' The officer addressed the waitress and the proprietor. 'Anyone slip out?' They turned their suspicious aggression to the café guests still huddled around Mia's and Christian's window table.

'There was a man sitting by the door,' said the proprietor, 'he must have slipped out ten or fifteen minutes ago.' The proprietor turned to the waitress for confirmation. Taking courage from her boss's words the waitress suddenly turned a pointing finger to Mia.

'She slipped out,' she emphasised the word 'slip' accusingly. 'About five minutes ago.'

The police officers immediately turned to Mia.

'We have a privy out at the back,' the proprietor put in quietly. Mia turned to him and held his eyes quietly for a moment, she nodded her head slowly. Christian's hands held hers firmly. The husband and wife backed away from them as the officers came over. Mia looked down self-consciously then turned an open gaze up at the officers.

'I went to the privy,' she concurred.

The proprietor took hold of the waitress and took her back into the kitchen, while the officers stood over Mia and Christian menacingly.

'What are you doing here?' An officer asked. Mia handed Christian her I.D. card and taking her cue he took his own out of his jacket pocket and offered them both to the policeman. The officer looked at them cursorily, taking in the man's smart clothes and the girl's beauty. 'What's your relationship?' He continued, his tone insinuating and offensive.

'This is my sister…' Christian broke into the questions.

Waiting to cut in over his words Mia said very deliberately. 'He's my cousin.' She conjured up a blush and pulled her hands away from Christian. Christian looked at her in alarm, but the officer was leering at them in the same way that the waitress had leered at Christian earlier.

'Sugar daddy eh?' The officer sneered. 'Find a quieter place for your assignations next time can you?' He was grinning nastily. Mia put her head down to hide a smile. Christian looked convincingly distressed and disconcerted.

The officers went out. 'Good luck, granddad,' one of them called out after them. Mia bit her lips to stop the laughter, Christian looked so uncomfortable. She stood up and leant over him.

'I think we can go now,' she said quietly.

They shuffled out of the café, heads down. As they walked off down the street a few officers looked up and watched them, dirty laughter easing the tension. Mia tucked her hand through Christian's arm and they were glad to hurry out of sight attracting nothing worse than derision.

**

Astrid sat for a while in the pleasant evening sun as it sloped into Petter's bedroom. She loved watching him sleeping, his mouth open, his face smooth and peaceful. He was nearly two! She could hardly believe it. She stood up and leant over his cot, rubbing a caressing finger over the soft skin, then she bent over and placed a quiet kiss on his forehead and went through to her own bedroom. Christian had gone out somewhere with Mia and had been uncertain about when he'd be home. She paused by the window and looked out. It was quiet in the street below. She wished she'd asked her mother over for the evening, but her mother was always so busy that Astrid found it difficult to ask her anything. She picked up a book from the bedside table and turning to go out she caught her reflection in the dressing table mirror. She smoothed her cardigan over the summer dress she was wearing and turned to look at herself in profile. She ran her hand slowly over her stomach and felt, or imagined she felt a small, new firmness. Her hands moved up to her breasts and she cupped them gently. They had grown a little heavy over the last week or so and her period was late. Astrid smiled a slow, secret smile, she was sure she was pregnant and soon she would tell Christian, perhaps this evening, if he wasn't home too late.

Her happy thoughts were broken by urgent knocking on the street door down below. Astrid turned from the mirror and put the book down irritably. Who on earth could it be at this time, she wondered? She glanced at her watch, it was after half past eight.

She opened the door cautiously. Tom! She might have guessed.

Tom pushed through the door without waiting to be asked.

'Is Christian back?' He asked curtly.

Astrid caught the words. How did Tom know Christian was out? So Christian and Mia's vague reference to 'going somewhere' had something to do with Tom! She shifted her cardigan in annoyance.

'He's out with Mia,' she said shortly, 'and I don't know when they'll be back.' She was still holding the door open behind Tom hoping he would take the hint and go. He took it from her grasp and slammed it shut.

'Dammit!' He exclaimed.

Astrid didn't know quite what to do. She would have to invite him in now. He also seemed hot and bothered, as if he'd been running and she didn't like the thought that this could have anything to do with Christian. She pushed the thought from her mind and turned to Tom calmly.

'You'd better come in then,' she said reluctantly.

Astrid made coffee – her mother's notorious mix – and Tom paced up and down the sitting room smoking. Astrid came in with the coffee, placed Tom's coffee on the table and sat down with her own, calmly and deliberately. After a few minutes of fretful pacing and strained silence Tom turned to pick up his coffee. His eye caught a large, brown package lying on the table next to his cup. He picked up the cup and jerked his head towards the package with a questioning look.

'The radio,' said Astrid, still calm. 'I presume you know that we are meant to hand in all radio apparatus to the authorities?'

'Yes, I had heard.' Tom said nastily, his mouth twisting ironically. 'I thought Christian might have managed to hide his away somewhere.

Astrid eyed Tom coldly and continued to drink her coffee primly.

The noise of a key turning in the door below caught their attention simultaneously. Tom clattered his cup down on the table and ran down the stairs. Astrid stood up and stayed awkwardly in the middle of the room. She immediately recognised Christian's voice and leant back against the mantelpiece relieved.

'Where the hell did you two get to?' She heard Tom demanding.

'And what the hell are you doing here?' she heard Christian reply, an unusual, cold edge to his voice.

'Checking you're all right,' was Tom's fierce response.

'Stop it you two,' Astrid heard Mia intervene.

'Where's Astrid?' Christian asked and the next moment he was striding across the sitting room floor. He joined her by the mantelpiece and put his arm around her. Tom and Mia followed him into the room. Mia's cheeks were flushed and her eyes glittered.

'We watched them storm up,' she was saying to Tom. 'Six vehicles and at least twenty men. They had the place surrounded hardly more than five minutes after I gave the warning. It was well planned,' she looked up at Tom a warning in her eyes.

'There's a new Gestapo officer, second in command, came a few weeks ago, he's intelligent and ruthless.'

Mia's eyes glanced up at him. 'That'll be a good match for you,' she said quietly and provocatively.

'But what have you two been doing? Where did you get to?' Tom asked again, ignoring Mia's last remark.

'We were…' Mia began.

'Stop it you two, that's enough,' Christian's voice cut in and his arm went tighter around Astrid's waist.

Astrid was looking up at him. 'You said,' she began. 'You said there wouldn't be any meetings, any meetings with Tom.' Her voice was heavy.

'There haven't been,' said Christian less than truthful, 'and there won't be,' he added firmly looking Tom straight in the eye.

Tom raised his arms and dropped them again. The gesture said, 'you fool', plainer than words. Watching him Mia suddenly noticed that his trousers were torn and a dark stain was spreading from the tear. She immediately dropped on her knees and started examining the wound.

'You got hurt,' she said.

'Just a barbed wire fence,' Tom snapped, irritated. 'I was last to leave. It was a close shave,' and unusually Tom's voice wavered. 'If it hadn't been for you,' he turned to Mia.

She stood up again and smiled. 'It was nothing. I didn't think about it,' she said.

Christian cut in again. 'Look, no post mortems and no gatherings here.' He glanced round at Astrid. 'You two had better go. It's getting late. I'll see you to the door.'

As they went down the stairs Astrid heard strained whispers.

'You will not, not do anything which implicates, or involves Astrid in any way,' Christian was saying.

Astrid remained standing. Darkness slowly invaded the confined space of the small sitting room. The rapid conversation of the last minutes confused her, but she had shut her ears and the cocoon of her new pregnancy had closed around her.

Christian came back up the stairs. He stood in the doorway looking at her awkwardly and self-consciously, wanting to apologise and yet not quite knowing what to apologise for. Astrid watched him and they both stood quietly facing each other.

After a while Astrid held out her hand to him gently. 'I'm going to have a baby,' she whispered softly into the gloom.

For a moment Christian looked stunned and a strain, obscured by the poor light, flitted across his face, then with one step he crossed the room and took her in his arms.

'Astrid, darling,' he said holding her tightly. 'I did

wonder…' he began, then stopped. The words caught in his throat and a slow, hidden tear formed in his eye.

October 1941

Tom was struggling into his white doctor's gown in the staff office at the end of the long men's ward. Christian was sitting with his feet up on the table smoking. He'd been visiting one of his patients, who'd been admitted the day before.

'You're late again.' Sophie said, addressing Tom. Her bosom bristled as if to draw attention to the watch pinned above it.

'And you don't smoke in here,' she added acerbically to Christian. Christian exchanged a wry smile with Tom, put his feet down and stood up slowly. He crossed over to the window and opened it, continuing to smoke.

'And now you're letting a draft in,' she said, hands on hips. The two men smiled at her and she pursed her lips enjoying their easy charm as the October fog drifted in through the open window. She had known these two since they were students and still thought of them as 'her boys'.

'We'd better get on with your round, doctor,' she said, now turning to Tom.

'I'll come with you,' Christian said suddenly. He stubbed out the cigarette and shut the window.

Sophie gathered up an armful of files and they followed her into the ward. As they stopped at each patient she gave a careful run down, giving Tom details of the patient's name, injury and age.

'Don't you remember any of this yourself?' Christian whispered across at Tom, surprise edging his voice.

'Nope,' said Tom shortly. 'In fact,' he added as they moved onto the next bed, 'I'm very careful not to remember any of my patients too clearly.'

He paused in the middle of the ward as if consulting with his colleague. 'Sophie makes sure that she is the only person who knows who all these people are. Her files are far more difficult to get hold of than anything held by the Gestapo in Victoria Terrasse.'

Christian looked puzzled. Tom examined another patient.

'They change,' Tom continued enigmatically. 'She shifts them around. This one for example,' he said moving onto the next bed, 'never seen before in my life.'

Sophie gave Tom the same full synopsis of his patient and the two doctors moved on.

'She has some kind of racket going on with that sister of hers, your mother-in-law, and any patients that may attract attention from the police get moved around.'

'Is that what they've been up to?' Christian said, understanding dawning on him. Astrid Maria and Sophie swapped patients so that it was difficult, if not impossible, for the authorities to keep track of them. If Sophie had a patient with dodgy papers she sent him to Astrid Maria before the authorities got suspicious and if Astrid Maria had a patient who needed hospitalisation she sent him to Sophie, quite ingenious.

They made their way slowly back up the other side of the ward and finally withdrew into the office again.

'No cigarettes,' Sophie commanded as Tom reached into his jacket pocket. He exchanged a look with Christian and put them away again. Sophie went out to instruct the waiting nurses shutting the door behind her.

Tom undid the buttons on his white coat. 'Actually I'm glad you're here I wanted to tell you something.' He went over to the door and checked no one was around, he then crossed to the far side of the room and stood by the window. Christian sat down and having nothing else to fiddle with took off his glasses and started cleaning them on his white coat.

'I've decided to leave,' Tom said looking out into the October morning. 'At least Tom Grobæk is going to leave.'

'And where's Tom Grobæk going to?' Asked Christian, mimicking Tom's wry tone.

'Sweden.' Tom paused. 'I'm going underground Christian and I think you should too.'

'But,' began Christian.

'Never mind but, Christian, just listen. It's not safe any more. None of us are safe and that goes for Sophie and your mother-in-law too. I've told you before, you join a proper organisation and you go underground, new name, papers, home, whatever. And you keep changing until we beat them.'

'You mean you keep running?'

'No, no one's running. You keep covering your tracks and changing your contacts, and you keep one step ahead all the time.'

'Look, Tom, maybe it's the right thing for you, and good luck to you. But I can't.'

'I haven't finished yet. We get Astrid and Petter safely off to Sweden.'

'And they spend the rest of the war in an internment camp?' Christian said derisively.

'Safe,' said Tom.

'Tom, she's expecting another baby.'

'I thought as much. All the more reason for getting her safely away from here. And you could go with them to start with, wait for the baby to be born and then come back.'

'As,' Christian paused, a smile playing about his lips, 'someone else?'

'Exactly.'

Christian put his glasses back on. The idea of Astrid being safe, of Petter and the new baby being out of all this was very appealing.

'I need to think about it,' he said, worry wrinkling his brow.

'Good man, I knew you'd come round, but don't think too long.'

Christian took a cigarette out of the usual crumpled packet in his pocket and played with it, he put it between his fingers then pushed it back into the packet.

'Ha!' exclaimed Tom, 'so you are frightened of her, and I thought it was only me.'

Christian smiled his slow smile, then a frown suddenly crossed his brow. 'What about the nurses?' He broke out.

'The nurses?'

'The nurses must surely notice when patients change identity mysteriously?'

'Ah, you mean Sophie's little game? Yes I thought of that too, and the nurses have all just been shuffled round so I've told Sophie to stop.'

'You told her to stop! You can't be that frightened of her,' laughed Christian.

'I suggested that smuggling out medicines might be less easy to trace. And I didn't want her little ruse getting me into trouble.'

'She fell for it?'

Tom nodded. 'You may as well remember, for future use, that your mother-in-law is going to be in charge of the most well stocked Red Cross centre in Oslo.'

'Now that really could be useful!' Tom and Christian were both laughing now. 'Well I've got better things to do than hang around here with you.'

'Yes you've got some decisions to make,' said Tom pointedly.

Christian walked down the long familiar corridors of the hospital and down the endless staircases, soon there wouldn't be anyone left to talk to, he thought wistfully.

***

Mia stabbed irritably at the typewriter. The editor had decided, for no good reason as far as Mia could see, to bring the deadlines forward an hour that day. Mia had been forbidden, which also chafed, by Tom, from messing around with her translations. 'You're in a good position,' he'd said, 'I want to keep you clean.' Mia carried on stabbing out the ugly words of rhetoric. She'd been in the group for over a year now and got no further than typing illegal newspapers, and neither had she made any contacts beyond Frank and, of course, Tom himself. She wondered if Christian had told Tom to keep her out of trouble, but that wouldn't stop Tom. She rubbed her temples to ward off a headache, she had also been up late with Frank the night before. Illicit relationships were rather strenuous. 'Dammit!' She burst out after her fourth mistake on one page. And, Siri kept pestering her to join her and the wonder police boy on a date. Mia did not want to meet Siri's boyfriend, who was obviously a Nazi.

***

Friedrich wiped a fleck of dust off the gleaming polish of the Beckstein grand piano with the sleeve of his black tunic and turned sharply away from the instrument to face the window. He hadn't come all the way from Germany to live in luxury and arrest people for sticking safety pins in their lapels and wearing red woollen hats. The long sweep of nineteenth century window looked out over Victoria Terrasse, which was a neat and orderly street, the buildings had gracious frontages and the few offices were small and exclusive. On one side of his spacious drawing room was a study, and on the other side his on-suite bedroom. All the rooms faced the front of the building and his kitchen was kept stocked and productive by an elderly Norwegian officer, who disconcerted him by using his title all the time, it being the only German he knew, or to put it another way, the only Norwegian which Friedrich understood.

In fact Friedrich was generally frustrated by a lack of personnel who were fluent in both Norwegian and German. He needed good interpreters, not the Norwegian police officers, who either twisted confessions to get convictions or spoke such bad German that sensible cross examination was impossible. Friedrich liked to do things properly, and if he was going to inflict punishment it had to be deserved.

He paced back through to his study and sat at the large leather topped desk, which filled it. On his desk were two confessions, which he should read, a telephone and a gold ink pen. He looked derisively at the first page of the papers. It was supposedly the words of some poor woman who'd been arrested because her husband had escaped to Sweden. Nonsense, thought Friedrich, expensive and messy if they were going to arrest and imprison all such people. However the real traitors, to those he would show no mercy. He brought a hand down on the desk with a force, which made the gold pen jump on the leather surface. The failed raid from the previous month still riled him.

The telephone, as if disturbed by the force of Friedrich's hand, started ringing with loud, persistent rings. Friedrich picked up the black receiver with an impatient gesture.

'Yes, hello?' The clicking of the telephone line and the voice could be heard in the room. As the voice rattled on a slow smile twitched at the corners of Friedrich's beautiful mouth and a satisfied gleam lit up his eyes. He sat down on the large chair behind his desk, still listening to the voice. *'I'll be down soon. Move the prisoner into an interrogation room,'* he responded when the voice had finished.

He leant back in his chair, satisfaction stealing around the room and blending curiously with the previous frustration.

'Yes! Now we have progress!' He said out loud.

Savouring the moment he sat up in his chair, took up his pen and began reading the depositions on his desk. He read the first one, straightened his shoulders and pulled open one of the desk drawers. He took out a sheet of clean paper and started to write on it. He wrote quickly but the words were precise and neat. He then opened another drawer and took out a tin box containing a pad of ink and a rubber stamp, he then stamped both his letter and the deposition. Taking an envelope from the first drawer he then folded the papers, put them in the envelope, addressed it and applied the rubber stamp again. He tidied his desk and stood up. He took the envelope and his desk was, as before, empty except now for the one deposition, his gold pen and the telephone.

With long strides he went out into the corridor behind his rooms and started making his way down the building. He passed through the police offices on the ground floor and proceeded down into the basement. Here he paused and went into a small office.

'The Eriksen woman,' he said handing the envelope over to a German officer, *'you can let her go.'*

'Her Kriminaloberasistent?' The officer questioned not understanding.

'Send her home!' Friedrich continued insistent.

'Yes, Her Kriminaloberasistent.'

'Now show me where this Jonsen chap is!'

'*Yes, Her Kriminaloberasistent.*'

The officer placed the envelope on his desk and led the way out of his office. They went down a further flight of stairs and stopped outside a small cell with a metal grid built into the door.

'*Her Kriminaloberasistent to see the prisoner,*' the officer said through the grill. A rattling of keys preceded the opening of the door and Friedrich went in. The room was about nine feet square and brightly lit by a single bare bulb in the middle of the ceiling. Friedrich had to move into the middle of the room to make space for the guard to lock the door behind them. He found himself nearly face to face with a tall spare man with thin grey hair and a tired but closed expression lining his face. Friedrich was taken aback for a moment by the man's age. He had been expecting to meet a younger man, someone closer to his own age, but this man was well into his fifties. The prisoner caught the surprise in Friedrich's expression and a pair of bright blue eyes looked sharply at him. Friedrich turned away, annoyed that he had been caught off guard. He had interrogated enough prisoners in the last eight years to suspect that this one wouldn't talk, at least not easily.

'*What do we know so far?*' Friedrich asked turning to the guard.

'*Nothing from the prisoner. You will have had the report from the arresting officer?*'

'*Only on the telephone.*'

Friedrich knew that the prisoner had been arrested the previous night at the Casino Theatre during a jazz concert. He had been found in a cellar underneath the stage, and when the arrest was made he was in the process of hiding a headset plugged into an illegal radio.

'*The radio was not active?*' Friedrich asked now. None-the-less it looked as though it might be a crucial arrest for them. He glanced at the elderly man who was watching them steadily. Was there any way they could get him to talk, Friedrich wondered. '*Did you try getting a signal with the radio set?*'

'*Yes, Her Kriminaloberasistent,*' the guard looked at the prisoner and lowered his voice, '*we got through to London.*'

Friedrich raised his eyebrows. *'Anything further?'*

'Not yet, Her Kriminaloberasistent.'

'How did you find him? Was it a tip off?'

'Yes.' At the suggestion of a tip off a slight movement from the prisoner attracted the attention of both the Germans.

Friedrich turned again to face him. *'Do you speak German?'* He asked fiercely.

'I can speak a little,' the prisoner responded in careful German, his eyes fixed on Friedrich.

'You understand the seriousness of your position?' Friedrich questioned him.

The man nodded his head.

'You will be aware that you can help yourself if you co-operate with us?' Friedrich continued. *'You were perhaps under orders? If you tell us who gave you your instructions we may look more leniently on your crime.'* But Friedrich felt the man closing up again. *'You are perhaps not aware of procedure here?'* The prisoner said nothing. *'If you don't co-operate you will be moved to Møllegate where your interrogation will be continued. You should understand that we will use all means at our disposal to make you talk.'*

A heavy silence stifled the small cell. Friedrich pulled himself up to his full height and looked unflinchingly into the Norwegian's face. His dark brows lowered over eyes which glinted coldly.

'If it is confirmed that you are a traitor to the Third Reich and your own government, you will be shot.'

The prisoner said nothing. He tried to pull himself up to return Friedrich's look, but he had been standing a long time and he could feel the strain in his limbs. His shoulders drooped and he instinctively tried to step back from the Gestapo officer, who filled the room with menace and determination.

Satisfied Friedrich turned sharply and indicated that he was ready to leave the prisoner.

'Give him some water, but don't let him rest,' Friedrich instructed the guard. We may well get him to talk in the end, he thought to himself. The key turned in the lock and Friedrich

made his way quickly back up into the light of day.

***

Astrid Maria pushed the last bottles of penicillin high up in her cupboard, well hidden behind some old bandages on the top shelf. She climbed back down from the chair she'd been standing on and brushed her hands together with satisfaction. 'Where there's a will,' she thought.

November, 1941
Nine

Frank pulled his cap down to reach the scarf, which was wrapped up over his ears and pulled up the collar on his black workman's jacket before stepping out of the coal lorry. He'd been promoted to driver this winter and had taken the opportunity to 'borrow' the lorry out of normal delivery hours. A November fog hung in the streets making the town dark even though it was only just past three o'clock in the afternoon. Frank slipped down a narrow alley and out into another street. There weren't many people about and, as he couldn't see far enough to spot anyone who might follow him, he presumed that he too was equally invisible. Cutting down a side street he found himself behind a row of shops fronting onto Tøyengata. Counting carefully he pushed open a wooden gate into one of the backyards of the properties where the sweet smell of baking encouraged him that he had found the right location.

He hammered on the back door. 'Delivery,' he called.

A large man in a white apron and baker's hat looked through the window then came quickly to the door.

'What are you doing at the back here? Did anyone see you come in?' The large baker stood in the doorway blocking Frank's entrance. 'Have I seen you before?'

Frank glanced up at him. 'Yes,' he replied, but not in these clothes he thought quietly to himself. 'The code word's Jonsen,' he added.

The baker stepped outside quickly and ushered Frank into the back of the bakery. 'They're all up at the top,' he said indicating the floor above.

Frank resisted the eager arms ushering him out towards some stairs. 'There isn't time,' he said. 'There's been a security leak.'

'Well, yes we thought so,' answered the baker, 'any news on Jonsen?'

Frank shook his head. 'We think he's still in Møllegate, but we're not sure. Look those guys up there – I don't know who, exactly, is sitting up there and I don't want to either – but I think you've got Lars Nygaard.' The baker made no comment.

'Well,' continued Frank, 'if he's up there send him down. He's to come with me now.'

'He wasn't due to leave until tomorrow,' said the baker suspiciously.

'Yes, I know,' Frank continued patiently, 'but as I said, there's been a security breach and we don't know who else knows he's planned to leave tomorrow.'

The baker sighed. 'I'll send him down then,' he said heavily.

'Thanks. Oh and better tell the rest of them to get out of here and disperse. Anywhere but not their current addresses.'

The baker nodded and turned to go up the staircase. Frank stayed behind in the back. He was obviously in a storage room and there was a quaint mixture of wood stacked neatly on the floor and an assortment of baking ingredients packed on the shelves above; flour, raisins, eggs, butter. Frank raised his eyebrows at the sight of all the butter and eggs. This baker was obviously well connected with more than just resistance groups. No wonder his colleagues who had gone underground and therefore had to give up their ration cards still managed to eat, and no wonder this was their favourite meeting place! Frank hoped the present debacle wouldn't put an end to this particular hide-out.

Hurried footsteps on the stairs broke into Frank's reverie and within moments he was joined by a distinguished looking man in his mid forties. Frank shook the man's hand then went on to give a clear, but brief outline of the plan. 'I've got a lorry parked a couple of streets from here. I can take you as far as Ski by which time there should be a car waiting to take you on to Kongsvinger. Hopefully you'll be a day ahead if there's been another security leak and you should be able to slip across the border before too many people are on your tail.'

The man nodded his acquiescence and the two men slipped out into the late afternoon fog. The lorry didn't seem to have attracted any attention. Frank passed out a spare black jacket and cap for the man to slip on over his clothes, it wasn't a very foolproof disguise, but hopefully, in the shadow of the evening, it would be good enough if they met with any routine checks.

The man climbed into the passenger seat, Frank started the lorry, and they drove on in silence for some time. Visibility was bad but Frank had done a lot of driving in and around the town for the last year and was able to find his way easily, despite the fog, and avoid the main roads.

'What's your cover if we do get stopped,' the man beside him asked suddenly, as if finally coming out of his own thoughts and alive to more present dangers.

'I've a requisition order for some wood to be collected out of town. I actually collected it last week, but the order got so smudged with coal that I thought it might come in handy for a few more trips.' Frank grinned across at his companion.

'And the journey back?'

'Not your problem.'

The man glanced at the young man driving him away to safety. He obviously wasn't a coalman by trade and his features bore much more the stamp of the intellectual than the worker; one knew so little about one's confederates. 'No,' he answered.

'I'll just say I got lost in the fog and decided to go home without the wood.'

The man smiled back at Frank and they returned to a more companionable silence as the lorry rattled and bounced along the back roads out of Oslo.

As Frank had hoped a car was already waiting for them. Frank retrieved the jacket and cap and swung back on his homeward journey. It was now late to be out in a coal lorry. Frank hoped that the cold had driven some of the policemen, who endlessly patrolled the streets, indoors. Anyway he thought he'd better not take any chances and wove another long and weary way back. His eyes were tired with straining to see in the fog and he was hungry. He wondered if Mia would call in later that night as she often did on a Friday, but, now he remembered it, she was probably going out with Siri, that girlfriend of hers who worked in a local police station. Mia had said something vague about a Nazi boyfriend of Siri's, who Mia had to meet.

He wished.

He wished what? That Mia was less restless? He'd always

thought that he was restless, but he'd learnt over the past year that he was actually rather steady, steady and careful. The risks he took were carefully calculated and he was proving to be an invaluable member of Helge's group. Typically a job like tonight's was assigned to Frank because Helge knew that Frank would not take unnecessary risks, but Mia, on the other hand, was more incalculable and less risk averse. Frank wondered if Helge had something planned for Mia or whether he just didn't like involving girls in risky assignments, not that Frank really believed that Helge had any niceties about using girls. He still wanted to come clean with Helge and tell him about his relationship with Mia, but Mia had insisted that it was between them and had nothing whatsoever to do with Helge. The problem was that he, Frank, was serious, more serious perhaps than Mia. When he held her in his arms and felt the soft honey of her hair against his cheek he wanted it to be for ever.

The perfect resistance fighter, he changed gear angrily, falling in love with the girl of his dreams in the middle of a war. Dammit, dammit, dammit.

***

Christian unlocked the car door and leaning in, threw his bag onto the passenger seat. Taking the keys from the lock he folded his long legs into the driver's seat. He was still wearing his white coat and hospital identity tag and had one more visit before he could go home. He usually walked or bicycled but he'd felt weary after the morning surgery at the apartment and a bitter fog was drifting in off the fjord. The lakes were icing over and the first snow had already fallen higher up in Nordmarka. Tom hadn't made any move to leave yet. They had just spent an uneasy five minutes together on the ward looking at each other through veiled eyes and dodging round the subject. Tom indicated that things had changed now and that, at least for the time being, he, Tom, would be staying as he was. Rumours of Jonsen's arrest had reached Christian and Tom's change of plan didn't surprise him. Christian, however, could still make an escape and he didn't need Tom to tell him that if he didn't make a decision now the snow would come and it would be too late.

Christian started the Ford Sedan. The fog had settled for the evening and it was going to be a slow journey home.

He'd been busy recently with an outbreak of November influenza amongst the elderly and young, on top of which he'd taken an increasing number of nameless calls. Astrid would normally have relieved him of much of the surgery work but she had been tired lately and had a haunted look which he didn't like. The rumours of Jonsen's arrest and the possible leak in security worried him. Although he was not actively involved in resistance activity he increasingly withheld information on the whereabouts of obvious resistance activists and was under no illusions as to the risk of eventual incrimination.

The last call was the inimitable Mrs Berg of the bunions. Christian smiled to himself as he parked the car in the street, gathered his doctor's bag and went to knock on the door.

The visit was reassuringly routine and his mind drifted away from the old lady and the long suffering neighbour, who had let him in. He paid no attention as the two women gossiped about the young couple next door, ration cards and milk shortages.

The more he became implicated in underground operations the greater the risk to his family. Sometimes he wished he could just spirit Astrid and Petter away to Sweden but he knew in his heart that Astrid wouldn't go without him, any more than he would leave the war for others to fight. An escape to Sweden looked too much like getting rid of Astrid. And what about the new baby?

'Well what's the doctor got to say?' Broke in the neighbour.

Christian smiled and started putting his instruments away. He hadn't a clue what the two women had been talking about but made the safe assumption that he could take the last comment as a reference to Mrs Berg's health.

'I think you'll survive another winter, Mrs Berg,' he smiled. 'I'll give you a prescription for a cough linctus which will help the congestion in your chest.' He made his way to the door and let himself out into the darkening fog. The car engine spluttered into life again and he made his way slowly home.

Yet what else could he do? He couldn't increasingly take

action that, despite all his caution, would implicate Astrid and his growing family. No, it was much better to risk her pain and disillusion than her arrest and separation from her children.

He paused, changing gear to turn off Bogstadveien. Surely he was painting too bleak a picture? But Tom's warnings were clear enough. Get Astrid into Sweden while it was still possible and return himself and operate, yes as a doctor, but under cover of proper anonymity.

He drew to a halt outside his garage and got out of the car to open the doors. Would Astrid ever forgive him? He drove the car into the musty darkness, shut the doors and went back down the street to the surgery. The house didn't look normal. There was no sign of either lights or blackout curtains. He tried the surgery door, but it was locked. He fumbled in his trouser pocket to find a key, hampered by the white doctor's jacket he was still wearing. All was quiet in the gloom of the unlit apartment. Perhaps Astrid and Petter were at her mothers? But she wouldn't usually stay out so late. He put his bag down in the surgery and stripped off the white jacket, he then bounded up the stairs taking two at a time.

'Astrid?' He called.

The living room and kitchen were devoid of life. He went to the foot of the stairs, which lead to the second floor.

'Astrid?' He called again. He thought he caught a movement or a faint noise coming from upstairs. He ran up the next flight of stairs and went straight into their bedroom. The room was dark, but his eyes were accustomed to the gloom and he could make out a huddled figure on the bed.

'Astrid?' He questioned softly and with one swift movement moved over to the bed and sat down beside her. The room was heavy with sorrow and as he put out a gentle hand to touch her he felt that her cheeks were sticky with tears. He kicked off his shoes and lay down beside her so that he could take her in his arms. She was cold and shaking and pressed her face into his shoulder. For a few minutes he just held her trying to control his thoughts as they raced from one disaster to another.

'Astrid, where's Petter?' He asked softly.

'He's with mother,' she mumbled into his shoulder. 'She took him for the afternoon so that I could rest.' Her breath choked on another tear. Christian waited. 'The baby,' she said, 'oh Christian, the baby.' Christian tightened his arms around her, a guilt and a dread clutched at his heart and he blinked to stop his own tears springing forth.

***

Mia peddled furiously to keep warm. She'd left Astrid Maria feeding Petter bread liberally spread with cod liver oil. She was meant to be meeting Siri and the wretched boyfriend later but she just thought she might pop by and see if Frank was at home.

She flung the bicycle down a side alley and hammered on the front door. A light was on in the downstairs apartment, but there was no indication that Frank was home. She hammered once more, then fearing that she might disturb the other occupants, she ran back round to the side alley and picked up her bicycle. Frank was probably out on one of his missions. He was always off somewhere, travelling and meeting exciting people, whereas she, Mia, had to spend the evening in some cosy, well stocked café with Siri and the dubious boyfriend, surrounded by Nazis and Germans.

Mia turned her bicycle towards the city centre and continued with her furious peddling. It was difficult to see where she was going in the ceaseless fog, but a café somewhere between Karl Johan and the Rådhus must be fairly easy to find. Mia put her bicycle in a rack by National Theatre and continued on foot. It wasn't the Theatre Café where Siri had said to meet but somewhere behind, in the vicinity of the Klingenberg cinema. Mia walked past the cinema keeping a sharp lookout for possible venues, but she didn't see anything that looked like a café. She should have either listened more carefully to Siri's instructions or agreed to go with Siri herself, she thought crossly.

Deciding that she would have to go back and ask at the cinema she flung herself around and walked straight into a dark figure wearing a greatcoat.

'Sorry,' she said.

The man stepped back quickly. 'Can I help you?' He asked

in broken Norwegian.

'*Sorry,*' she repeated in German. Dammit, she'd probably just winded some high ranking Wehrmacht officer, or worse some Gestapo chief. She bit her lips to stop a sudden urge to laugh bubble out. '*I'm sorry,*' she continued. '*Actually I'm looking for the Café Royale, but it's so foggy I can't see a thing.*'

'*The Café Royale? I'm going there myself. May I accompany you?*'

This was no private, the man was obviously officer material. '*That's very kind.*' What else could she say?

He indicated that they should proceed along the pavement and Mia turned to join him. The café was just a few yards further up the street and Mia couldn't see how she had managed to miss it. The man opened the door and she preceded him into the lobby. The café had a plush interior and the atmosphere was warm and heavy with cigarette smoke. They paused at the cloakroom and the man took Mia's coat. He handed over his own and Mia's coat with such an air of authority that the man behind the counter gave a slight bow as he took them.

The German now indicated that they should go on into the café together. Mia was beginning to wonder how she could slip away from her new companion. The last thing she wanted to do was enter a room, as it were on the arm of the most striking man she had ever met, and to boot a German officer of some rank. And he was striking, the civvies did little to diminish his impact. She took in the lithe physique, the steely passion in the brown eyes and the refined and beautiful features. He, on the other hand, was enjoying acquaintance with one of the most attractive women he had ever met, and a Norwegian who seemed to speak flawless German.

Plunging into the busy café Mia looked around desperately, trying to spot Siri. Thank goodness, she was there already, sitting at a table in the middle of the room with a rather awkward looking young man with thin dark hair. Siri saw Mia straight away, in fact not many people had failed to notice the striking couple who had just walked in. Siri was waving frantically and, with relief, Mia turned to her companion.

'*Thank you, you've been very kind, my friends are already here,*' she said indicating the waving Siri.

Mia moved towards the centre of the room aware that her new friend was still following her. Siri met Mia's look with a question and moved her gaze to the German with obvious approval. The German pulled out a chair for Mia at Siri's table and helped Mia sit down. He then bowed to Siri and her boyfriend. Turning to Mia he held out a strong, but immaculate hand with long tapering fingers, and not knowing what else to do, Mia placed her own hand in his and he held it for a moment longer than etiquette allowed.

'*Enchanted,*' he said and bowing away from her he made his way briskly to the other side of the room.

'Well!' Exclaimed Siri. 'Where on earth did you find him?' She leant over towards Mia and lowered her voice. 'He's gorgeous!'

The dark-haired boyfriend was staring at the retreating back of the German, and then at Mia, open-mouthed.

'That's the Kriminaloberasistent,' he said, his voice husky with both shock and awe.

***

A sharp knocking on the surgery door down below roused Christian. Putting Astrid gently from him he ran down the stairs barefooted, and feeling his way in the gloom he cautiously opened the door out onto the street. Astrid Maria was standing there, hand raised to knock again and the two year old Petter was standing by her side and looking up at his father.

'Mamma didn't come,' the child said accusingly.

Christian opened the door and scooped the child up into his arms. 'Mamma isn't well.'

'It's freezing in here,' said Astrid Maria, deciding not to take her coat off.

'Come upstairs and we can put some lights on.' Christian led the way up into the living room. He switched the electric light on and drew the heavy curtains closed. Astrid Maria blew the turf, smouldering on the fire, into life and added some precious pieces of coal. Christian put Petter down next to her.

'I'll just go up to Astrid,' he said.

In the bedroom he also switched on a small lamp and drew the curtains. Astrid stirred on the bed.

'Are you sure about the baby?' He asked, his voice sounding loud in the quiet room.

Astrid nodded from her pillow.

'Here put your pyjamas on and get properly into the bed.' He helped her undress and get into the bed and propped her up against the white pillows. Her face was bruised with loss and tears.

'I started bleeding about a week ago, and then today...' she stopped, swallowing more unbidden tears.

'You didn't tell me.' Guilt made Christian sound accusing.

'I thought, I hoped it would just go away. And then you've been busy and...'

Christian sighed heavily. He sat down on the bed and rubbed her cold hands between his own. She leant back on the pillows. Christian stood up.

'Astrid Maria and Petter are downstairs. I'll make a hot drink and come back up.' He paused. 'I'd like to examine you, Astrid,' he said quietly.

She nodded her acquiescence and Christian went back down the stairs. The fire was now glowing healthily in the grate and Astrid Maria had already set water to warm on the small electric stove in the kitchen. Petter was playing with a toy truck on the hearthrug. Christian went through to Astrid Maria.

'She's lost the baby,' he said, hating the heavy words hanging in the gloomy kitchen.

'I'm not stupid,' Astrid Maria said looking at him sharply. Christian should have recognised the signs before now.

'Is she all right?' Astrid Maria questioned. Christian opened his mouth to reply but she interrupted him. 'I mean physically?'

'I don't know. I'm going to look at her now. I wondered...I mean what about Petter?'

'Petter's fine. I can take him home again if need be, but she may want him near her. Go up and check her over while I make some coffee.'

Glad that someone else was taking charge Christian went down to get his doctor's bag and then made his way slowly back up to Astrid.

Astrid Maria came up with some coffee a little while later. Petter crawled up the stairs behind her and stood next to her in the bedroom clutching onto her skirt. Christian took the coffee and put it by the bed. Astrid was calmer now. She turned when she saw Petter and stretched out her hand to him and he ran over to her and climbed into the bed beside her. Astrid Maria indicated to Christian that they should leave mother and child, and Christian followed her back down the stairs.

'Here, I made you a sandwich as well,' she said to Christian handing him coffee and a plate of food.

Christian put the food and drink down on the table and stood awkwardly in the middle of the room. 'I think she's okay, but there's a slight swelling and she has a fever. I should probably try and get her some penicillin in the morning.'

'You can leave that with me,' said Astrid Maria, not without a small amount of self-satisfaction.

Christian managed a wry smile. 'I won't ask you how,' he said.

'Now warm yourself and eat something.'

'What about?' He jerked his head in the direction of the stairs.

'I expect they're both fast asleep by now.'

Christian smiled again and sat down gratefully with his sandwich.

'Well I'll be going then,' said Astrid Maria. She let herself out and Christian sat munching his food.

He sat looking into the dying fire. His family, which had been growing and blossoming, in his imagination safe in Sweden, was now small and vulnerable. Christian no longer had the heart to cast them loose in a landscape of war, even if it were possible that Astrid would be well enough to travel.

Rousing himself he went quietly up the stairs. Mother and child were sleeping and their measured breathing filled the room with a soothing calm. He leant against the doorframe and stood watching them for some time.

***

Friedrich strode down the dark, empty streets, strains of Schubert echoed in his head. The murky fog of the day was finally clearing and, as Friedrich reached the harbour, a magical expanse of water was just coming into view, glimmering and dancing in the light of the moon, which was slowly revealing itself.

Friedrich had stood at the bar in the Café Royale drinking a slow beer and watching the Norwegian girl. He had traced the line of a slim wrist as her hands expressed some point she was making, he had followed the line of her slender neck and shoulders, he had imagined the lively intelligence, which her demeanour suggested.

The music came to life in Friedrich's thoughts. His fingers touched the delicate keys of imaginary notes and a soft refrain escaped his lips.

> *Ich hőrt' ein Bächlein rauschen*
> *Wohl aus dem Felsenquell,*
> *Hinab zum Tale rauschen*
> *So frisch und wunderhell.*

> *Ich weiß nicht, wie mir wurde...*

'I don't know what came over me...'

Friedrich paused and turned to walk along the harbour front. The song still dominated his thoughts and his feet skipped a few light steps. He now had a face for his *Schőne Müllerin.*

24th December, 1941

Ten

Christian stamped his feet to keep warm. It was a beautiful day, but cold. He lit a cigarette and watched the motley crowd of people weave their way out of the church. Christmas bells were ringing out with a rather defiant air. Petter was stamping up a snowy bank beside him and sliding down the hard packed snow with gurgles of delight.

'Pappa, Pappa, look at me. See how fast I can go.'

He was wearing a snow suit, which they had managed to get in exchange for an old winter coat of Christian's.

Tom emerged out of the church into the brightness of day. 'Might have known you'd be here,' he said. 'Here, lend me a cigarette.'

Christian offered the packet to Tom then lit the cigarette for him. 'You can have it,' he smiled, 'as it's Christmas.'

'Uncle Tom, Uncle Tom,' called out Petter and as Tom turned to greet the child he was met with a powdery snowball which spattered over his greatcoat. Tom laughed and drew deeply on his cigarette.

Mrs Berg of the bunions was approaching them. She looked askance at Petter.

'Don't throw any snowballs,' Christian admonished the child and Petter contented himself with hurling himself down the now icy slope he had made.

'Happy Christmas, Mrs Berg,' Christian said to the old woman.

'And to you too,' she answered.

'I hope you managed to get the linctus?'

'Yes I did, but it wasn't easy, Marit had to queue for two hours!'

'It's sad times,' commented Christian.

'Yes, Doctor, it is indeed.' She turned to leave them and Tom moved nearer to Christian.

'The old witch, she's obviously as bad as ever. I can't understand why you haven't killed her off years ago.'

Christian burst out laughing. 'What are the others doing?'

He asked, stamping his feet again as the cold crept insidiously through the thick soles of his shoes.

'Ah, here's the delectable Mia with my plump cousin.'

Siri and Mia came towards them and Siri waved a door key up at them. 'Mummy said we could go on ahead. The others are coming in a minute.'

Mia exchanged a greeting with Tom and turned to take her nephew into her arms.

'Come on little man,' she said, 'now we can go to Auntie Siri's house and make dinner.'

'Will there be presents?'

'Oh well, we'll have to see about that. What do you think, Pappa,' she said turning to Christian, 'do you think Petter deserves any presents this year?'

Tom came up and took the child from her. 'Well, I don't think there should be presents for little boys who throw snowballs.' Petter looked into Tom's face uncertainly and his lower lip began to quiver.

'Here, give him to me,' said Christian laughing, 'you're frightening the child.'

'Great bedside manner you must have,' Mia joined in, smiling provocatively.

Christian lifted Petter onto his shoulders and they all turned to walk long the crisp snow on the pavements towards the Grobæk's house.

***

Astrid Maria, Siri's mother and Astrid busied themselves preparing boiled cod. In combining resources between the two families they were looking forward to quite a feast this Christmas. Christian had been given a large cod by a grateful patient, Astrid Maria had a generous supply of potatoes smuggled in from her brother in Hønefoss and Mrs Grobæk had been saving sugar rations for the last two months, and, after some astute bargaining with the local baker, had managed to make a large cake stuffed with dried fruit and heavily spiced. The final addition to the festivities had been a bottle of aquavit, which Tom had produced with a flourish. Its provenance was unknown.

The kitchen was awash with steam and condensation ran down the cold windows. The pungent smell of the fish mixed with the heady Christmas spices lifted the women's spirits as they worked together. Astrid was at the modern stainless steel sink washing up kitchen utensils and Astrid Maria was telling Mrs Grobæk how to cook the fish. Mrs Grobæk, a large contented woman, not unlike her daughter, remained unoffended and was happy to tend to her cake. Astrid Maria cast an occasional glance towards her eldest daughter, but Astrid was in good spirits today. Christian had been at home much more this month, and Astrid seemed to have recovered well after the miscarriage.

Astrid Maria lifted up the lid, as it bounced and rattled over the steaming potatoes, and jabbed a sharp knife into the soft golden flesh. Five more minutes, she thought.

'Have those girls set the table yet?' She asked Mrs Grobæk.

Mrs Grobæk wiped sticky fingers on her patterned apron and went to the kitchen door.

Siri and Mia were flirting with Tom, who was leaning against the mantelpiece in the dining room, a cigarette in one hand and a tumbler of aquavit in the other. Siri had put out wine glasses in the hope that her father might open one of his home made bottles of wine and was now counting silver forks. Mia was sorting through an old box of Christmas decorations and decorating the table with a random assortment of trinkets, which was giving them all an inordinate amount of amusement.

Christian was sitting in the drawing room listening to Mr Grobæk. Petter was on his knee playing with the buttons on his jacket. Christian was glad to have a day off, a day off from the endless winter round of work and a day off from Astrid's furtive need for his physical presence and his reassurance.

Mrs Grobæk despaired of getting anyone around the dining table before the food was all spoilt. Siri had rushed off to find her old highchair for Petter and Astrid Maria and Tom had started a heated debate on the efficacy of voluntary groups.

'You completely undervalue, not to mention underestimate, a whole army of women out there, actively and silently resisting,' Astrid Maria was saying.

'I don't mind the silent resistance but interference will just cause trouble,' responded Tom, his lip curling.

Astrid Maria made a noise somewhere between 'puh' and 'nonsense'.

'I've treated too many Mrs Berg's to have any faith in either the resilience or the community mindedness of such women,' Tom continued cynically. 'Come, Christian, what merit could you possibly ascribe to Mrs Berg,' he said turning to Christian, who had just walked into the dining room holding Petter.

'Resilience perhaps,' Christian said, smiling, 'but don't go dragging me into it.' He put the child down and Petter ran over to his mother, who was standing quietly on the other side of the table.

Mia came in with heated plates and set them at the head of the table.

'Do seat everyone dear,' said Mrs Grobæk to her husband, 'the food is spoiling.'

Mia came back with a large dish laden with the boiled cod and placed it next to the plates. Mr Grobæk cleared his throat and started rummaging around in the sideboard. Siri reappeared bearing a highchair, which meant everyone had to rearrange themselves again and a space had to be made next to Astrid for Petter.

'Least course of resistance eh?' Tom said rather nastily in reply to his friend's reluctance to join in the argument with Astrid Maria.

Mia reappeared with two steaming tureens of potatoes.

Mr Grobæk emerged triumphantly from the sideboard bearing a bottle of home made wine. Siri winked at Mia and her father began graciously positioning his guests.

The wine and the food, coupled with the decadence of a blazing fire filled the room with a repleteness only out-matched by Petter who, after glutting himself on fish and potatoes, laid his head on the highchair table and promptly fell asleep.

Astrid took the child down from the chair.

'I'll just put him down on a sofa in the drawing room if that's all right, Mrs Grobæk,' she said softly. During the commotion of the men standing as she left the room Mr Grobæk opened another bottled of wine.

'Well here's a toast to us all,' he said heartily, 'we'll just wait for your wife to return,' he said raising his glass slightly to Christian.   Christian bowed his head in acknowledgement. Astrid returned with a slightly apologetic air and sat down quickly.   The wine had flushed her cheeks and a hesitant smile had relaxed the anxiety which had set new lines around her eyes and mouth.

Mr Grobæk stood up behind his chair and raised his glass. 'To better times', he said solemnly.   'Happy Christmas to you all.'   A chorus of better times mingled with happy Christmases echoed round the room, and toasting one another they all drank from the freshly filled glasses. A slight giggle escaped from Siri. Mia wondered, with a certain amount of interest, how long it would take for the wine to go to Siri's head and what the consequences would be.   She had drunk sparingly from her own glass and noticed that Christian, as was his wont, had left his wine untouched apart from joining in the toast in courtesy to his host.

Mrs Grobæk was still waving her glass at everyone.   'Why don't I bring the cake in?'   She announced.

'Yes, yes, dear,' agreed her husband expansively.

Siri and Mia stood up obediently to help remove the dirty dinner plates, clearing up around the replete guests.   Christian stood up and stretched and Tom went to the sideboard to re-fill his tumbler with aquavit.   Christian walked round the table and put his hands on Astrid's shoulders and lowered his head down towards her.

'All right?'   He asked softly, bending down to whisper quietly in her ear.   She nodded gratefully.   'I'll check Petter,' he added.   Astrid leant back in her chair.   The warmth from Christian's hands lingered on her shoulders and an air of contentment crept over her.

The party re-assembled and Mrs Grobæk presented the cake with a flourish.   Astrid Maria was starting to fidget and make discrete glances at her watch as she intended to spend at least part of the day at the Red Cross centre.

'Well, eat up everyone,' announced Mr Grobæk as plates of the heavy cake were passed around the table. 'You could do with putting a bit of flesh on those bones of yours,' he said after sending a particularly large piece of cake towards Mia. 'You're not going to get a boyfriend if you go around looking half starved all the time.' The drink was obviously loosening Mr Grobæk's tongue.

Several responses flitted through Mia's thoughts, mostly along the lines of war time offering limited opportunities for fattening up. She felt Tom make some derisive noise from the other side of the table and Christian, who was sitting next to her, turned to her with a smile and a slight wink as his eyes met hers. Siri, however, cut in on all their thoughts with a flourish of her now empty wine glass.

'Mia has a secret admirer!' She announced, and banged the cut glass goblet down on the table so hard that Mrs Grobæk winced.

'Do be careful, dear!' She couldn't help exclaiming.

'A secret admirer!' Persisted Siri looking round the table triumphantly.

Mia looked across at Siri with a warning expression, but Siri was now incapable of picking up subtle hints. Mia hoped to goodness that Siri wasn't going to say anything embarrassing about Tom. She glanced across at him, but he was studying his tumbler with studied indifference and with a slight sneer on his face.

'Well that rules out the extra portion of cake,' said Christian with an easy laugh. 'Perhaps the admirer likes slim girls, and we don't want to put him off,' he continued lightly.

Mr Grobæk looked confused.

'And I know who it is,' continued Siri trying to regain her audience. 'He's very good looking,' she said, this time with a sly glance at Tom. Mia groaned inwardly, willing her friend to shut up. 'And he's a very important person!' Now Siri had got everyone's attention, except Tom who continued to play moodily with his empty spirit's glass. 'He met Siri at The Cafe Royale last month and couldn't keep his eyes off her.'

Everyone still looked blankly at Siri, then Mia suddenly remembered the handsome German she'd bumped into when meeting Siri and her boyfriend. Relieved that Siri wasn't going to say anything compromising about Tom, or worse, had somehow found out about Frank, she burst out laughing.

'Oh that!' She said, 'that was ages ago. I'd forgotten all about it!'

'Well I bet he hasn't,' continued Siri, put out by her friend's easy dismissal of the story. 'He couldn't keep his eyes off you all evening!'

Mia moved impatiently in her chair.

'Nonsense,' said Astrid Maria looking at her watch.

'Well, I think that's enough now,' said Mr Grobæk weakly. His wife was looking at her daughter with an eagerness she struggled to disguise, a little bit of romance never did anybody any harm.

'How important?' Tom's voice cut in quietly.

Pleased to be able to make her announcement, Siri spoke loudly over the various murmurings.

'He's the second in command of the police force,' she said triumphantly. For a moment no one understood, except Mia, who still had a calm expression of dismissal on her face. 'The Kriminaloberasistent,' Siri finished dramatically.

The implications were immediately clear to Christian and with an unusual energy he pushed his chair back and leapt to his feet. 'That is no joking matter, and certainly no matter for idle gossip,' he said sternly. Siri looked at him open-mouthed. Mr Grobæk coughed.

'Well, no harm done,' he said.

His wife could scarcely veil her excitement. Astrid Maria was still muttering nonsense and looking at her watch. Astrid had her eyes fixed on Christian, who slowly sat down again. Tom was apparently unmoved by the declaration, but there was a dangerous glint in his eye. Mia stood up. She put a light hand on Christian's shoulder.

'Come, Siri, let's do some clearing up,' she said brightly.

Siri rushed after her into the kitchen and burst into tears.

'Come silly,' said Mia, 'it's no big deal. You can wash up all these dishes, that'll sober you up.

Astrid Maria seeing an opportunity to escape began to make her excuses, but was met with the full reproaches of her eldest daughter. Astrid felt that her family had all disgraced themselves quite enough.

'Come into the drawing room,' fussed Mrs Grobæk, 'I'll bring coffee. Astrid, dear, why don't you take the cake through then we can all have more with our coffee.'

Glad to escape Astrid took the cake and went to sit with Petter in the drawing room. Astrid Maria took a tray and began to clear up noisily around the men.

'I'm afraid there's no port!' Said Mr Grobæk in a weak attempt at a joke. Christian offered his battered packet of cigarettes to the other two men.

'Well, I think I'll join the ladies,' said Mr Grobæk, refusing the cigarette.

Christian drew one of the lit candles towards him and lit the cigarette. He pushed the light over to Tom who also lit a cigarette. Astrid Maria stomped out of the room dangerously rattling the cut glass on her overloaded tray, and left the two younger men on their own in the dining room. A log rolled over on the dying fire and little sparks flew into the air like small explosions, vanishing before they hit the hearth.

Tom drew heavily on his cigarette. He seemed wrapped in thought, but his eyes were fixed on the empty seat where Mia had sat, with a hungry fire consuming them. Christian watched his friend closely. He collected an ash tray from the sideboard and set it on the table between them. Becoming aware of the intense scrutiny of his friend Tom looked up and returned Christian's gaze steadily. Christian could now see the glint burning restlessly in Tom's eyes.

'Whatever it is that's fired you up, forget it,' Christian said quietly, drawing on his cigarette.

A cold smile distorted Tom's handsome features. He got up and helped himself to more aquavit.

'You know what I mean,' Christian said quietly. He turned his own eyes deliberately towards Mia's empty place at the table and looked back at Tom. 'She's just a kid, Tom.'

'She doesn't look like a kid,' remarked Tom.

'Her whole life has been turned upside down by this damn war, don't make it any worse.'

'Whose hasn't?' Challenged Tom.

'I'd like to think that there'll still be some innocence left after it's all over.'

'Then I hope you're not looking to Mia for your innocence,' said Tom nastily. Christian shot him a quick glance. 'Your little sister-in-law is not as innocent as you would like to think.' Christian pushed his chair back and half rose up from it. Tom waved his hand indicating that Christian should sit back down. 'Don't get so irate. I haven't touched her. Maybe in happier times,' he glanced up at his friend with a half smile, but Christian was not so easily appeased. 'She's been dating one of my best workers for the last sixth months or so,' continued Tom.

Christian's surprise reassured Tom that Mia had been very careful in her arrangements with Frank. If they were lucky no one else knew about it.

'Ordinarily it wouldn't be any of my business of course, but in the circumstances I'll have to put a stop to it sooner or later.' Tom adopted a more conciliatory tone.

'So why now?'

'If she's going to participate in anything serious it will have to be on my terms, not hers.'

'And is she?'

Tom paused, gathering his thoughts. 'Yes, I think perhaps she is,' he said cautiously.

'Then I hope to God she refuses.'

'Then you don't know your sister-in-law very well,' responded Tom with the same crooked smile.

Christian dare not contemplate what Tom had in mind for Mia, but Tom was right, if there was something to be done then nothing would stop her.

'What's the risk?' He asked, his throat tightening on the question.

'Enormous,' said Tom simply, 'but don't worry my risk is as great as hers. She's the only person who knows, as it were, where I come from.' He paused. 'Thank goodness you never got to that meeting,' he added more quietly.

'I don't like games, Tom.'

'This isn't a game.'

'But why Mia?'

'Simply?' Questioned Tom.

Christian nodded.

'She's got two unique properties. A, she's a beautiful woman and B, she speaks German.'

Christian played with his wine glass then pushed it away from him. A drop of wine spilt out of the glass and ran down the stem leaving a small stain of red wine on the white table cloth. Tom couldn't really be contemplating what Christian feared he might be. Could he?

'You can't do this Tom,' he said.

'I'll do whatever I have to do,' replied Tom. 'We're going to win this war.'

'Whatever the cost?'

'Whatever the cost.' Tom stood up and stretched out his legs. 'I'm going to join the ladies and see what dreadful coffee concoction my aunt has managed to come up with.'

Christian watched Tom leave the room. He remained still for some time looking abstractedly at the pale stain of wine spreading under his glass. Whatever the cost. The words pricked at his conscience, tearing at his peace of mind. What right had he to preach restraint? He, who did nothing but protect his wife and child? He stood up heavily, his moral surety faltering. He realised, with some alarm, that he had always retained a certain moral superiority over Tom. Tom, who'd seduced nurses and pocketed small amounts of hospital supplies for personal gain. Tom, who now put everything second, his personal safety, his friendships, everything, to winning freedom for his country.

When Christian walked across the hall to join everyone in the drawing room he met Astrid Maria struggling into her coat. Mr

Grobæk was standing by the front door regretting that she had to leave so soon.

'Someone has to look after the poor fools who burn their fingers on Christmas Eve,' Astrid Maria pronounced stoutly, as she escaped through the door into the growing winter dusk.

Someone has to look after the poor fools. And who are the poor fools? Christian thought sadly, those who are cared for, or those who do the caring?

The atmosphere in the drawing room was heavy with false gaiety. Mia was flirting with Tom and Siri was playing noisy games with Petter, who had woken up. Astrid was studiously ignoring Mia and smiling indulgently at her son. Christian accepted a cup of coffee from Mrs Grobæk and wandered over to the window. He just caught a fleeting glimpse of Astrid Maria as she bustled out of sight escaping to her Red Cross centre. Christian took a sip of the coffee, a strong smell of chicory caught in his nostrils and he put the cup back down on the saucer. He turned back to face the room and, as ever, Astrid's eyes were seeking him out. His smile came slowly, hesitantly. He put the cup down and crossed the room to join her.

'I think we should get Petter home before it gets too late,' he said as he reached her. Astrid nodded her assent gratefully. She had been eager to leave the party for the past half hour.

'Come, Petter, time to go home.' The child, over excited by Siri, made as if to resist her. 'Perhaps the Julenisse's been while we've been out,' said Astrid wheedling him away from Siri. 'Shall we go home and find out?'

'The Julenisse?' Asked Petter, his voice rapt in childish wonder.

'The Julenisse,' joined in Christian. He seized the child up in one arm and led their thank yous as they left the room.

Having lost her distraction Siri was forced to listen to Mia and Tom bandy words. Their current discussion was alternatives to tobacco. Mia wasn't enjoying the tense air of over excitement, which had pervaded the company and now that Astrid was no longer there to shock, her own part in it felt rather hollow. Nor did she like the more than usually dangerous glint flashing in

Tom's eyes. She would have liked to make it up with Siri somehow and spend a cosy evening listening to Siri's harmless chatter and opening Christmas presents with Siri's family, but as there didn't seem to be any sign of Tom leaving she thought she would follow the others home, although Astrid Maria would be out and their apartment cold and dismal. She could have spent Christmas with Frank. He was with his uncle in Holmenkollen. Frank had wanted to invite Mia and introduce her to his family but Mia had refused. She still hoped to do something with Tom's group and once she and Frank were openly engaged she could say good bye to any involvement with resistance operations. Tom might even carry out his threat and send her to Sweden. The last place Mia wanted to spend the war was in an internment camp in Sweden.

Pulling herself away from the fire, she refused Mrs Grobæk's offer of a second cup of chicory coffee and said that she thought she'd better get home.

'Well, if we can't persuade you,' said Mr Grobæk, as she made for the door. 'The night's drawing in and I don't like the thought of you girls out on your own in the dark.'

Mia smiled weakly and slipped out to get her coat. In the middle of her thank yous she noticed that Tom had joined them in the entrance hall and was putting on his coat behind her.

'I'll walk you home,' he said.

'That's very considerate of you, Tom, I'm sure,' said Mr Grobæk. 'Will you be joining us later?' He addressed the question to Tom.

'No, but thank you,' Tom replied tersely.

Mia struggled into her galoshes wondering how she could get rid of Tom and deciding that she had better just resign herself to the company, besides it was only a few minutes to her home. Tom took her elbow and led her across the square at a quick pace. He glanced back at his uncle's house. The curtains were safely drawn closed and no giveaway beam of light showed that anyone was watching them.

Mia was fiddling with the door lock and Tom was standing close beside her. She could smell the aquavit on his breath. At least soon she'd be on her own. She opened the door but as she stepped inside Tom put his foot in the doorway. He checked the street for casual observers and, satisfied, followed her into the apartment building.

'What the...' began Mia.

'Not here. Get us upstairs as quickly and quietly as possible before any prying eyes see us,' Tom hissed softly.

Alarmed, but not knowing what else to do Mia led them quickly up the stairs and into the apartment. She hoped he wasn't going to embarrass them both by making a pass at her. He hadn't shown any especial interest in her before, but he had drunk a lot this afternoon.

The apartment was cold.

'I'll see if I can get the stove going in the kitchen,' Mia said and Tom followed her into the kitchen at the back of the building. He halted Mia's hand on the light switch and with a swift step drew the curtain closed first.

'Now you can put the light on,' he said.

He watched her quietly as she blew life into the embers in the stove. She put a little of the precious wood and coal onto the fire, then sitting back on her heels she stood up and faced Tom.

'I've got a job for you,' he announced abruptly.

'Oh?' A ripple of excitement caught in Mia's chest.

'That German officer, how much was Siri exaggerating the story?'

'The German?' Mia responded, not understanding at first.

'The Gestapo officer. Is there any truth in Siri's words?'

'I, er,' Mia hesitated, wondering where the conversation was leading. 'Look I didn't pay it any attention and I can't understand why Siri should suddenly bring it all up now. I met him on that one occasion, over a month ago.'

'But you did meet him?'

'I bumped into him while trying to find my way to the Café Royale to meet Siri and her boyfriend. He, the, er, German, took me there. That's all there is to it. I don't see why it should arouse so much interest.'

'How did Siri know his title?' Asked Tom. 'You do know

what that title means don't you?'

'Second in command of the central police station here in Oslo,' Mia replied reluctantly.

'Second in command of the Gestapo in Oslo,' elaborated Tom. There was a pause. 'Well, how did Siri know that?' Tom asked again, a slight irritation tensing his voice.

Mia spoke slowly. 'Siri's boyfriend works at Siri's police station. He's Norwegian, but he's obviously a sympathiser,' she said carefully. She didn't want to get Siri into trouble. 'Anyway, he recognised the German, and I don't doubt his knowledge. Besides,' she continued, 'the man had an air of authority. He was certainly an officer, and a high ranking one at that.'

'Gestapo?'

Mia nodded. 'He was in plain clothes, and, as I say, I felt no need to question Siri's boyfriend's assertion.' She looked at Tom warily, he was gazing at her with a burning intensity.

'And did he fancy you?'

'Well, I wouldn't know,' responded Mia lightly.

'To hell with that, you know perfectly well whether a man is interested in you or not.' For a moment an unbidden pain flashed across his face and was hidden again.

Mia paused. 'He was interested,' she said simply.

'Good,' Tom stepped back a little, relaxing. 'Good.' He looked steadily at Mia before continuing. 'You get back to the Café Royale, meet him again and,' a slight pause, 'do what ever you have to do to get him interested in you.'

Mia looked at him blankly, not wanting the words to make sense.

'For goodness sake, Mia, you develop a relationship with this man,' Tom burst out.

Mia blinked, for a moment stunned. 'You're telling me to date him?'

'You'll have to do more than date him,' broke in Tom crudely. 'I'm telling you to have an affair with him.'

'But,' the words died on her lips. What about Frank? If she told Tom about Frank now he would have to drop the whole silly scheme and she would end up in an internment camp in Sweden. Whereas if she stayed here? 'Explain to me what you have dreamt up,' she said coolly.

Tom flashed her an approving look. 'I've been waiting for an opportunity to infiltrate Victoria Terrasse and this could mean not only Victoria Terrasse, but the Gestapo as well.'

'You want me to be a sort of spy?'

Tom nodded.

'You can't be serious!'

'Try me!'

'What if it doesn't work? It can't possibly work!'

'Then there's no harm done. Nothing ventured...' he added more lightly.

'And what makes you think I'll do it, or even be able to do it? If I'm arrested I could bring the whole movement down!' She suddenly exclaimed.

Tom nodded. 'The stakes are high,' he said quietly.

'I need time to think.'

'There isn't time.' Tom continued to watch her closely. 'I'm going to move Frank undercover,' he said. Mia caught his eye and saw that he knew perfectly well about her relationship with Frank. 'You have to stop seeing him.'

'What else do I have to do?'

It was a step towards agreement, and Tom was well aware of it.

'You have to drop the group, everything. Keep your job, which is good cover in itself. You'll do nothing. I'll arrange for someone to contact you in the street, ride next to you on a bicycle, you know the arrangements. This will be the last time you have any contact with me, or anyone else for that matter. Don't try to leave messages yourself. Always wait, whatever the consequences.'

Mia nodded, stunned and dumbfounded. She had got herself a job at last, and like a sleep walker she could already feel herself walking into it.

'I need your answer now,' pushed Tom.

She nodded again. She lifted her head up and looked him

squarely in the eye. 'I'll do it,' she said.

A painful crack swept across Tom's face, then his lip curled into a cynical smile. 'You're a natural,' he said, but there was a bitter edge to his voice.

Mia was too rapt up in her own thoughts to pay Tom any further attention. What was she thinking of? Tom was already leaving and in a few moments there would be no going back. A rush of confusion pounded round her head. First, whatever Tom said, she would have to see Frank, and then?

Her agile mind was already planning how she could meet up with Oslo's Kriminaloberasistent for a second time.

Eleven

Astrid finished writing up her notes on the last patient and placed them carefully in the file. Thinking she had better check that no one else had come in late, she went through to the waiting area where it was wonderfully quiet. She put some turf in the stove and turned it down, then went over to the outside door and locked it. The floor was a mass of melting pools of snow so she collected the cloth and bucket from the back hallway and mopped up the mess. She then went back to the consulting room, took off her white doctor's coat, put away the patient files and, after checking that everything was in order, she went up to the flat above the surgery. It was cold and unusually silent because no one else was at home. She plugged in a small electric heater that she had managed to acquire from her Aunt Elisabeth and Uncle Gunnar, the couple who ran the hardware shop in Bogstadveien.

She looked at her watch and noted that it was already one o'clock, by which time Astrid Maria and Petter were usually home. Astrid Maria had taken Petter out on the Holmenkoll banen, her plan being to take the train to the top of the hill and play in the snow as, despite the bitter cold, the sun was shining brightly. Christian was out on home visits. Astrid didn't keep a check on home visits and Christian's record keeping was deliberately inadequate and muddled. Prompted by Astrid Maria, who had offered to look after Petter for two mornings a week, Astrid had offered to do morning surgery those same two mornings, which gave Christian more time for hospital work and visits. She suspected some collusion between Christian and her mother, at least on her mother's part, but she enjoyed working again as it gave her a sense of usefulness beyond the home.

A sharp tap at the surgery door down below broke into her thoughts. She hoped it wasn't a patient or some mysterious, urgent call for Christian. She went down the stairs to the waiting room and opened the door cautiously. Mia was standing outside stamping her feet impatiently and knocking her gloved hands together to keep warm. For a moment the two sisters eyed each other uncertainly before Astrid opened the door wide to let Mia in. She noticed with dismay the fresh trail of wet snow left by Mia's boots as she crossed the room.

'Is Christian home?' Mia asked.

Astrid shook her head. 'He does visits on Mondays and Wednesdays,' she said.

'Oh.' Mia wondered silently what the visits entailed.

'He usually goes onto the hospital on Mondays and isn't back until four.'

'Oh,' Mia said again.

'Do you want to come up? I was going to have a hot drink and a slice of bread,' Astrid said by way of invitation.

Mia wasn't quite sure what she wanted to do, having feigned sick at work she had gained free time, which she didn't know what to do with. She had spent a fraught evening with Frank the night before and for no logical reason had decided she wanted to see Christian. Not that Christian would approve of what she was planning to do if he knew, just that somehow things always felt normal around Christian.

She struggled out of her galoshes and followed Astrid up the stairs.

'Isn't Petter home?'

'No, he's out with mother.'

'Oh?' Mia questioned.

'She looks after him on Mondays and Wednesdays so that I can take morning surgery.'

'Oh!' Mia repeated, this time surprised. She didn't really think of her sister as a working mother.

Astrid came out of the kitchen with some bread spread with a little fish based margarine and two cups of Astrid Maria's coffee mix. 'Let's sit in here, it's a bit warmer.'

Mia noticed the electric heater. 'Where did you manage to get that from?'

'Aunt Elisabeth. We did a sort of Christmas exchange, I gave her some pills for her back and she reduced the price of the heater.' Astrid blushed slightly at the implied irregularity, but as everyone else swapped things all the time why shouldn't she?

'Good for you,' said Mia. 'I don't think I've got anything out of her since my confirmation.'

'I didn't exactly get it out of her, I did pay for it.'

'What on earth does Mother do with Petter all morning?' Mia asked, changing the subject, 'Take him to her Red Cross centre?'

'They were taking the train up to Frognerseteren to play in the snow.'

Mia burst out laughing, playing in the snow, now that was normal. 'Petter will be freezing by now. She's had him all morning you say?'

Astrid nodded, unable to resist a smile herself. 'Actually she's wonderful really. I'm not sure what I'd do without her.'

'I know what I'd do,' Mia said jokingly, 'I'd keep the apartment warmer! She's taken to marking the fuel and counts how many logs, pieces of coal and turf we can use each day!'

'Well at least I've warmed up now,' Mia continued after a pause.

'Shouldn't you be at work?' Astrid asked suddenly.

'Yes. I sent a message to say I was sick, but maybe I should go in now.' Mia stood up to leave.

'Shall I give Christian a message?' Astrid asked.

'No, no, it's all right, I'll catch him later.' There was, after all, no message, but surprisingly Astrid had provided the normality and Mia left in a happier frame of mind.

She had finally caught up with Frank the previous evening after having despaired of ever finding him. He had vanished from his flat before the New Year and there'd been no sign of him at the coal yard. Tom was a fast operator. As a last resort she had frequented a dismal café they had occasionally met in and he had finally turned up there the previous evening. It had been a difficult and unwise meeting. Frank had thought that Mia had been sent away and his delight on first seeing her had soon dissolved to fear; they both knew that they had been banned from meeting. Then as Mia had sketched the plans that Tom had for her Frank became angry. He had tried to persuade her that it was suicide and wouldn't do anyone any good. Blow Tom, he Frank could get Mia out of Oslo, she didn't have to go to Sweden, he could get her to England. Mia had to steadily persuade Frank that she wasn't going anywhere. She had agreed to the plan, and, if at all possible, was going to follow it through. Frank couldn't understand. How could she? How could she so calmly contemplate being with another man? It was the same way that he could contemplate blowing up a building even if it risked people getting hurt, Mia had responded, frustration and uncertainty edging her voice. They had sat silently together for some time. Frank realised that she was beyond persuasion and could only hope that the diabolical plan would come to nothing.

The scene had been more or less what Mia had expected, but she had been shaken by his final calm acceptance and his ultimate unselfish concern for her. When it was all over they would get married he had promised. He had reminded her that the key to his apartment would remain hidden in its usual place with the thought that, as no one would be using it, it could provide an escape for her one day, if things went wrong. Frank, unusually mute, had been depressingly certain that things would go wrong.

Mia trudged up the snowy streets towards the newspaper offices persuading herself that there really was no going back now and the thought that there should be no more attempts to meet Frank, or even Tom, made her feel horribly lonely, despite Astrid's brief comradeship.

***

Friedrich tapped his fingers impatiently on the polished desk in his office. He had read through yet more badly translated depositions, but soon all that was going to change. They had started to get decent translators now, but not satisfied, Friedrich had requisitioned his own personal translator. It had taken him nearly two months to find her, but now, at last, he was sure he had found the right girl. The face of his 'Schöne Müllerin', although idealised, was still recognisable in the original. That his motives might be questioned had not disturbed Friedrich's single-minded search after perfection. The girl was called Maria or, more familiarly, Mia Gram. She lived with her mother, and further investigation had revealed a sister, who was married to a doctor and had one child, a boy aged about two years. The mother worked as a volunteer in a local Red Cross outfit. The girl worked as a translator for The Post, a pro Nazi newspaper which had been under German control since the occupation. All her family and herself had been thoroughly checked out and nothing suspect had been found, apart from some initial suspicion over the number of home visits made by the doctor, but during close scrutiny during December they had found nothing untoward. The home visits were easily explained by the fact that his wife was also a Doctor, who practiced her profession, and was thus able to provide her husband with the opportunity to do more work outside the surgery. It all seemed an estimable set up.

Bored with the routine paper work Friedrich rose from his desk and went through to his drawing room, where he surrendered to the felicity of his music. He lifted the lid off the piano keys and, revelling in a first few lazy chords, abandoned himself with a passion and a fury to the final movement of Beethoven's Moonlight Sonata.

Mia Gram was to be moved from her job at 'The Post' as soon as possible and work as his personal assistant and translator.

***

Mia plodded up the stairs and over to her desk. The desk was empty, the drawers were empty, and all trace of her last activities there had been removed. The editor was looking across at her unpleasantly, fuelling the sudden fear which gripped at her heart; she had somehow been found out.

The editor came over to her, leering. 'You're being moved,' he said.

'What do you mean? Where? How? I can't just be moved!'

'Should've come in this morning then shouldn't you,' he replied unhelpfully.

'Have I been moved to another office or something?'

'You could say that.'

'For goodness sake! You can't just move me around without asking!' Mia was trying to control the panic rising in her throat.

'Maybe I couldn't, but it's not me who's doing the moving.'

The man jerked his head towards the boss's office. 'You'd better go and ask him.'

'I will!' Mia said indignantly. What was going on? This had been their perfect cover and now it was all going wrong. She banged on the boss's door, caught between her fear and a frustrated anger.

'Ah, Miss Gram,' he said as she went in, 'sit down please.'

'I hope someone's going to tell me what's going on!'

'I'll be sorry to lose you, good translators are hard to get.'

Mia bit her lips to control any further outbursts and concentrated on producing a calm and nonchalant exterior.

'But you're being moved where it would seem good translators are even more sought after, and it's not the sort of request that any of us can refuse. In short, I am to congratulate you on a most prestigious promotion.' The man continued.

Mia presumed he was eventually going to unravel the riddle, and remained silent.

He looked her up and down. 'Hum, well, as I say, we none of us have much choice, but I can't say I envy you. You're being moved to Victoria Terrasse where the Kriminaloberasistent wants you for his personal assistant and translator.'

Mia gaped at the man. Luckily he took her reaction as quite natural in the circumstances.

'Your things have already been sent over and you should report for duty in the morning.'

'At Victoria Terrasse?' She questioned dumbly. 'The police headquarters?'

'That's the orders.'

Fearing that she might dissolve into a fit of hysterical laughter, Mia turned quickly and walked out of the man's office, forgetting normal courtesies. In a daze she collected her coat and walked back out into the cold.

She was stunned. It was impossible. It couldn't possibly be that easy!

From the turmoil of the previous days she found herself suddenly washed ashore in a strange new landscape. This wasn't Tom manipulating her life, selfishly or heroically, but an unknown being or agent. She walked quickly from the newspaper's offices and, needing time to collect her thoughts, decided she would walk through the Park to get home. Her steps lead her through the monuments crafted by Vigeland some ten or fifteen years earlier, the stone already coloured with time. There were monuments to love and eternity, fertility and the iconography of love and sex. Snow clung to the statues and her feet made crisp imprints on the frozen ground as she wove her circuitous way home.

Her pulse was still racing and she felt the heat of a nervous sweat despite the cold, but was it fear or excitement? With some reluctance she turned from the Park and left the bright winter starkness to head home. Fear, because she was now on her own, and excitement because she was suddenly free from Tom, free from them all and able to enter a new, blank world. She would be no victim of circumstance, she thought fiercely, manipulated by opposing forces, she would run this her own way and not be oppressed by Tom and his crude, perverse demand for seduction and sacrifice.

Lost in her thoughts as she continued on her ambling walk home, Mia didn't sense the familiar presence until it had almost caught up with her.

'What are you up to?' Questioned the well known voice, warm with its habitual humour.

Mia swung round, her expression still dazed with contemplation. 'Christian!'

They both paused on the pavement.

'I might ask you the same thing,' Mia said, happy that he, of all people, should be the one to disturb her solitude. 'I was looking for you earlier, but Astrid said that you were at the hospital,' she smiled, edging her voice with a playful suspicion.

'I was at the hospital.' Christian raised his hospital bag as if presenting her with evidence, 'and if you don't ask me what I've been up to I won't question you any further,' Christian laughed.

He looked good, Mia thought, perhaps action suited him.

'Come I'll walk you home,' Christian said, taking her arm with his free hand.

Mia took the proffered arm gladly. Enjoying Christian's warmth Mia let go of the trauma of her former thoughts until a sudden, unbidden guilt crept over her heart. However much she wished, or wished not to, she couldn't tell Christian what she was up to. Her unreserved trust and admiration for him would now be shadowed. It was a foolish thought, but she suddenly realised that he was being taken from her, both because he would never approve of her chosen course of action, and because she would never again be in a position to seek his approval.

For the first time amidst all her fear and excitement, Mia wanted to cry.

'You're very quiet, Christian commented as they turned into the square where Mia lived.

Mia moved her hand from his arm and turned her face away from him, then, on a sudden impulse, stopped and flung her arms around him. Christian put down his doctor's bag and held her gently. The lightness of his previous mood gave way to sadness. Poor, beautiful child, he thought, she had agreed to Tom's plot.

March, 1942
Twelve

An order from the Kriminalsekretær requiring instant execution lay untouched on Friedrich's desk. Friedrich knew that the order came from the Reichskommissar's office and that similar orders had been despatched to all central police stations in Norway. Friedrich, alone, had a list of nearly two hundred teachers who were to be arrested, which suggested that over the whole of Norway it could amount to more than a thousand arrests. Friedrich didn't like it. Arrests of criminals and traitors were one thing and lead to orderly governance, but political arrests because of incompetent government just lead to unrest and bad feeling. Friedrich pushed the papers away and rose from his desk. He went through to his drawing room and stood uncertainly in the middle of the room. He paced across to the window restlessly and looked down onto the street below, a flurry of spring snow drifted in the air and the pavement was slushy and wet. Distracted for a moment by the timeless flakes floating past his window he allowed his thoughts to wander.

They wandered, as they usually did, to his new assistant, Mia Gram. The ideal had taken form, and the form was beautiful. Having brought her within his reach, Friedrich was now caught between a desire to perpetuate the idyll and a growing need to cement the reality of her presence with more intimate contact. That he had had her watched just to be certain that she was as impeccable as she appeared was a detail, which didn't trouble his present thoughts.

A further delight and confusion was her own possible indifference to him. Friedrich didn't like keen girls and Miss Gram had had the presence of mind to remain alluringly aloof. The courtship game was pleasurable. However, partly through her professional competence, and partly because of her obvious quick intelligence, Friedrich had come to crave something more from her. He wanted her respect.

He looked down over the few figures hurrying along in the snow, Norwegians, as it were, cowering before the face of German oppression represented by Friedrich and his fellow

Gestapo officers. Although not adverse to his position of power, neither did Friedrich enjoy it, especially as it brought with it frustrated responsibility, responsibility not just to follow instructions, but to do the right thing. Friedrich bit the beautiful lips and the passionate eyes clouded with doubt; arresting two hundred teachers was not the right thing.

He swung back into the room angrily and crossed back into his study. Right or wrong he would have to issue instructions and approve immediate arrest of the people on his list. He paused for a moment by his desk. He would have liked to have told Mia that, although he followed instructions, it was not willingly done. He would have liked, somehow, to secure her approbation.

***

Mia typed the last sentence of the deposition she'd been working on that morning. The Kriminaloberasistent usually came into her office and took any work she'd finished, but he hadn't been in to her since giving her instructions at the beginning of the day. If he didn't appear she thought she might take it through to his office. He hadn't encouraged her to go into his quarters, but Mia had been looking for an excuse to gain more regular access to the Kriminaloberasistent's private rooms.

She centred the carriage return, released the roller bar and pulled the last page out of the typewriter. She then gathered the pages together and pinned them with a paper clip. She pinned the original Norwegian document behind her translation and put the papers in a folder together with two others she had typed that morning.

There was still no sign of the Kriminaloberasistent. Mia pushed her chair away from the desk, straightened her skirt and gathered up the papers. Here was an opportunity, she thought, as she walked swiftly across the corridor, and knocked firmly, but lightly, on the door which lead into the Kriminaloberasistent's suite of rooms. There was no immediate response. Mia was about to knock for a second time when she heard footsteps in the room on the other side of the door.

A cross voice barked out. *'Come in.'*

Mia opened the door and walked quickly in. The Kriminaloberasistent was standing by the window, a deep frown furrowing his brow.

'Well?' He said, not very encouragingly.

'I've finished the work you brought me this morning,' Mia said, indicating the folder she was holding.

'Already?'

Mia nodded. The Kriminaloberasistent remained by the window, his eyes fixed on her. Mia paused for a moment uncertainly, then stepped resolutely towards him, her eyes holding his steady gaze. Once in the centre of the room she paused again and smiled a little uncertainly. The Kriminaloberasistent stepped swiftly towards her, took the folder from her and walked towards his study.

'Wait, please,' he said before turning away from her and leaving the room.

Friedrich stood on the other side of the door, as it were, transfixed. As an apparition giving sudden substance to his thoughts, she had appeared before him.. There was some meaning, some compliance, in her gesture, and Friedrich stalled on the edge of the precipice. Did he take that next, irretrievable step?

Mia stood in the centre of the room watching his departing back as he closed the study door behind him. She spun around slowly, taking in her surroundings. There was a table under the central light with a piece of fine china placed on it. Against the wall facing the two sets of double windows was an elegant sofa, possibly regency, Mia wasn't sure, with two matching chairs. A romantic painting hung between two wall lamps above the sofa and a side table with a lamp on it was placed between the sofa and one of the chairs. Against the wall leading to another room was an elegant marble fireplace and to the side of it was a small cabinet, while an antique mirror was positioned over the mantelpiece. The floor was of highly polished wood with a large Turkey rug positioned in the centre. The dominating piece, the highly polished ebony gleaming, was the grand piano, standing in a corner by the lavishly curtained windows. The piano, and the music she occasionally heard emanating from it, were anomalies which both confused and attracted Mia in her task of seeking some kind of intimacy with the musician. Mia turned from the piano and stepped back towards the sofa and leant over to examine the painting, which was a Norwegian landscape. In the growing confusion she felt in her attitude towards her boss she could have wished for something more Germanic and less sympathetic. There was a book on the occasional table with a page neatly marked by a book mark. Mia picked it up just as the study door opened and the Kriminaloberasistent came back into the room. She turned to face him still holding the slim volume.

'*Hermann Hesse, do you know his works?*' The Kriminaloberasistent had paused in the room some way away from her.

'*Yes.*' Mia looked at the title. '*This is one of my favourites.*' Mia turned to place the book back on the table and moved as if to leave the room, but an interest, a question made her turn back to the German; she couldn't quite believe that a good Nazi was encouraged to read Hesse.

'*Wait!*' Her hesitation was enough to encourage Friedrich to take that little step towards his precipice. '*You will take some coffee?*' He asked rather awkwardly.

Mia looked at him steadily, then inclined her head by way of assent. '*Yes, thank you.*'

'*Please, sit down.*' Mia sat down on the sofa. Friedrich regarded her for a moment then crossed the room to the fireplace where he pulled on a bell rope. He then came back to where Mia was sitting on the sofa and sat on one of the chairs. It seemed that his eyes never left her.

A discreet knock on the door interrupted Friedrich's level gaze and his Norwegian servant stood in the doorway.

'We will have coffee,' Friedrich demanded in rather awkward Norwegian.

The Norwegian bowed his head in supplication. 'Very good Herr Kriminaloberasistent. Will there be anything else?'

'No.'

The man bowed his way out of the room and Friedrich turned

his attention back to Mia.

Mia had used the opportunity to discretely study her admirer while his gaze was averted from her, for admire her he certainly did. She wondered why it had taken so long for him to make any move, and was puzzled, now, that he should approach her so formally and awkwardly. That he was handsome Siri had already broadcast to anyone who would care to listen, and setting herself up to be his mistress had been an assignment that she had accepted without much thought to the consequences. But all her machinations had been blown away when he had confounded her by having her moved from the newspaper to his own personal office and from the start it had been him slowly inveigling her into a relationship and not the other way round, as she and Tom had planned. A slight smile played about her lips as Friedrich's gaze returned to her. Caught in her reverie she looked down for a moment and a slight blush crept over her cheeks before she raised her eyes again in a gentle challenge. Friedrich's breath caught in his throat and the conversation he was trying to formulate vanished into air.

Mia smiled more openly. *'I was studying Hesse when the war started,'* she said. *'I was studying German at the university.'* There was too much about this man which intrigued her.

'I know,' Friedrich responded shortly. His brown eyes fixed on her with a longing and a sadness. *'I would have studied music,'* he shrugged and his eyes moved from her to the Beckstein in the corner, *'but music wouldn't pay the bills.'* As if sensing her sympathy he suddenly turned back to her and added fiercely, his eyes glinting dangerously. *'You must understand, Miss Gram, that I am happy and proud in my chosen profession. It is...'* and there he stopped as suddenly as he had started.

'It is a great passion of mine, the history of my people,' as if collecting his thoughts, Friedrich changed the subject. *'Do you like History, Miss Gram?'*

'I must admit I prefer literature.'

'But you have studied the history of your own people?'

'I'm afraid not!' Mia smiled again. *'Unless you count the*

Sagas! But I can't think they contain much serious history!'

'On the contrary, the myths and legends of a nation are what makes its history! I love the stories from our past inheritance and the literature of the ancients,' and now Friedrich was smiling as well. Mia nodded her head in assent to the verity of his remark and for a moment found herself smiling into his eyes.

Well this should please Tom, she thought dryly to herself, as she withdrew slightly from Friedrich's intensity.

A discrete knock on the outer door announced the return of the servant with the coffee, which he placed on the table between Mia and Friedrich before departing in silence. Mia felt a moment's discomfort at the man's studied avoidance of her, but such studied avoidance was perhaps to be her lot if she continued to pursue Tom's plan.

The Kriminaloberasistent was pouring coffee from a silver coffee pot into delicate bone china cups and the smell of real coffee drifted out into the room. Yes, there were a lot of things Mia was going to have to get used to, she thought with a certain amount of irony, as she took the fragile cup from the Kriminaloberasistent. She hoped she was refined enough for the German's tastes.

'So you read Hesse?'

'Yes.'

'You should also read your own Knut Hamsen.'

'Yes, I have.' Mia put the coffee cup down on the table.

'He is a great National Socialist. Perhaps one day he will help make Norway into a great country, rightly holding an honoured position in our Third Reich!'

'He's an old man,' Mia said quietly, beyond that Mia didn't know anything about Hamsen. She had studied 'Marken's Grøde' at school and, if she remembered rightly, he had written some articles in 'The Post' recommending a National Socialist Norway, and she and her friends had dismissed him as a Nazi.

'An old man with much wisdom,' continued the Kriminaloberasistent. This man was going to measure everything she said and Mia was acutely aware that she would have to be careful. She looked at him steadily before weighing

her words and replying.

'I'll read some more of his works.'

An awkward silence ensued.

'You will take more coffee?'

'No, thank you, I think I should go home now.'

As she rose from the sofa Friedrich also stood up, and in one, deft movement was by her side helping her up with a courteous hand under her elbow. He moved her towards the door then stepped back. His mind was racing, and a fear of losing the moment paralysed his thoughts.

'There is a concert tomorrow night. Some of our best musicians are joining your own city orchestra. They are playing Beethoven. You will come with me,' he said in a nervous rush.

A command or a request? Mia smiled.

'I will go with you,' she assented.

Friedrich stepped towards her again and with another neat movement took her hand and raised it to his lips, his eyes were on hers, bright with the passion awakened by her acquiescence.

Mia left the room quietly. She returned to her work room to collect her things and left the building quickly. Once outside she breathed in the sharp, spring air with relief and went round to the side of Victoria Terrasse to collect her bicycle. For the moment she just wanted some action, and she peddled through the slushy streets spraying up the dirty water onto her poor coat and skirt.

For nearly three months now she had worked for the Kriminaloberasistent. For nearly three months she had had no contact with Frank, or with Tom, neither had any one approached her for information. She saw Siri, who was the only safe friend she had these days, and she limited her visits to Christian when she was sure that Astrid and Petter were also at home. In fact she was being so bloody careful that the war would be over before she'd had chance to carry out her mission as an informer. She also wondered how many organisations were watching her. When she had first started working for the police she had noticed a discrete presence which shadowed her journey home. She wondered if Tom's people were also watching her and if they had seen the other discrete shadow. Recently, however, she had felt that the shadow had left her and it was probably no co-incidence that the Kriminaloberasistent had now made his first move.

Mia's thoughts were too confused, too disturbing to dwell on, and it was too easy simply to blame Tom if she now encouraged an intimacy with her German boss.

Mia peddled round to the back of their apartment and pushed her bicycle into a small lean-to. Astrid Maria was probably already at home doling out the sardines and spreading the endless cod-liver-oil fat on the grey bread she made from flour scrounged from the bottom of the local baker's bins.

May, 1942

Sophie rammed Christian's poor little Ford Sedan into third gear and the car lurched into the reluctant ascent of a small hill on the journey back to Oslo from Hønefoss. Sophie had taken a free weekend and persuaded Astrid Maria to do the same. She had then commandeered Christian's car and organised what she called a 'foraging' trip down to the farm at Hønefoss. It had been a long winter and more and more things were getting rationed. Astrid Maria had decided that Christian and Astrid needed a few days on their own and had taken Petter with them. The car was laden with contraband and poor Astrid would never have let them take Petter if she'd known what they were really up to.

It was early May and spring had come with a vengeance. The sun was heating up the contraband in the boot of the car and the sweet smell of ham hung in the air around them.

Astrid Maria opened the window. 'I still think we should have driven over Lommedalen, the patrols won't even need to search us the amount of smell we're making.'

'If you're going to do something illegal do it as openly as possible,' Sophie replied, lurching the car over the brow of the hill and proceeding at a formidable speed down the other side.

Petter was sleeping in the back of the car.

'That's all very well, but it can't be advisable to drive through the patrols smelling like a butcher's shop.'

'Smelling like a butcher's shop used to,' responded Sophie with grim determination. 'Besides which the big chiefs won't be working on a sunny Sunday and I reckon I can manage the underlings!'

'That's as may be.'

The car was now hurtling down the hill, it's speed completely unchecked and heading for a double bend.

'For goodness sake Sophie,' exclaimed Astrid Maria.

Sophie rammed on the brakes, the car struggled to lose speed and Petter fell off the back seat. Astrid Maria turned to organise Petter, who was now wide awake and Sophie drove straight into a patrol waiting on the other side of the double bend. The two sisters exchanged long looks before Sophie wound down the window on the driver's side. Astrid Maria couldn't help thinking that Sophie wound down the window with a certain relish.

A Norwegian police officer approached them. Sophie studied the group as he approached and noticed that only one of them had the black uniform of an SS Gestapo officer, and he seemed to be engaged in a conversation on a field telephone. If they were quick, she assessed, they'd sail through.

'Good afternoon,' said the young officer, a little too hesitantly for his own good. Sophie pursed her lips and adjusted her bosom in true matronly fashion. She looked at the young man coldly and waited.

'Um, I wonder if you'd be so good...'

Sophie put out an open palm to Astrid Maria. 'Be so good as to hand me our papers,' she said, her eyes still coldly scrutinising the young officer.

Astrid Maria handed permits and I.D. cards to Sophie without a word. The permits to travel, which Sophie passed on to the young man with a majestic flourish, were covered with official hospital stamps.

Petter, now wide awake, was standing up in the back of the car and leaning over the front seats. He gazed at the young man with rapt attention then announced with the piping clarity of a two year old. 'We have ham.' For a moment a shocked silence struck the assailants, until Astrid Maria saw the officer's nose begin to twitch, and Sophie set her bosom again with grim determination.

'The child has a ham sandwich,' she said facing the officer with cold disdain. 'Would you like to take it from him?'

The words 'take it from him' registered with Petter. His eyes got rounder and rounder and his bottom lip began to tremble. Astrid Maria quickly taking her cue turned to Petter and with an indirect appeal to the young man said. 'No of course the young man isn't going to take it from you.' Feeling confused and frightened Petter began to cry.

The officer cleared his throat and handed the papers back to Sophie. He cast a nervous glance at his Gestapo superior and Sophie and Astrid Maria waited with baited breath. The Gestapo officer had obviously finished his telephone conversation and his beady eye now turned to the awkward group. The young officer desperate to come to a conclusion, and fearful of the consequences of involving the German, suddenly stood back from the car and said in a loud voice. 'Well everything looks in order, you'd better get the child to the hospital as quickly as possible.'

Even Sophie was dumbfounded by the last remark, but not needing a second invitation started the car. She'd just managed to ram the wretched thing into gear when a black-gloved hand hit against the windscreen. The Gestapo officer turned to his underling angrily.

'*Why have the correct procedures not been followed?*'

'The boy, er sir, a er...' the poor young officer floundered on in Norwegian while his captain looked on uncomprehendingly, and then inspiration came to him. 'Suspected case of Scarlet fever, sir. They're going, er, to the hospital as quickly as possible.'

The German caught the words 'fever' and 'hospital' and backed away from the car. Sophie and Astrid Maria turned steadfast worried faces of concern to the policemen. The German beckoned over another officer.

'*Try and get some sense out of someone,*' he commanded.

The third policeman turned to the young officer and

addressed him in Norwegian. 'What's the problem, Bakken?'

The young man gave him a meaningful stare. 'It's a suspected case of scarlet fever and these two women are nurses on their way to the hospital.'

'In a private car?' The third officer turned a sceptical eye to Sophie and Astrid Maria. Petter, at least, looked all red and blotchy sitting on the back seat, his little face crumpled up with tears.

'Yes sir, but their papers are in order and approved by the hospital authorities.' The poor young man was getting desperate now, he was going to be in serious trouble if anyone else smelt the ham and he was regretting his moment of weakness.

Thankfully the mention of disease, hospitals and scarlet fever had sown enough doubt and fear into his senior officers' minds, and, after a quick consultation the Gestapo chief pronounced his judgement.

'*We'd better send an escort and get them to the hospital then! But for goodness sake get them away from here!*' He commanded.

Sophie and Astrid Maria listened with growing dismay as this order was translated for the benefit of the young officer. The young man then came over to them, looking rather relieved and not a little sheepish.

'I will accompany you through any further road blocks,' he said indicating a gleaming, dark grey Zündapp motorbike. 'When we get into Oslo I'm sure you will be able to find your own way,' he coughed self consciously, then added stiffly, 'but you must tell me if you need any further assistance.'

Sophie rallied with her accustomed aplomb. 'Thank you, that's very kind I'm sure.' She found a gear and, with a large amount of encouragement from the accelerator, launched them back onto the road. Within a few minutes their new friend caught up with them, he had attached a flashing light to the back of the motorbike and they proceeded at a speed which made Astrid Maria feel quite dizzy.

'Well,' said Sophie, 'what did I tell you?'

'For heaven's sake, don't talk, just concentrate,' Astrid

Maria replied. Then, after a pause, as the road seemed to straighten out for a while, she added. 'I hope we won't have to give him any of our ham.'

***

The May evening was delicious. Spring, as was its wont, had come with a breath-taking frenzy and Mia and Friedrich were reluctant to leave the quiet walks of Bygdø and return to the city. Birch trees flirtatiously revealed the first, fresh green of newly unfurled leaves, and the buds on the oak trees were so fat that one was filled with a constant expectation of their suddenly bursting into leaf, or song.

Mia lead the way down the wooded path until they came to an opening in the undergrowth, which gave them a sudden and delightful view of the open sea. The warm light of the early evening gave the water a lustre and an allurement only matched by moonlight. Mia moved towards the water, feeling the uneasy pull of the shingle beach under her feet. Friedrich followed quietly. He put out a hand and took hers in gentle reverence. Reluctant to break the mood with words, they leant lightly towards each other until their shoulders brushed, and Mia returned the gentle pressure of Friedrich's cool fingers. A slight breeze fluttered over the fjord, sending the orange light of the setting sun into a myriad of fragments over the water.

Mia finally let go of Friedrich's hand, and stepped back from the light.

'I'm going home.' Her voice sounded edgy in the still evening.

Friedrich remained standing, looking out over the water.

'I'll take you home,' he said, he was still turned away from her and didn't see the shake of her head.

'I'll get a bus.' She was backing away from him, the growing solemnity of the evening lightened by a smile playing about her eyes.

Friedrich watched her retreating figure, relishing every last ray of her departing presence. When she was out of sight he turned back to the sea, his heart full of innocence and longing.

***

Mia helped herself to a thick slice of ham. 'You've got to be joking! They can't really have had a police escort all the way to Oslo?'

'True as I'm standing here,' replied Christian, a rare smile playing about his lips.

'You're not standing you're sitting,' said Mia joining him in the sitting room of the flat.

'Please stop talking about it you two,' Astrid's voice followed them from the kitchen where she was feeding Petter with some of the prize ham, 'you'll only encourage them.'

'I wonder what we can send them for next time,' Mia continued.

Christian started to laugh, the lines of pain and anxiety lifting from his face. Mia smiled across at him. 'Mrs Berg saw them,' he added his laughter filling the room.

'Mrs Berg?' Mia questioned.

'You know, old Mrs Berg of the bunions.'

'Stop it Christian,' said Astrid standing in the doorway, but she was looking at him fondly.

'Mrs Berg,' Christian tried to continue with his story but couldn't stop laughing.

'You mean escort and all?' Questioned Mia.

Christian nodded. 'She thought...' then suddenly the laughter died in the room. 'She thought we'd all been arrested.' Astrid had returned to the kitchen and the last words were said softly so that only Mia could hear them.

Mia gave him a long look. 'Well at least those two are having fun,' she said.

Christian looked back at her steadily. 'And aren't you having fun?' His face twisted on the last two words and a look of sharp betrayal shot from his eyes. Mia held his gaze for a moment then dropped her eyes, confused by a sudden feeling of anger and embarrassment.

August, 1942

Mia drew the carriage return on the heavy typewriter with a deep sigh. It was hot with the dusty heat of late summer. The windows in her small office were jammed with old paint and she'd opened the door to the corridor to let some air into the stuffy room.

The endless routine typing was stretching her patience and her nerves. She'd had two encounters with people on bicycles, people sent by Tom to see if she had any information to impart yet. Her negative response made her feel inadequate and vulnerable. She felt that she wasn't managing to fulfil her commission correctly, and yet the risk of arrest was just as high whether she had contributed anything or not. She didn't mind the risk if she could achieve something, but to take enormous risk and still be outside the action was frustrating and meaningless.

She stopped typing and leant back on her wooden chair. Through the open door she heard Piano music seeping into the corridor and disturbing the sultry heat. Mia got up from her chair and went to the open door. She leant against the doorframe and listened. She didn't recognise the music, or the composer, but the music struck her with its haunting beauty.

Friedrich was a puzzle. He was a confusion of sophistication, even effeteness, idealism and male passion. Sometimes his artistic gentleness confounded all her machinations and at other times his awkward formality and repressed passion both frustrated and bored her. She could still walk away, or at least withdraw, from any further involvement with him, after all such involvement hardly seemed necessary to her position and the furtherance of Tom's ambitions.

The music continued, its cadences like moonlight, subdued and yet redolent of passion.

However there were moments of intimacy, moments of intense harmony, which Mia stored like fragments of gold in the sand. Friedrich's intrigue and attraction grew with each meeting, such that she hardly knew which of them was trapped in the spider's web.

The piano had taken a long slow decline into silence.

At times she was so sure of Friedrich's complete adoration, and at other times she was faced with emptiness, lack of resolve, or an other worldliness, which left her stranded in a real world of objections and difficulties. She remained framed in the doorway, watching and listening in the silent corridor. What was it she wanted from this strange man, this cultured and beautiful foreigner?

The door to Friedrich's apartment suddenly opened and Friedrich himself emerged, standing before her, as stunned and uncertain as she herself was. They looked at each other with a long question. Mia smiled sadly, a smile reminiscent of the haunting music she had just been listening to.

'I heard you playing,' she said by way of explanation for not being at her desk.

'Ah, yes.' Friedrich continued to look at her awkwardly.

She turned as if to get back to her work.

'No, don't move,' he said, still watching her, *'you are like a painting, a modern painting, something maybe by Modigliani.'*

Mia turned back to look at him.

'Do you know Modigliani?'

She shook her head.

He sighed. *'One day,'* he said, and then he paused, and continued as if to himself, *'perhaps one day...'* he said inconclusively.

She hardly knew what to say, and remained still and silent, just watching him. He took a sudden step towards her and took her hands in his. He raised them both to his lips and then turned as suddenly away from her and walked with hurried resolution down the corridor towards the entrance to the building.

Friedrich walked quickly, fearing that any hesitation would further cloud his decision. Through many agonising months he had come to increasingly admire and respect Mia Gram. He wondered, now, what his motivation to employ her had been. Had it been to furnish the Gestapo with an intelligent and able secretary, or had it been to fuel his own idealistic ardour? His desire had been both tempered and matured by his respect for her.

Friedrich ran down the stairs and went straight out through the front entrance. His car was already waiting for him, the chauffeur standing to attention. Friedrich pulled on his black SS tunic and re-adjusted his officer's hat. He had a meeting with his superior, the Kriminalsekretær, in Møllegate. The meeting was merely routine, except that this week Friedrich was determined to fulfil his duty and recommend that Miss Gram be promoted to more sensitive operations.

Friedrich's problem was that he felt that such a promotion meant the cessation of any possible impropriety in his dealings with Mia, that such promotion was at the expense of his own burgeoning relationship with her. Thus he had agonised over the past months, did he keep Mia for himself, or did he promote her to duties more commensurate with the invaluable contribution she could make to the Third Reich? Mia's very skills as secretary and translator, which had made her proximity possible, now meant a permanent withdrawal from any intimacy with him. Whether the conflict of interest was real or not was immaterial, that Friedrich felt it was real was sufficient. She couldn't both belong to the Third Reich and to him.

But how he had struggled. The evening they had spent looking out over the sea at Bygdø had nearly turned him from his resolve to submit her to his country's needs. If she had stayed with him that evening he would have kept her for himself and lived with the guilt. He supposed he was pleased to have been saved the temptation, pleased to be able to offer her services now, uncluttered by personal involvement.

He walked slowly into Møllegate 19, which was a sombre, dirty, yellow building with a forbidding frontage and gloomy outlook.

If only Friedrich had known how little the Kriminalsekretær cared whether Friedrich had an affair with his secretary or not! The Kriminalsekretær wanted results not inner debates about duty and honour. Miss Gram's clearance and promotion to more sensitive, high security work was no more than a piece of routine protocol. He was far more worried about the increased involvement of the United States of America in the war in Europe than whether Friedrich had dishonourable intentions towards a native Norwegian, be she on the nazi payroll or not.

September, 1942
Thirteen

It was the 25th of September 1942 and Petter's third birthday. Astrid looked across the surgery desk at the tired looking woman facing her and pulled out yet another patient file: Nora Nygaard, thirty eight years old, with four children, and a husband in the merchant navy, missing presumed dead somewhere in the Atlantic. The woman was undernourished and badly clothed and had probably been giving too much of her rations to the children. What she really needed was a job, not a doctor.

The occasional patter of feet, muffled chuckles and the distant clatter of baking tins from the floor above interrupted Astrid's thoughts. Astrid smiled weakly at the woman still silently waiting, wondering how she could tell her that there wasn't actually anything wrong.

'If you,' she paused, 'if you worked in the hospital kitchens you would be entitled to one hot meal a day and you would also have a little extra money for...' Astrid flushed slightly, she could hardly say for black market produce.

The woman raised herself in the chair, her mouth setting into a thin angry line. 'I have a lung infection that's all, our family have always been prone to lung infections!'

'I'm sorry,' was all Astrid could think of saying. She opened the drawer, pulled out the note pad and wrote a prescription for some fairly benign and easily available cough medicine. 'This will help a little,' she lied to the pacified patient, 'come back if you...' If you what? Astrid thought helplessly. If you change your mind and take on the kind of menial work you wouldn't even have asked your maid to do three years ago?

The woman left in her cloud of silence and Astrid paused a moment before calling the next patient in. Soon she would be able to join her mother and Petter in the happy business of cake baking which was going on upstairs. Christian was at the hospital this morning, safe, as Astrid always though of it, safe from the mysterious telephone calls asking for 'the doctor'. Tom had even volunteered to cover for Christian that afternoon and Christian had promised to be with them for supper. A little cloud of guilt tried to worm its way around the thoughts of eggs and flour being mixed upstairs but it didn't get very far. Astrid found it hard to feel guilty about domestic pleasures; she fought too hard for them.

In the small kitchen above the surgery Astrid Maria was trying to activate old yeast with some of her precious sugar and Petter was jabbing a large wooden spoon into a deep bowl of flour. The yeast suddenly went molten under the influence of the sugar and Astrid Maria mixed it together with warm water from the kettle and covered the pot with a kitchen cloth. She then turned to Petter's bowl of flour to which she added more of the precious sugar, a little margarine, which was not cod-liver-oil based, and a large spoonful of cinnamon. Petter jabbed at the little grey blob of margarine and Astrid Maria added a pinch of salt and a beaten egg. What riches she had procured! She then retrieved the bubbling yeast mixture and poured it over the flour.

'And now for the fun part,' she said to Petter as they both dived their hands into the sticky mess.

***

Mia had forgotten it was Petter's birthday. Astrid Maria had confronted her that morning, her voice heavy with sarcasm. 'You have, of course, remembered that it's Petter's birthday today, which means that you won't be going out to any concerts.' She had then made one of her dramatic pauses before continuing. 'We are making a cake to have this evening and Astrid is expecting us all to be there.'

Mia smiled at the memory. She was planning to buy something new, not made over, after work, as she earned good money working for the Gestapo.

She hung her coat on the back of the door and went over to her desk where, unusually, there was no work waiting for her. She was fairly familiar with the upper offices of the police headquarters now and thought she would go along to the main office and see if there was anything there. It was also an opportunity to poke around a bit. She still hadn't got further than the Kriminaloberasistent's private quarters and her own little office where she typed mundane confessions surrounded by the less sensitive files. The only information she had sneaked out of the building was about an English woman married to a Norwegian, who had been detained and held in the Grini prison, but if her family would vouch for her and she would take on Norwegian citizenship she would be released. The information was hardly sensitive and the family probably already knew procedure from official sources anyway. What Mia had done, however, was to establish a whole chain of drop off contacts, small owner run shops and cafés, particular streets and meeting points where she could exchange passwords and information. Tom had obviously been busy setting up a network around her and none of the locations seemed to have any connection with any of the others. Tom was clever, she appreciated that, and now all she had to do was get into a position where she could acquire more sensitive information. Unfortunately the Kriminaloberasistent didn't seem to like mixing business with pleasure, and although her romance with him seemed to be blossoming it was strangely slow and inconsistent, and as yet she had seen neither his bedroom nor his office.

She went down the main stairs towards the offices below. A familiar figure was coming up the wide staircase, the black boots taking long strides up the shallow stairs.

'Miss Gram, good.'

'Herr Kriminaloberasistent.'

'You will follow me.'

The Kriminaloberasistent turned on the stairs and re-traced his steps downwards. Mia felt a sudden rush of adrenaline as she followed him. He went past the administrative offices, down to the ground floor, then taking a smaller flight of stairs continued down into the cellars of the building. Suddenly something was happening. Mia followed, her heart racing.

They stopped in a low stone room on what was probably the lower ground floor, two narrow windows, with heavy iron bars across them, looked out onto the pavement. The room was unheated and lit by the stark light of two unshaded light bulbs. For a moment the breath caught in Mia's throat, perhaps she was being arrested! Then she noticed that there was a table with a typewriter on it and a simple wooden chair.

'*You will wait here,*' said the Kriminaloberasistent, indicating the table and chair. He then left the room through another door leading out to the back of the building.

Mia went over to the desk and touched the cold metal of the typewriter. There was a neat pile of paper with a box of carbon paper next to it. She was going to type and take copies, she surmised. But type what? She sat on the chair and waited. Her hands started to get cold, she was still wearing cotton dresses and her cardigan was thin. Tomorrow she would come better prepared.

The door at the back of the room opened. The Kriminaloberasistent came into the room followed by two police officers, who stood on either side of a chained prisoner.

Mia recognised the man. A surge of panic set her heart pounding. She had seen him in Thomas Heftys Street; he was one of 'Helge's' group. And if he recognised her? He dragged his chained legs across the floor and stood to the side of her desk. The police officers fastened the chain which was round his leg to an iron ring fixed in the wall behind her. He gave her a long dull stare, but there was no glimmer of recognition in it. Perhaps his senses were too dulled and beaten to recognise anyone, but as Mia came to think of it she realised that although she had observed many meetings Tom had kept her out of sight typing up illegal newspapers in the little room at the back. Had he foreseen this? Planned it all along? No, it wasn't possible! But she felt he was capable of anything.

The police officers now retreated a modest distance from her desk and left the prisoner standing by her. The Kriminaloberasistent turned to her.

'*You will type his confession, firstly in Norwegian, then you will translate it into German. Take a copy of both the originals, which the prisoner can then read and sign. It may take some time, you will not mind if you finish your work late this evening?*'

Mia thought briefly of Astrid Maria's sarcasm and Petter's birthday cake. She shook her head.

His voice became less formal and he inclined his head gently towards her. *'You must tell the guards if you need to take a break.'* He carried on looking at her for some time. The prisoner shuffled uncomfortably and one of the guards coughed. *'You are cold! I will send something down, a jacket or perhaps a sweater?'*

'Thank you.'

He then turned to the guards, returned their salute, and left the room.

Mia turned to the prisoner. The poor creature was cowed and broken and he had obviously been tortured; by the Kriminaloberasistent? A cold little dread hung about her heart, how could she equate such thoughts with that beautiful and cultured man, who was wooing her so ardently, even successfully? She turned quickly to the typewriter and arranged the papers, carefully placing the carbon between two sheets of blank paper with the ink downwards to make a second copy. There was no room for pity for prisoners and she wouldn't expect any herself if chained to a wall confessing all her secrets. She must concentrate, and control all these morbid thoughts.

She turned to the drooping figure next to her. 'Shall we get it over with?' She said encouragingly.

He raised his eyes to her a second time and then looked back down on the floor. He opened his mouth to speak. At first his throat was so dry that he couldn't form words, and then he began his slow steady stream of declamation. Mia was glad he hadn't recognised her, as he certainly wouldn't have shown her any mercy.

Her fingers flew over the typewriter keys until they ached and finally she interrupted him.

'You'll have to go more slowly,' she said.

A bitter look escaped his downward gaze. It was going to take a long time as he was giving a full account of anything he could think of since he had joined 'Helge's' group a year and a half ago.

'There was a girl in a back room typing illegal newspapers, but I can't remember what she looked like,' the voice droned on. Mia's fingers flew with cold irony.

There was a lot about Helge, but the man seemed to know nothing about him apart from the name 'Helge' and that name probably changed with each new group and each new venue. From what she could gather from the man's confession there didn't seem to be much left of the original group and he had made no mention yet of other locations, such as the warehouse in the east end of town where they had nearly been busted. What if she and Christian had met him there?

Mia's fingers typed and the man confessed. She scrutinised the text with avid concentration looking for clues and allusions, which might endanger others. There was a reference to Frank, but it was vague and ill-informed.

Still Mia's fingers typed. The chill was seeping into her back and shoulders and her hands were getting stiff and awkward with the cold. She was starting to make typing errors, which was very tedious as she had to stop the droning voice and cross out the mistake before they could continue.

How strange that she felt so little for the forlorn figure before her.

She would have to take a break before her fingers froze. She finished the sentence and indicated that the man should stop.

'I'll take a short break,' she said turning to the guard.

The guards looked uncertain and cast each other uneasy glances. It was most irregular to pause in the middle of taking confessions and yet this girl was obviously the Kriminaloberasistent's personal assistant, which confused their sense of hierarchy.

'The Kriminaloberasistent said I should take a break when I needed to,' Mia explained, thinking that the two policemen hadn't understood her exchanges in German with the Kriminaloberasistent.

Not waiting for a decision Mia left the room by the door through which she had entered. Just along the corridor, by the stairs which went back up to the ground floor, there was a small lobby containing a table and a couple of chairs. On the table was a flask of coffee and on one of the chairs was a dark blue sweater, hand knitted in a soft wool. A small card was folded on the sweater. Mia picked it up and opened it out. '*I have not forgotten you,*' was written on the card in black. The script was small, but the letters neat and clear.

Mia picked up the soft wool and pressed it against her cheek. The wool felt warm and there was a faint smell of clean man about it, mingled with a subtle cologne shaving scent. Mia pulled the sweater on over her head, it was much too large and she had to roll up volumes of sleeve. She then poured herself a cup of coffee from the flask which had been left out for her. It was real coffee.

Back in the cellar the guards paid no apparent attention to Mia's unconventional dress and the unmistakable whiff of coffee, which followed her into the room. They and the prisoner were standing as she had left them, although, if possible, the prisoner looked even more bent than before. Refreshed and warm Mia felt a vague feeling of guilt stirring in her.

'Can't you get the man a chair,' she said abruptly to the guards.

'The prisoner must stand,' was the terse reply.

'Well then at least get him some water,' she continued confrontationally.

Unused to disobeying orders the guards responded to her tone and, with a quick glance to check the compliance of his fellow officer, one of the guards disappeared out of the door at the back of the room and returned moments later with a cup of water. The prisoner took it and drank it, but he showed neither gratitude nor dignity in the action.

Mia suppressed a sigh and sat back down at the little desk.

And typed.

The droning voice finally came to an abrupt end. Mia paused for some time waiting until she realised that he had finished. Without asking him she removed the type sheets from the typewriter and stood up from the desk to stretch out her back and arms. As far as she could tell the light outside seemed that of late afternoon, perhaps as late as five. She glanced at her watch. Yes, it was half past five. Incredible, how could it have taken so long? She had typed eight or nine sheets and it would take her at least a further two hours to translate the pages into German. She thought she would take another cup of coffee while they removed the prisoner.

'He's finished,' she said to the guards.

'He has to sign all the documents,' was the dogged reply.

'But surely he doesn't have to stay here while I type up the translation.'

This time the guards were not going to be manoeuvred by this girl, whatever her relationship was to the Kriminaloberasistent.

'We all stay until all the papers are completed and signed.'

Mia thought longingly of the flask of coffee, but some pity for the poor creature by her desk finally smote her conscience and she felt she should make some show of solidarity. Besides which the guards might not take kindly to a second coffee break and she wasn't in a situation where it was a good idea to make too many enemies.

She sat back at the desk and began the long, dreary business of typing up a translation of what seemed to be a fairly meaningless confession. The packed information was irrelevant and out of date, but she knew that the Gestapo kept immaculate files and any information in this confession they could cross reference with other confessions; many references to 'Helge', for example, would indicate that 'Helge' played some kind of key role. Details of events and places could also be cross referenced against other confessions enabling the Gestapo to assess the truthfulness of other confessions. They were a formidable enemy.

Mia shook her fingers out, stretched her shoulders and sat back down at the desk. Translating was concentrated work, but she'd done so many similar documents now that she had a formula for most of the phrases and at least she didn't have to listen to the wretched man's broken voice any more.

The guards took to pacing up and down the room to shake some life back into their own limbs. The prisoner stood chained to the wall, his head fallen on his chest as if in sleep. Mia typed and the hard rattle of the keys hitting the paper echoed round the room.

Mia finally turned to the last page. It was nearly eight o'clock and the windows to the world outside were black with the encroaching night. Somewhere in the distance there was a rumble of guns but Mia took no notice, concentrating on feeding the last papers onto the typewriter drum. The guards, however, paused in their pacing about the room and cast each other uneasy glances. Mia looked up at them with a question on her face.

'Anti-aircraft guns,' one of them said.

'Oh, that's not usual is it?' Mia questioned.

'No, it's not usual.'

Mia shrugged and got back to her typing, with any luck they'd all be out of here in half an hour.

The guards, though, were now alert to the sound of heavy aircraft bombers, somewhere in the neighbourhood a siren went off and they rushed to the windows, craning their necks to see out into the dark. Mia looked up from her typing but the prisoner remained inert.

And then there was chaos. A bright burning flash lit up the black windows, the guards rushed for the door into the back of the building and then the whole area seemed to explode. The impact knocked Mia off her chair and into the wall. Somewhere something was burning and smoke started to seep through the door out to the stairs and then all the lights fused. Mia rushed after the guards.

'For God's sake someone unchain the prisoner,' she shouted after them.

She staggered into a narrow corridor. It was fast filling with smoke and it was unlit. She pushed forwards shouting for help, then turned back to where the helpless figure was trapped, but the smoke was stinging her eyes and she could feel it catching in her lungs. At first she thought she was trapped as well, then she saw a faint glimmer of light further down the corridor. She rushed towards it trying to hold her breath. The light came from a torch which someone had dropped on the floor in their haste to leave the room. A filing cabinet had fallen over and papers where strewn all over the floor. Mia picked up the torch and shut the door behind her, then she picked up some of the files to shove under the door to stop the smoke spreading. The torch light picked out the harsh black print of lists of names, lists and lists of names. Mia shone the torch on more papers. There were more names and each list was categorised according to full blood, half blood or quarter blood. Mia looked at lists and shoved papers under the door. She knew she should find a way out but the lists had frozen her thoughts. She stared, mesmerised by the German headings and subdivisions, the light from the torch making a smoky spotlight on the papers. Names, names she said into the smoke, names, and then she understood; they were Jewish names.

Get out, get out she urged herself. She took the torch and felt her way towards another door leading away from the room. It was open and smoke was everywhere. Crawl, crawl, the smoke goes up, stay down, she encouraged herself, controlling the surge of panic and adrenalin which shook through her heavy limbs.

Now she could hear voices. She tried to call out but her voice was too choked up with smoke. She held the torch out in front of her and continued to crawl forwards, she knew not where. The voices got louder and she could hear the sound of feet running. The noise came closer and then attracted by the light of her torch the person was upon her, arms scooped her up and the last thing she remembered was the heavy thud of the torch as it dropped onto the concrete floor.

Waves of fresh, cold air hit into her lungs and with a gasp she found she could breathe again. She was held tightly in someone's arms and a silver button was cutting into her cheek. They were outside in a street full of people, flame and the acrid smell of smoke.

'*Over here, quickly, someone find me an ambulance,*' the command came from the person whose arms were around her. He then started moving again, but it was heavy carrying a limp body and his feet stumbled as he tried to get down some steps. Mia moved slightly in his arms.

'*Thank God, she's alive. Help here now, someone.*'

Mia pushed out one of her own arms and put it round her rescuer's neck. He was then able to shift the weight and it was easier to carry her. Breathless with exertion he paused and looked into her face.

'*Friedrich,*' she said.

Why she should suddenly use his name at that particular moment she hardly knew, but it was as if all barriers between them were suddenly broken down. They were neither invader nor resister, German nor Norwegian. They were a boy and girl in a broken world and, as it were, falling in love.

Friedrich spotted an ambulance and rushed towards it. He put Mia gently on the stretcher and covered her with the thin grey blanket.

'*Get her to the hospital as quickly as you can.*'

Doors were shut, more distant shouting and then the smoke seemed to fill Mia's mind again.

Any thoughts of divided duty or correct procedure had vanished from Friedrich's mind as his entire being had propelled him into rescuing Mia. At that moment he would have risked everything to save her, and no longer bound by position or imagined protocol the unrestrained joy of love overwhelmed him. The feel of her body in his arms and her breath against his threatened to unman his very being. Friedrich loved her, and the delight, the pain and the horror sent his thoughts reeling from tears to laughter. He stood amongst the splintered ruins of a façade of German oppression and thought only of the girl he had clutched from the flames.

***

Petter was sprawled on Astrid's knee fast asleep, his little tummy a satisfied hummock of sweet, doughy cake. Christian sat in the chair opposite them, his long legs stretched out to the empty hearth, puffing on a pipe. The pipe was a new acquisition; he said that bad tobacco didn't seem so bad in a pipe. Astrid Maria was clattering about in the kitchen and muttering to herself. Astrid allowed her eyes to close and began to relax into a comfortable doze.

Astrid Maria appeared in the doorway. 'Well I don't know what's become of her! She promised she would come this evening and I reminded her this morning.' Astrid Maria had been complaining about Mia most of the evening.

'Perhaps she's gone out to a concert or something, she's always going out,' Astrid said sleepily and unconcerned, the party had been so much more peaceful without Mia.

The faint, but distinct sound of anti-aircraft artillery caught Christian's ears. He drew up his legs and laid the pipe down on the hearth. Astrid Maria caught the gesture and fussed over to the window. She flicked off the light and opened the blackout curtain to hear better.

'Bombers,' she said, 'we haven't heard any of those around for a while. I don't know what these supposed allies of ours are doing. I wonder who they're going to kill tonight? A few innocent households and the odd German soldier loitering around in the wrong place?' She rambled on cynically. Christian shot her a warning look hoping she would stop going on. 'She'd better not be out in all this, that's all I can say. I'm not hanging around waiting for her much longer, I'm doing the night shift at the Centre tonight.' She turned grimly to face Christian who had joined her at the window. 'Looks like we might be busy!'

Christian shut the curtains with a gesture of irritation, and switched the light back on. Astrid had woken up and had fixed her anxious eyes on him.

'They'll have a specific target,' he said, 'it's nothing to worry about, but I think you should wait for a half hour or so,' he added turning to his mother-in-law. 'We'll wait and see if it calms down before you go out.'

'What about Mia?' Both women turned to him.

'I'm sure she's inside somewhere, safe and sound,' Christian reassured them. 'Take Petter up to bed and I'll make sure your mother doesn't go anywhere until it's quite safe,' he added to Astrid. He took his pipe back from the hearth and tried to adopt his former ease. Astrid took Petter up to bed and Astrid Maria stood irresolutely in the middle of the room. Neither of them felt inclined to speak, they were too busy straining their ears for further sounds from outside. When the sirens started Christian's heart fell as it indicated that the bombers had made a strike, which would mean casualties. He should go to the hospital, but

Astrid wouldn't like him to leave her on her own and there was no way he could keep Astrid Maria away from the Centre. If only Mia had turned up!

After some long uneasy minutes Astrid Maria sat down and they both continued to listen.

'No more gun fire or the sound of aeroplanes,' announced Astrid Maria after several minutes. They could both hear the steady sound of Astrid's voice as she read to Petter up the stairs.

'I'm off,' Astrid Maria continued, but as she prepared to leave the silence was rudely disturbed by the urgent ringing of the telephone down in the surgery. Christian pushed Astrid Maria to one side and charged down the stairs.

When he came back up both women were standing, waiting anxiously in the middle of the room.

'It's Mia,' he said heavily.

'What Mia? On the telephone?' Astrid Maria said, shouted almost crossly.

'No, in the hospital.'

Astrid gave a little gasp.

'It was Tom. He must still be on duty. He just happened to see her come in. Look I'm sure she's alright, I think he said she didn't look too bad, but I'm not sure...' Christian's hands were shaking and he stuffed them in his pockets. They all started speaking at once, and then stopped. 'I'll go over there. You stay here with Petter, Astrid, and don't wait up. Try and get some sleep. I'll ring if there's anything, er, urgent.'

'Well I'm...' began Astrid Maria stridently.

'Go to the Centre,' said Christian cutting through her indignation. It was much better to get her off doing something before she drove them all mad with her pent up frustration and anxiety. 'I'll get word to you as soon as I have more news.'

***

Mia leant back on the clean, white pillows, she'd been sick several times and looked rather green. Two doctors had listened to her breathing, and then rushed off without saying anything, surely someone she knew would turn up soon, she hoped. She felt she was going to be sick again and leant over the side of the bed trying to find the metal bowl. Someone reached it before her and propped her up holding the bowl while she wretched over it. Fumes stuck in her throat and up her nostrils and exhausted she leant back against the pillows.

Tom gave the bowl to a passing nurse and Mia recognised him with a start of surprise.

'What are you doing here?'

'Specifically now? Looking for you. Generally? I work here if you remember.'

'Yes of course, I'd just...'

'Don't say anything.'

'Tom, I...'

'Don't say anything, I'm going to listen to your breathing.'

Mia stopped trying to struggle and lay back quietly while he examined her. There was something she needed to say to him but it kept slipping from her mind. The prisoner? The confession? But she was sure there was something else.

At that moment Christian came hurrying up the hospital ward, his white jacket flapping round his knees as he hadn't taken the time to fasten it. A few casualties from one bomb blast and the whole place was in chaos! He'd been going round in circles trying to find Mia, but here she was at last. He paused and took a breath, Tom was already with her and he saw that Tom was examining her, almost tenderly.

'At last,' he said. 'This place is a mad house. How is she?'

'Right lung's badly blocked and she seems to be suffering from some mild poisoning from the fumes, but other than that?' He smiled down at Mia. 'Fighting fit.'

'Good, good, maybe I should ring and tell Astrid before it gets any later.'

Christian bent down and ruffled Mia's hair fondly. 'Your mother's been clucking over you like a mother hen all evening.'

Mia laughed rather hoarsely. 'That's because I didn't show up, not because she was worried about me!' Christian smiled wryly. 'And now, don't tell me, she's at the Centre, waiting eagerly for an influx of minor injuries.'

Christian laughed. 'You old cynic. I shall report to both her and Astrid that you are quite your usual self.'

This fond scene was broken by a sudden hush descending over the ward and the careful tread of booted feet could be heard ringing out on the polished floor and the whole ward watched as a Gestapo officer, in full SS uniform, marched down the room. He soon picked out Mia and the three men stood round her bed in an awkward silence.

Friedrich stepped forward and in one deft movement was on one knee by her bed, his hands enclosed round both of hers. Christian, slightly taken aback, looked across at Tom. For a split second he saw a look of unveiled hatred pass over Tom's face, his eyes fixed on the German. And there was something else, some smothered pain clouding his eyes.

'*You are all right?*' Said Friedrich, bending over Mia.

Mia nodded. '*I seem to be getting the all clear.*'

Relieved, Friedrich stood up and confronted the two friends facing him. A look of command on his face left them in no doubt that they were expected to explain themselves.

Tom stepped forward, thinly disguised disdain curling his lip. '*I'm the senior consultant on duty here tonight,*' he said coldly, '*and the hospital is closed to visitors. You may have noticed that we are struggling with an influx of casualties after a bomb blast in the city.*'

'*I am surprised, Herr Doctor, to hear that you are struggling,*' Friedrich replied with equal coldness. '*It is my headquarters that have been bombed and I am here, quite naturally, to check that there are no fatalities or serious injuries. I presume that meets with your approval, Herr Doctor?*'

Tom made no further comment and Friedrich turned to Christian.

'*Doctor Christian Krogvold,*' Christian said levelly. '*I'm this patient's...*'

'*You are Miss Gram's brother-in-law and I'm very pleased to meet you,*' Friedrich held out his hand, '*Herr Kriminaloberasistent, Friedrich Hirsch.*'

Christian took the proffered hand and then stepped quickly back. There were a lot of things about this particular scene that he didn't like and as far as he could see Tom was the cause of most of them.

Friedrich turned back to Mia.

Mia looked from one to the other of them. 'Friedrich saved my life,' she said simply.

Tom moved towards Christian and the two of them retreated.

'Isn't life just full of little ironies,' said Tom, a little too loudly.

And they both turned to find themselves facing Sophie, striding up the polished ward, prepared and armed to give battle.

'I gather that my niece is somewhere on this ward and that someone has let loose a senior Gestapo officer in my hospital.' She announced fiercely to the whole room.

Christian didn't know whether to laugh or cry and Tom turned to her with undisguised glee.

'Your niece is in bed number 34 and the second in command of the German police force currently stationed here in Oslo, is by her bedside.' Tom then put his arms round the indignant matron and planted a kiss on her astonished cheek.

Some time later everyone finally went and Mia managed to get some sleep. During the night she slept uneasily and there was a sharp pain in her chest, but the following morning she fell into a deep and dreamless sleep and woke from it clear headed and feeling much better.

Friedrich was by her side and looked up eagerly when she awoke. Friedrich! What had she done? There was no going back now. She had encouraged, no, worse, had responded to him in such a way that his passion for her had now given in to his restraint and he would expect a full and uncompromising response from her. And hadn't she already given him that response, or at least the promise of it? It would be an all consuming and possessive passion and she only hoped it wouldn't be a violent one as well.

She had also remembered what she had to tell Tom. She had remembered the careful lists of Jewish names she had stuffed under the door in an attempt to stop the smoke.

She had even remembered the prisoner, chained to the wall,

who had, no doubt, suffocated to death.

She turned to Friedrich, who was tenderly holding her hand. *'I need to see the doctor again, there's something I'd like to ask him.'* She looked self conscious to imply that it was one of those private matters between doctor and patient. Friedrich immediately obliged.

'I'll have him sent for,' he said. *'I'm afraid I should go back to headquarters again, there has been some damage to the building and we have lost some files. I'll come back this evening.'* He carried on holding her hand, reluctant to leave her. *'You will, you will rest,'* he implored her, his eyes full of tender concern.

Mia smiled. Friedrich rose slowly and placed a reverend kiss on her forehead.

'I can't lose you now,' he said softly, his throat tight with emotion and his eyes glistening with unshed tears. He moved away from her and she followed him with her eyes.

She listened to his boots tapping down the ward and then heard his voice of command insisting that the senior consultant, the one who was on duty last night, should attend to Miss Gram as soon as could be arranged.

Tom appeared remarkably quickly.

'Examine me and lean over me a lot, I need to talk to you,' Mia said quietly. 'I was taking down a confession last night, when the bomb went off. It was Lars Underdahl and he's confessed everything, although most of his information seemed out of date, but I would think they're onto 'Helge'. Actually the typed script is probably lost and I don't think he survived the blast.' Mia paused, remembering her own narrow escape with a sudden jolt.

Tom shone a light in her eyes and leant close to her face. 'They've had him for some weeks, poor chap, but he didn't know much. He didn't, er, recognise you did he?'

'No.'

'Good. And by the way 'Helge' has been many people since 'Helge'.'

'I thought as much.'

'Put your tongue out please Miss Gram.'

Mia obliged. Tom then listened close to her chest and put his ear to her lung cavity.

'But there's something else, I found files, lists, lists of names, all Jewish names, Tom. Do you think they're going to do something? I mean round them up or...'

Tom paused. 'We've had other indications that something is being planned,' he said heavily. 'We've even sent some groups round warning those most at risk, but we've only managed to send a handful of Norwegian Jews to Sweden, as most of them can't, or don't want to believe the implications.'

'But what does it mean, Tom?'

Tom paused again. 'It means arrests, maybe mass deportation to Germany. I don't know, Mia.' And then he suddenly turned on her. 'Why don't you ask your friend, I expect he knows all about it.'

Mia rose up from her pillows indignantly. 'Don't you start preaching to me about my friend.'

For a moment she thought he was going to apologise, but he stepped back from the bed and eyed her coldly. 'Everything seems to be quite in order, Miss Gram,' he said and left her.

November 1942

Another wave came crashing over the bulwarks and Frank clutched at the low beam in the cabin as the small fishing vessel reeled over yet again. Helge had sent him to Scotland and he was now on the so called Shetland line in the middle of an autumn gale. Helge was sending him on a training course in Scotland from where he was to await further orders from central command in London. Was Helge getting rid of him for his own sake or Helge's sake? Or was it because of Mia? And if it was because of Mia it meant that Helge's diabolical plan had worked.

***

Mia sat on her knees, hands stretched out to the luxury of the open fire. With happy disregard for all the shortages they suffered at home she reached for the log basket and tossed another log on the cheerful blaze. The dry white bark of the birch log sputtered into life and the flame immediately licked and danced around its new fuel.

Friedrich watched her from the sofa. He was no longer obsessed with the proprieties, just with the girl.

'Leave the fire and read the poem,' he said. He loved listening to her read German.

Mia leant her back against the fire surround, picked up a book which lay beside her, and turned a smiling face to him.

'I'll read the poem, then you have to play the music.'

'Okay,' he agreed.

They were reading the poems by Wilhelm Müller from Schubert's lieder 'Die schöne Müllerin' and Friedrich was teaching Mia the music.

'Then we must eat. Shall we go to the Theatre Café or the Café Royale?'

'Spoilt for choice,' laughed Mia, there were few restaurants in Oslo, even for the Germans.

Ich sah nach keinem Monde,
Mach keinem Sternenschein,
Ich schaute nach ihrem Bilde,
Nach ihtem Auge allein.[3]

Mia put the book from her and returned Friedrich's earnest gaze. The fire crackled and roared like Christmas.

'Friedrich, last week,' she paused, looking at him steadily, feeling for the right words. *'We deported,'* but that didn't sound quite right, and if there was guilt Mia wasn't sure how to apportion it. *'Last week Norwegian Jews were deported weren't they?'*

A slight strain came over Friedrich's features. He nodded.

'Where were they going?'

'They are being relocated.' There was a tense edge to his voice, yet part of him warmed to her question, there should be no secrets between them.

'But what does that mean?' Mia's voice was still gentle, redolent of the poetry she was reading.

---

[3] I was not looking at the moon, nor at the shining stars, I was looking at her image, at her eyes alone.

Friedrich stood up. *'You know there are many issues and problems which have to be resolved before Europe can unite.'*

He walked across the room towards Mia where she sat against the fire surround, then he turned away and paced back to the sofa.

'The Jewish question is one of those issues.'

'But I don't understand why it is a problem, aren't these people Norwegians?'

Friedrich shook his head wisely, sadly, and turned back to face her.

'They are Jews.'

'But...'

He held his hand out to stop her words.

'My music teacher was a Jew. He was married to a German, she was a Catholic in fact, and they brought their children up as Catholics.'

'So isn't your music teacher a German, hasn't he chosen to be a German?'

'You can't chose to be a German, you can only be born one,' Friedrich said shortly.

'Do you still see him?'

A frozen calm descended over Friedrich.

'He and his wife, with two of their children went to America in 1933. It was a wise move, in America it is all right to be a Jew.'

'And the other children?'

'I don't know,' Friedrich looked uncomfortable.

'But you knew these people, they were your friends?'

'Yes, I knew them, but one doesn't have Jewish friends. Do you have Jewish friends?'

Mia shook her head.

Friedrich came back to the middle of the room.

'They will have been re-located, proper procedures must be adhered to.' He held out his hands to her. *'What are Jews to us?'*

Mia stood up and came over to him. *'I need to understand,'* she said softly.

Friedrich cupped her face, flushed with the fire, in his hands. *'I like it that you are interested in my country, that you want to understand it, want to be part of it.'*

Mia looked down, away from the brown eyes, imploring her with their passion. She wished that she could deserve his trust and love all of him, not just bits.

July, 1943
Fourteen

Mia examined the shop window casually. Through the window she had a perfect view of the shop's interior from where she could watch and wait until the assistant got involved with the last customer giving Mia an opening to make a fast transaction with the owner. The opportunity soon arose, and she slipped in quickly through the door and went straight to the counter.

'A small bottle of blue ink, please,' she said to the shopkeeper but before he turned to find the ink she continued, 'I hope the weather holds, it is perfect for a boat on the fjord.' The man tensed as he heard the words. The current code was 'boat on the fjord'.

'A white boat,' the man hissed under his breath.

'Blue ink, please,' Mia repeated.

'Yes, of course, Miss.'

The assistant was still involved in a noisy transaction. Mia leant over the counter as if to watch that she got the correct ink.

'Blaafarge,' she said quietly down into the shelves where the man was bending, 'Arne Blaafarge.'[4]

The man straightened up. 'The blue colour?' He asked, holding up a bottle of ink.

'Yes, exactly, the blue colour,' Mia replied as she took her purse out of her handbag.

'That'll be two kroner and twenty øre.'

Mia paid and left the shop quickly with her unwanted purchase, but the message was delivered. Somewhere, somehow a man going under the name of Arne Blaafarge was under suspicion and was likely to be arrested within the next twenty four or forty eight hours, but Mia's message would now pass on through a rapid circuit of various resistance networks and Arne Blaafarge would be warned not to go home that night. He would probably either change his name and residence or escape to Sweden, or he might join resistance groups working in the woods and mountains. None of that, however, was Mia's concern, her

---

[4] Blaafarge means blue colour in Norwegian. It is a typical example of a cover name used by the Resistance.

job was to give as many people as she could a chance to escape. Her main impact was to stop mass arrests. Tragic though any individual arrest might be, the knock on effect of any one arrest could be catastrophic, as through torture one person could endanger many others, even whole organisations and their plans.

Mia retrieved her bicycle and pushed off into the road. She was looking forward to an hour's peace at home as Astrid Maria had finally been persuaded to join Christian and Astrid at Hvitsten where they had rented a cottage by the sea for a couple of weeks.

Mia was looking forward to following her usual routine of washing, changing and then bicycling back to Victoria Terrasse, where she would meet Friedrich and they would spend the evening together. Having betrayed the Kriminaloberasistent's secrets during the day Mia would then spend a harmonious evening with her lover, Friedrich. Routine had an alarmingly normalising effect on the most bizarre of circumstances and guilt about the cruel world she had led herself into was a rare indulgence.

Mia became aware of the irritation of another cyclist trying to overtake her. He was coming in much too close and before she had time to shout out a warning her wheel caught in a tram line, Mia lurched to the side and fell off her bicycle. She stood up examining her dress for tears and eyed her assailant crossly.

'What on earth...'

The assailant rushed over to her and tried to help her up while Mia shook him off furiously.

'Just look where you're going next time!' She said.

'I should've taken a boat on the fjord,' he said quickly, bending over her.

'A white boat,' Mia responded, catching her breath.

The man picked up Mia's bicycle and held it for her to climb back on. 'Message from H.Q. There's a tip off that there'll be mass arrests within the police force. The boss says be on your guard mid August and get out of town if you can, in case of repercussions.'

Mia said nothing, balancing on her bicycle.

'No damage I hope,' the man continued loudly.

'No, not yet anyway,' Mia responded ironically. She pushed off from the pavement and turned to say loudly. 'Watch where you're going next time,' then she peddled away.

A pedestrian idly watching the scene paused by the man. 'Can't blame you for trying, quite a looker isn't she.'

Mia's thoughts were racing as she peddled home. She hadn't had any contact with Tom since the explosion nearly a year ago now. He was obviously still keeping a close eye on her, but was he protecting her or watching his own back?

Her thoughts drifted on to Frank, the sudden, unexpected contact with the group making it seem suddenly near again. Frank, her fiancé! The incongruousness of the thought startled her. What had Tom done with Frank? She wondered. No doubt he'd disposed of him one way or another. He'd probably sent him to England to keep him safely out of the way, she thought, propping her bicycle against the wall of the lean-to behind the apartment house.

***

Frank stretched himself out on the heather and looked up into a cloudless summer sky. He could hear the laughing voices of two friends from the training camp down in the valley below him; Frank seemed to be the only Norwegian in the camp who didn't have a Scottish girlfriend.

Rough twigs from the heather found their way under his shirt and he sat up. He must be ridiculous to go on dreaming about Mia, but dream he did. Besides which the Germans were going to lose now, perhaps the war would be over in a year's time. Frank wouldn't be surprised if it ended even sooner, as the Americans seemed to be supplied with limitless arms and ammunitions power, added to which the Germans were enduring crippling defeats on the eastern front. Of course Frank was acutely aware that his chief source of information was the British radio and as far as Frank could see the BBC was little more than a propaganda machine. None-the-less there was no doubting the presence of the Americans and the extra fire power that, among other things, was renewing their relentless bombardment of

Germany. A desire for revenge in Frank was gratified by the crippling of German cities, after all the Germans had taken his fiancée from him in more ways than one.

But vicarious revenge was rather thin compensation. Frank felt that it was time he got a posting back to Norway.

The two couples had walked up the path and were now in sight. Frank stood up to meet them. One of the girls put her hand through his arm.

'You'll come to the dance tonight, won't you Frank?'

He smiled distractedly. 'Yes, if there is a dance, I'll come, as long as I don't have to dance.'

The others laughed and Frank enhanced his reputation as the lone wolf.

***

Astrid stretched her toes in the warm sand. The late afternoon sun lit up the sea and ripples from the occasional boat lapped lazily up the beach. She propped herself up on her elbows and watched Christian and Petter with fond indulgence. Petter was playing in the water and Christian was teaching him to swim, drawing him into the deeper water and reassuring him with a firm hand under his tummy while Petter splashed and laughed with delight.

Astrid Maria sat on a deck chair fiddling with some knitting.

'Can't you put that down, Mother? You can't possibly knit when it's so warm.'

'I've nearly finished,' said Astrid Maria stubbornly.

'What are you making anyway?'

'Just leave me alone for five minutes and I'll show you.'

Astrid turned her attention back to Christian and Petter. They were now coming up the beach towards her dripping little rivulets of salt water onto the sand. Petter ran on ahead and plumped a wet, naked bottom onto his mother's lap. Astrid wrapped a towel around him and held him close, watching Christian as he picked up another towel off the back of an empty beach chair and dried his face and hair, then flung the towel around his shoulders. He still had a handsome figure, tall and lean.

'Two strokes today without aid,' he said proudly.

Astrid turned a glowing face up to him and passed up his glasses, which she'd kept safely away from saltwater and sand. Christian put them on just in time to bring Astrid Maria into sharp focus as she stood up wielding a dowdy looking woollen object.

'Good heavens,' began Christian.

Astrid interrupted him quickly. 'Mother's been working on it all day,' she said.

Astrid Maria held out the wool and holding it up let a small, vest like garment unfurl from her hands, a long woollen thread dangled from one of the seams. Muttering to herself Astrid Maria lifted the garment up to her teeth and bit off the offending strand of wool.

'Er, what is it?' Ventured Christian.

'It's a bathing costume,' Astrid Maria announced proudly.

'Er?'

'For Petter,' she continued less patiently.

Astrid and Christian glanced at each other uncertainly. Petter wriggled free from his mother's embrace and stalked up to his grandmother in all his splendid nakedness.

'Let's try it on,' said Astrid Maria filled with the excitement of creation.

She helped the child climb into the costume. Petter scratched irritably at the wool and cast a rebellious look at his parents.

'It looks lovely, darling,' intervened Astrid hastily.

'Come on,' urged Astrid Maria, 'let's go and try it out.' She and Petter ran down the sand to the water.

'Don't go where it's deep without your father,' Astrid called anxiously after them.

'They'll be fine,' said Christian clearing a space next to his wife and lying down beside her.

Astrid watched her mother and Petter as Petter launched himself into the water and Astrid Maria held up her skirts and waded in after him. Petter splashed around happily for a short while then a look of puzzled annoyance crossed over his face. He stood up in the water revealing the costume, now saturated with water, as it slowly stretched itself out until it hung below his knees. Astrid Maria looked on thwarted and Astrid dug Christian in the ribs.

'Look, quickly, look at Petter,' gasped Astrid and they both fell into paroxysms of laughter.

***

Another report had just come in, confirming that the heavy bombardment of Hamburg had continued into the previous night. Friedrich, frustrated with the tardiness of the news reports switched the radio off and wondered if there was anyone he could ring. He had received his usual monthly letter from his mother earlier in the day, but of course it was written long before the bombing started.

It was barbaric to purposely go for civilian targets. Hamburg was Germany's second largest city and the Allies must intend to cause as much destruction and loss of civilian life as possible. And what of all the history, centuries of culture destroyed in a few days? Friedrich hardly knew whether to succumb to the impotence of anger or the uselessness of tears.

He moved from the radio apparatus and stood over his desk, troubled by a new report he had just opened. If only this Hamburg business would come to an end, but if anything had happened to his parents he would have to apply for leave and go home.

The highly confidential report on his desk was the outline of a serious crack down on the Norwegian police force. The force was riddled with traitors and informers and it seemed that all Norwegians were under suspicion. Arrests could be random and in-discriminatory. If Friedrich had to leave Mia on her own in Oslo she would be vulnerable to arrest without his protection. He had to get her out of Oslo until the crisis had blown over.

Could he take her to Hamburg? Would she come?

The telephone started ringing, its urgent tone startling him. He grabbed the receiver crossly.

'Yes, hello?'

Friedrich's face slowly crumpled into horror and disbelief. He put the receiver down on the desk from where the voice at the other end of the line could still be heard speaking. He walked from his study into his drawing room and automatically sat down on the piano stool, but the lid remained closed and the fingers, which may have found some consolation in music, wove into his dark hair and pulled, pulled until his eyes started with tears and his throat hurt with the block of pain and rage.

***

Mia, still shaken by her sudden, albeit remote, contact with Tom and her thoughts of Frank, was late setting off for her pre-arranged rendezvous with Friedrich. Despite the man's unpredictability and passion, there had become an element of routine in the relationship and Mia was still young enough to interpret routine as boredom. She dressed carelessly and rode her bicycle back through the evening streets slowly.

She showed her night pass and went up the stairs to Friedrich's rooms. How was she going to manipulate a holiday in August, she wondered. Wouldn't a blunt request for leave arouse suspicion by its suddenness?

She knocked on the door to Friedrich's apartment. There was no reply, and finding the door to be unlocked she went cautiously in. The drawing room was empty, and yet there was a heavy air of sadness hanging imperceptibly in the light room.

'*Friedrich?*' She questioned softly.

There was still no response, but the telephone started ringing from the study. Mia heard the click of the receiver being raised and then recognised Friedrich's voice as he answered it, although his voice sounded thick and tired and lacked its usual precision.

Mia waited in the drawing room, not knowing what to do. She heard the receiver click back onto the telephone and then nothing. Should she go to him? Should she call out and make her presence known?

Before she resolved on any line of action the study door opened and Friedrich stood before her. His shirt was open at the neck, the stiff collar only attached at the back, and his hair was untidily framing his head like something out of a gothic melodrama.

'*Friedrich, whatever's...*'

'*Hamburg is burning. Tens of thousands of people are dead or dying.*'

He took a step towards her and she ran forwards to support him.

'*Friedrich, your family?*'

'*I know, I mean I don't know,*' he tried to speak. '*I have to go there.*'

He rested in her arms, slowly allowing his shattered nerves to find some calm.

'*I must take some leave and go home.*'

He moved from her and put his hands on her arms. '*Mia will you come with me?*'

The yes caught in Mia's throat and an unhappy guilt made cold inroads around her heart. Refusing to cry she bit her lips and cleared her throat.

'*Yes, I'll come with you,*' she said, her voice sounding loud, almost course, in the room heavy with sorrow and oppressive summer heat.

August 1943
Fifteen

It was still hot, oppressively hot. Friedrich reluctantly changed his light summer clothes for his SS uniform. Mia pressed her face to the small porthole in their cabin, but she couldn't see anything, just the harsh light of the sun rebounding off the water.

The distant noise of an anchor chain running out caught their attention.

'Well, we seem to be stopping,' Mia said, turning to Friedrich. She looked distastefully at his black uniform. *'Do you have to put that on?'* She asked.

Friedrich shrugged. *'It has its uses,'* he said vaguely, his thoughts concentrating on the horrors that awaited them.

'Can't we go up on deck and see if we can find anything out?' Mia asked, turning back to the porthole.

Friedrich paused, he knew he had to come to Hamburg, he knew he had to try and find his parents, but he was reluctant to face a reality so far removed from his current posting and to experience the combative horrors of war.

'Yes, we'll go and see what's happening,' he finally agreed.

They took a small bag of belongings and made their way silently up towards the rear deck. The ship had dropped anchor out from the city's harbour and the reason why was immediately apparent. The first thing they made out was the blackened metal of bombed out boats and the second the grime and confusion of the shattered quays.

Friedrich caught his breath and Mia took his hand. Little plumes of black smoke forced their way up towards the heavy, hot air of the August sky, little plumes of smoke which covered the entire city. Friedrich and Mia held hands and looked out over the ruin of his home, they had neither experienced, nor imagined, destruction on such a large scale before.

'Perhaps...' Mia started, then stopped again, and they both stared out at the blackened city, stunned and shocked.

After some time, neither of them were aware whether it was a short time or a long time, one of the ship's officers approached them.

'There's a boat waiting to take you on shore,' he paused, *'we have orders to move further up the coast.'*

Friedrich and Mia remained silent. The man cleared his throat.

'You do still want to disembark?' He questioned.

Friedrich shook himself. *'Yes, yes of course.'*

He picked up their bag and taking Mia's arm followed the officer briskly to where a small boat waited to collect the few passengers, who were heading for the burning city. The sombre journey took half-an-hour, and the acrid smell of smoke and charred wood oppressed their thoughts, getting ever worse as they approached the city and left the open sea behind them. Mia took Friedrich's hands and held them tightly to stop them from shaking.

The boat pulled into a make-shift jetty and the few passengers alighted in silence. Still holding hands Friedrich and Mia picked their way through the charred rubble and headed towards the city centre. It was hot. Mia had a pair of light summer shoes on and she could feel the burning heat of the pavement through the thin soles. She glanced at Friedrich, who looked suddenly slight and vulnerable, a boy coming home to a shattered existence, not a man daily wielding power and justice, or injustice depending on the point of view. He was walking quickly and his hand was hot, feverish. Mia pulled him back gently.

'Change your things,' she said.

They were walking down a quiet street, eerily silent and whole apart from the overbearing heat and stench of fires all around them.. This was not the place for symbols of authority and power, it was a place to hide and hurry along unseen and unobtrusive. Neither was it practical to wear the hot, oppressive black uniform. Mia pulled Friedrich into an open porch and he took off the heavy woollen garments. Mia smiled, strangely relieved. Friedrich, the boy coming home, was something she could relate to.

'Okay?' She questioned.

He nodded, and they continued their eerie journey along the

deserted streets. Questions half formed in Mia's mind, then vanished before she found words or voice to ask them. Friedrich seemed to know where he was going and she just followed.

Mia had been in a bomb blast, but she'd never seen or experienced a bombing campaign. It was like being on a film set as the macabre reality of what she saw couldn't be real. There seemed something bizarrely planned about the whole spectacle; untouched streets, burned out housing blocks and sudden gaps, gaping empty spaces like missing teeth in a child. And where the pavement still burned, and black fires still sent up plumes of smoke there were other more lurid smells, the rancid, choking smell of incinerators.

Mia clutched Friedrich's hand and followed, keeping her questions unformed. Friedrich looked neither to left nor right, but walked on doggedly and undeterred. As they approached the city centre there was more activity and at one corner a fireproofed army vehicle stopped and questioned them . There was, however, no real will to detain them, neither was there any useful information to give them other than that the city had been evacuated and that there were orders that all civilians must vacate the centre. Friedrich saluted the officers, but otherwise ignored their instructions. He held Mia tightly by the hand and continued their awful journey towards the Alsterarkaden.

The city centre was the same mangled mess of smouldering pyres, rubble and apartments, still extant, but sad and empty. Wanting to avoid further patrols Friedrich took them through side streets, and shortcuts until they found themselves on a maze of streets behind the Alsterarkaden. Friedrich took a couple of sharp turns then came to a sudden stop and Mia found herself looking through the shattered window of a bookshop. Glass and printed pages had blasted onto the street and the once neat and packed shelves were a riot of torn and heat damaged books. Friedrich stood in the hot, desolate street and stared at the ruins of his father's livelihood.

'They're not here,' he pronounced suddenly and decisively. He moved forward and picked up a torn fragment of an unidentifiable book. He turned it over in his hands then let it drop back onto the splinters of glass. *'They're not here,'* he repeated.

'But how, how do you know?' Mia asked. She was standing in the middle of the street, shock and helplessness overwhelming her.

'Because,' Friedrich turned briskly from the fragmented chaos and started walking again.

'Friedrich!' Mia implored him.

He stopped and turned to face her. *'I'm sorry. I'm not ...'* He didn't say any more, but the crushed pain in the brown eyes was words enough. *'Because if they were here my father would have cleared up the mess,'* he finished simply.

Mia gave him a quick glance, or if they were here they were dead.

'Friedrich, there are a million refugees from Hamburg scattered God knows where, we can't just keep on walking...'

'We won't,' he interrupted her, *'at least we won't if we can find a boat. Come, if we're lucky we can take a boat and cross the Alster. They'll be home.'*

Friedrich's words made no sense to Mia. She wondered whether to make further protests, but perhaps that was what it was like to lose family, suddenly and violently. Perhaps one carried on hoping, carried on believing that somehow, somewhere life was carrying on as it always had done. She kept quiet and they continued on their silent journey.

To Mia's surprise within a few minutes they were standing on the edge of a large lake, its calm aspect and unrepentant beauty a monument to the city's former splendour. Friedrich headed straight for an undamaged boathouse where small rowing boats still bobbed innocently on the water. After some haggling with a rather more belligerent patrol Friedrich managed to commandeer a pleasure boat to take them across the Alster lake. It was ridiculously romantic and embarrassingly unscathed by the surrounding devastation.

The lake was the restless colour of a summer storm. Mia sat in the back of the little rowing boat, clutching their small bag of belongings, and trying not to think about the unavoidable question, what next? Friedrich flung off his light summer jacket and rolled up his sleeves. Mia burdened with too much thought and confusion, watched the slender strength of his arms as they pulled the oars in the water making calm, steady strokes. He smiled at her, a slight nervous smile, but it was a smile. There was still hope.

The end of their journey was as bizarrely mundane and real as the beginning had been as unreal as a nightmare. Just a few streets away from the northern perimeter of the lake Friedrich lead them up the neat path of a modern suburban villa and a smaller, heavier version of Friedrich opened the door and welcomed them in.

'Mother's in the bunker down the garden, I'll tell her that she can come in now,' Friedrich's father said.

He looked at his son, the same brown eyes glowing with pride and delight, then he turned their welcome to Mia. Mia halted on the path controlling a sudden and hysterical urge to laugh.

'Mia, my dear, we're so glad to meet you at last.'

Mia took the proffered hand and looked at Friedrich. Friedrich was recovering his poise. This time they had all escaped, but forty thousand other people hadn't, not to mention another forty thousand who were wounded and over one million who had been made homeless.

That evening they sat up in candlelight, feasting on beans and salad from Mr Hirsch's garden. War was a confusing muddle of extremes, Mia thought, as she watched the cheap candle wax splutter and smoke in the still August night.

***

The boat home was hot and crowded with troops. Mia was confined to their cabin because of heightened security. It was claustrophobic in the confined space. The lights were all turned out and the ship had waited until the dark of the late August evening before leaving Hamburg's bombed harbour. They lay together in the narrow bunk, comforted by the presence of another whole human being and protected from the fear and tension which pervaded the ship.

'How long does the war have to go on, Friedrich?' Mia asked, her open eyes looking blindly into the dark cabin.

Friedrich put an arm around her and held her tightly and the silence of the night sea settled over them. A deep sigh, like some creature stirring in the deep, escaped from Friedrich.

'The war,' he began, his voice sounding loud and rough. He paused and continued quietly. *'It won't end; they'll never give up,'* he whispered.

'But it's crazy,' Mia said, turning in his arms.

'Yes, it's crazy.'

Friedrich was silent again.

'Mia?'

'Yes?'

'Mia, we can't ever have this conversation again.' His voice sounded distant and sad as if oppressed by the weight of the silent sea beneath them.

Mia turned in his arms again. There was nothing more to say, but she held him thankfully, for once loving him without regrets and betrayals.

December 1943

Christian muffled himself up against the bitter December wind blasting through the streets, picking up the swirling white powder of a thin snow fall and a few fragments of autumn leaves still lurking in the gutters. He'd taken to walking his rounds, it was more anonymous, besides which petrol was impossible to come by. He'd taken an opportunity on a quiet Sunday to make some unofficial calls and just wanted to make one more before spending the afternoon with Astrid and Petter. His last patient was a young lad who he'd treated for concussion a few days ago. The boy had also had a nasty gash on his thigh which looked like a tear from a wire or barbed wire fence. Needless to say the youth had no papers or ration card and if no one had found or fed him Christian may have to risk sending him to Astrid Maria's Red Cross centre. Checking the street was quiet Christian stood close into the shadow of the door and knocked as loudly as he dared. After a painful silence he heard the muffled shuffling of carpet slippers in the passageway and the door was opened the width of a security chain. An old man peered out from the gloom of the hallway and eyed Christian suspiciously. Relieved that the youth was not, after all, alone, Christian held up his medical bag by way of identification.

'Is it the doctor then?' The old man asked warily.

'I treated Per a couple of days ago. Is he still here?'

The old man didn't answer but fiddled with the chain on the back of the door and finally let Christian in.

The old man jerked his head in the direction of the basement. 'I've been feeding him up,' he said.

'He hasn't been sick or dizzy or complained of headaches?' Christian asked the man.

'I should say not, he's been eating like a horse. Do you want to have a look at him?'

Christian paused, he should say no. This time the boy would be alert and remember 'the doctor' who had treated him.

'Yes. I'll just check that the wound on his thigh is healing.'

'Wound?' Questioned the old man. 'I didn't know anything about any wound!'

'Then it's probably not been troubling him,' Christian said levelly looking at the old man and wondering how far his allegiance went.

'I'd have got him more help if I'd known there was a wound,' the man continued stoutly.

Christian gave a quiet sigh of relief, the allegiance obviously went a long way. Christian changed the dressing and left as quickly as he could before the boy blabbed any more secrets in his eagerness to make contact. The old man followed him to the door.

'Ring if there are complications, but I don't expect to have to come again.' Christian scribbled the word 'doctor' on a piece of paper and his telephone number and handed it to the old man. How many times had he compromised himself in this way, he wondered? He heard the rattling of the security chain as the man shut the door behind him and he stepped out into the street, relieved to breathe the bracing air and have a little time to himself as he strode home.

Astrid and Petter were sitting at the kitchen table surrounded by the debris of a cutting and gluing session. They had cut up one of the old red hats that Astrid Maria had made and were making Christmas decorations with the red wool, fir cones and bits of wood. Christian sat down happily with them and proceeded to admire the various sticky offerings. The surgery telephone started ringing downstairs. Astrid gave Christian a long look; the surgery telephone was always ringing. Christian stood up and ran down the stairs to take it.

'Hello,' he said cautiously.

'Christian?'

'Tom?' Christian questioned, surprised, as Tom now made no contact with him outside the hospital.

Tom rushed on. 'There's been some kind of explosion down on one of the keys, Filipstad we think. First casualties are coming in now but by all reports it's carnage down at the site.'

There was a long cool silence from Christian, the telephone line crackling between them.

Quickly reading his thoughts Tom carried on. 'It's not resistance activity, Christian. At least it's not us,' he added carefully. 'I think it's an ammunition ship, which must have exploded after docking. I don't know any more than that.'

'So it's mostly civilians?'

'Yes, and we have to assume the ship was well guarded so there must be German military personnel as well, but we've only seen civilians so far.'

'What do you want me to do? Come down to the hospital?'

'No. I want you to commandeer one of Astrid Maria's Red Cross vans and get down there, to the quay, as quickly as possible, and take some of her stash of first aid kit.'

'I'm on my way.' Christian put down the receiver. A great heaviness and reluctance overcame him. Carnage, the carnage of war, he shuddered, as his mind's eye depicted the scene for him. He went back up the stairs to Astrid and Petter.

'Call out I'm afraid,' he said.

'Oh no!' Astrid exclaimed. 'You can't be the only doctor

around here!'

Christian hesitated wondering how much to tell her. 'It's an explosion down on one of the quays. I've been asked to help.' He tactfully left Tom out of it.

'Explosion? But isn't that dangerous? I mean mightn't there be more explosions?'

'I don't know Astrid,' Christian said tiredly. He turned to go, Astrid's alarm and frustration following his steps out of the house.

Christian turned hasty strides towards the Red Cross centre. The bitter wind was now at his back, pushing him along in great gusts. He reached the centre in just over five minutes, noted with relief that a couple of Red Cross vans were standing in the yard, and pushed open the door. An icy blast followed in the wake of his entrance and a familiar voice met his ears.

'Close that door, damn you!'

Astrid Maria came sweeping out of the office Sophie style. 'Oh?' She stopped in her tracks, 'Christian?'

Christian snatched his breath back so that he could speak calmly. 'I've had a call from the hospital, from Tom in fact.'

A look of alarm spread over Astrid Maria's face. 'Mia?'

'No, none of us. There's been an explosion down on the quays, he thinks somewhere round Filipstad.' Astrid Maria now gave him her full attention. 'It's, er, mayhem down there and he wants me to go down to the scene.'

'With one of my vans?'

Christian nodded.

'We'll take both. One can bring back less serious casualties here for treatment and the other can act as a field base.' Astrid Maria immediately turned to give orders to the small group of helpers who had now gathered round them.

'Bless you,' said Christian.

Astrid Maria despatched him out to the vans with two boxes of bandages. 'I hope Sophie can organise me some fresh supplies,' she said under her breath.

Within ten minutes Christian found himself driving one of the vans with Astrid Maria sitting stubbornly beside him and two nurses in the back. The other van was following with a driver and medical orderly. Astrid Maria had left her other two nurses in the Centre to deal with any casualties.

'Switch the bloody lights on,' shouted Astrid Maria, 'to hell with blackouts, the whole seafront's lit like a beacon anyway.' Her voice trailed off as they reached the water front. They charged through huddled groups of spectators and stopped on the edge of the devastation. Christian swung out of the van and into the barrel of a rifle. He reached in to get his medical case and heard the click of the safety catch being released.

'Doctor,' he said.

'This is a forbidden zone. We have instructions to shoot any trespassers on sight.' The soldier positioned his gun meaningfully.

'I've been sent by the hospital,' continued Christian desperately.

'He's with me, Red Cross.' Astrid Maria was waving various passes and documents at the soldier. 'For goodness sake get out of our way and do something useful like keeping those sightseers back. I can see we've got work to do here,' she finished grimly.

Doubt stayed the soldier's hand and the team got prepared. Astrid Maria and her two nurses filled field bags with first aid items and the two stretcher bearers joined them.

'We'll stick together to start with, more effective that way. Christian you diagnose for us and we can mop up.' She turned to the soldier. 'And if you've got nothing better to do you can guard these vans. We don't want any plundering do we!'

Either because still confused by the right course of action or because he'd understood the necessity of guarding the vans the soldier remained in position and intentionally or not secured their safety.

Unable to take in the scale of the devastation before him Christian dived towards the first area where soldiers and medics weren't already taking the dead and injured off in military vehicles, which must have been commissioned for the purpose. There was no sign as yet of any regular ambulances.

Their first stop was a small group of passers-by who had been caught by the blast and who were sitting amongst the rubble more shocked than injured. There were signs of minor burns on the adults and a child with a deep cut that had bled too much and needed cleaning. One of the nurses was assigned to deal with the group.

'The child is probably better at home if the wound has stopped bleeding, but get them out of here as quickly as possible before they also suffer from exposure to this deadly wind,' Christian instructed the nurse.

They then moved into the torn fabric of a building, the front had been blasted off entirely and walls and ceilings had fallen into each other. Christian could see at least one body in the debris. He indicated that the others should stay out and went into the mess. The man was not dead and miraculously neither was he unconscious. Christian felt his limbs carefully, he definitely had a broken leg and Christian suspected that his back was also broken. He beckoned the stretcher bearers to come into the building.

'For God's sake be careful, there's nothing holding this place up. Broken leg, possibly the back as well, by rights we shouldn't move him but I can't see any other way to save him. Find a vehicle on its way to the hospital and send him with it.' Christian turned to the patient. 'Was there anyone else in the house?' He asked. The man's eyes were burning with pain and his mind was overcome. 'Is there anyone else in the building?' Christian asked again.

The man tried to focus on Christian as he leant over him, then with a huge effort of will he brought his shattered thoughts together. His lips moved soundlessly as he tried to make one more concerted effort. 'My wife,' he whispered and then fainted.

Christian left the man to the stretcher bearers and stood up carefully surveying the blasted building around him. Astrid Maria was at his shoulder.

'His wife,' said Christian, 'his wife's somewhere in this mess.'

'Christian, you can't!'

Christian looked at her steadily. 'I have to,' he said, 'but not you.'

He moved towards the back of the building, carefully putting aside torn planks of wood which blocked the way. The building creaked around him, swaying with every fresh blast of the wind. He ventured deeper into the chaos and then he saw her foot, still in its warm woollen slipper, the rest of the body was trapped under the debris. Carefully Christian started pulling the torn planks from the body. He reached a hand and felt for the pulse, there was no life. Less carefully now he threw the last planks away so that he could pull her out. Her grey hair was matted with blood and her woollen cardigan was torn and tangled in a wound to the gut, blue eyes, wide with shock gazed up at him, glazed with death. He picked up the poor broken body and carried her out of the wreckage of her home. Behind him the structure gave one last groan against the wind and finally fell in with a blast of torn timber and a cloud of dust and dirt.

He put the body down, grimly holding back his tears. The stretcher bearers had returned. 'Find out where they're putting the dead and take her there,' he said and turned away from the body.

Astrid Maria and her nurses had carried on without him and he moved on to catch them up. They were moving closer to the quay side now and in the remnants of fires around them they could make out something of what had happened. It would seem that a ship had exploded taking with it most of the quay and the surrounding buildings.

'Carrying ammunition,' said Astrid Maria looking up from a patient and reading his thoughts.

Christian moved further towards the heart of the blast and stumbled over another body. He stepped back quickly and bent down to examine it. It was a soldier, in the familiar uniform of the German Wehrmacht. It was just a private, probably on guard duty. Christian knelt down beside him and instinctively felt for the pulse. The man was young, not much more than eighteen. His body had probably been thrown by the blast. it was limp and strangely unmarked, but a trickle of blood from the mouth suggested severe internal bleeding. Christian felt a faint pulse and started pulling open the soldier's tunic so that he could breathe better. Haunted eyes suddenly focussed on his own as the boy tried to speak, but too much blood stuck in his throat. Christian put his arms round him and lifted him gently. The boy continued to search his face, as if looking for some familiar features. He struggled to speak again.

'Father?' He gasped, his eyes blurred and his torn thoughts stumbling homewards. More blood gushed from his mouth and his body relaxed into death. The eyes gazing into Christian's were filled with a momentary false hope of recognition and delight. Christian held the body to him and his tears fell unchecked.

'I can't do this,' he whispered into the cruel wind, 'I can't repair all these broken people.'

He let the soldier's body fall from his arms and staggered to his feet. For a moment he struggled to find his bearings then his eyes searched for Astrid Maria, weaving her way through the carnage. He soon spotted her, strapping up wounds and giving orders, in her element and grimly resilient as though a veteran of many campaigns. Christian shook himself and went to join her and so take what small comfort he could from using his skill to comfort, even save, more lives.

***

Yet another air-raid warning. Frank ignored it for a few minutes, hoping he might reach his friends before the familiar drone of heavy bombers met his ears, but it was too late. Reluctantly he spotted the familiar entrance to a street shelter and dived into it as the first fires of bombs lit up the night sky.

Frank had been in London for three months now, shuffling papers, assigning groups of young men back to Norway to face either death or glory. Anything must be better than this, he thought surveying the damp interior of the bomb shelter. It was empty save for himself and was just a simple dugout in the bowels of London. The tin roof was wet and rusting and dripped the sodden dampness of an English winter into the far corner of the shelter.

This shelter was obviously little used as there were none of the usual signs of intermittent habitation such as stubs of candles, old packing cases or scraps of blankets. Frank squatted against the wall and listened to the whine of bombs, the dull thumps of blasts shaking the city interspersed with the inadequate volleys from anti-aircraft guns, and waited, without much optimism, for the all clear.

He had spent a year in Scotland, first as a recruit on a training course and latterly as an instructor himself. He had then been sent on down to London to work for H.Q., paper pushing. He had been applying for transfers back to active service for over sixth months now. Was Helge blocking his return? Well if he didn't get an official transfer soon he would follow unofficial routes and get himself back home come what may, although such was idle thinking. His best course of action was to keep pressurising more superior officers here in London. He guessed that a first sniff of victory would move central command from its position of containment to a more active realisation of its objective, and Frank was fairly confident that any change in the winds of war would fulfil his ambition and get him back to Norway.

The sound of footsteps running in the street outside roused him and a dark figure propelled itself headfirst into the shelter.

'Cor blimey, it's like Guy Fawkes came back with a vengeance out there tonight.' The speaker had a crack to his voice and Frank suspected the kid was hardly turned sixteen. He was sticking his head back out of the shelter as if looking for something. Apparently satisfied he came back into the dripping hole and leant against the wall opposite Frank. He reached into his pocket and Frank heard the familiar sounds of a cigarette packet being opened.

'Got a light gov?'

Frank obliged and was rewarded with a cigarette.

'Good tobacco, where did you pick these up?'

'Least said soonest mended,' responded the boy. Frank saw the trail of smoke from the cigarette as the boy tapped the side of his nose. 'Good pickings tonight, gov.'

August, 1944
Sixteen

Mia was pushing her bicycle along the pavement, enjoying the August sunshine warming her back and drawing deeply on one of Friedrich's cigarettes. She had nothing to report that evening and was happy to relax her guard for a few, precious minutes. She caught the sound of footsteps on the pavement behind her and felt someone walking just by her shoulder. She resisted the temptation to look round and concentrated on her cigarette and holding her bicycle up.

'Blueberry jam,' a woman's voice spoke just behind her.

'My tin's empty,' Mia responded quietly to the current code.

'We need information on the next issue of ration cards, as the boss wants to get his hands on them.'

Mia continued to walk up the road. She sensed that the unseen woman was no longer with her. Puffing the last tobacco out of her cigarette Mia threw the stub to the ground and grinding out the glowing end with her shoe she used the movement to look about her. A woman with a child in a push chair was looking in a shop window, and a couple of men were walking in the other direction, otherwise the street was quiet. Mia mounted her bicycle pensively and peddled on home. What did they want with ration cards she thought? And what could she find out? It made much more sense to use someone in the Government offices. If police headquarters had any relevant information it would be to do with security back up, so she supposed that she could find that out. If she feigned help with a broken heel in the morning down at reception she could probably check out the week's duty rosters, where anything out of the ordinary would come below the usual lists and should be fairly easy to spot.

She took her Bicycle to its usual wall in the backyard and caught the unmistakable smell of fish drifting down from their kitchen through the open window. Her mother must be at home, eating their endless supplies of sardines.

***

Frank pulled up the Ford van as arranged in the maze of

streets in Oslo's East end. Noise from the gas generator fixed to the back of the van made it impossible to hear if anything was going on, it also made the vehicle rather unwieldy with a tendency to swing to the left. His fellow driver was loitering against the far wall of the street where he had a good view of the crossroads below them. Frank, watching the man, saw his head suddenly rise and his body quicken with action. The signal had obviously come, although it was earlier than expected. The other man ran across the street to the van and got in beside Frank. They took one look at each other and set the plan in action. As expected a transport lorry came towards them from the next street and, also as planned, had to wait while they pulled into the road and turned to the right. Frank then pulled up onto the curb and, as the lorry drove past them, both he and his companion craned their necks to see in the driver's compartment.

'Are there two or three people in the cockpit?' Frank asked. It was planned that one of their team would hijack the lorry while it waited for Frank's van to pull out into the road.

'Three, I think.'

'Our chap's on board then.'

'We can assume so.'

Frank let out the clutch and the van lurched forwards, the gas roaring in their ears. Keeping the lorry within sights, about thirty or forty meters in front of them, Frank followed behind. The lorry was heading towards the central post office, which meant that everything was still going as planned. Keeping close to the lorry Frank watched as it drove on past the post office and on in the direction of the waterfront. His companion was keeping watch on the post office in case any extra guards had been sent to keep a look out. There was no sign of anything untoward. Frank drove on past the post office, still following the lorry. After swinging into a couple more streets the lorry came to a standstill outside a large gate which opened directly onto the street. A couple of other men came out of the shadows, made contact with the lorry, then beckoned to Frank to reverse the van up to the back of the lorry. People on their way to work were now heading along the pavements in various directions. Frank took a deep breath and leapt out of the van, his companion opened the back of the van and Frank went to look inside the back of the lorry.

'What on earth?'

'Ration cards.'

'Well, we were told that, but there must be over a ton of stuff here, it'll never fit into that Ford!'

'Never say never, come on let's get loading, one of our chaps is sitting in there with a loaded pistol and I'm sure he doesn't want to get picked up by anyone!'

Frank swallowed his dissent and all available hands switched the cargo from the lorry to the van. The passers-by showed remarkably little interest and they managed to transfer the load within ten minutes. Frank leapt back into the van and his companion climbed on top of the heap of ration cards which had had to be crammed into the passenger seat to get them all in the vehicle.

Frank set off and headed back east again. The streets were now busy with people going to work, but within ten more minutes Frank and his consignment were safely in a large warehouse north of the city centre.

***

Friedrich stood at the window in his study looking down at the pavements, blistering with a final blast of summer heat. It was obvious from the first that heads were going to role after the double embarrassment of yet another failed policy on the part of the Government and the scarcely restrained delight on the part of the Resistance after its successful hijacking of a whole consignment of ration cards, which could now be used by illegal operatives or by those refusing to follow the latest government initiative. The Reichskommissar's office had scarcely contained its delight over evidence of yet further incompetence on the part of Quisling's Norwegian government. Terboven would not willingly give up his control of Norway and such bungles on the Norwegian side only made his position stronger. Friedrich feared that this time the police could be caught between the two rival factions and someone somewhere desperately needed a scapegoat, which could mean more mass arrests and further depletion of his force. And at the same time the resistance in Norway was growing in strength and confidence every day, thus this was not a good time for an internal crackdown.

Friedrich turned from the window, trouble clouding his vision, understanding the politics wasn't ultimately going to be much help. There were two issues on his desk, one was a promotion which he had looked for in the last two years, and the other? He walked over to the desk and leant over it looking at the second piece of paper again, willing the typescript before his eyes to change. He covered the paper with the first order and sat down at the desk.

In the wake of an assassination attempt on the Fuhrer his commanding officer was being transferred back to Germany and he, Friedrich, was to be appointed Kriminalsekretaer in his stead.

Friedrich read the order again, his ambitions before him, yet it seemed to him that they were impossible to realise. He reached out his hand towards the telephone, then drew it slowly back where it lay palm down on the desk. It was possible that his commanding officer wished to stay here in Norway, in which case Friedrich could persuade the authorities and apply for the transfer back to Germany himself. If this was the case they could both use what little influence they may still have in Berlin.

Friedrich put his other hand on the desk, palm down. He looked at the long fingers, examined the clean nails, neatly trimmed, the strong, lean fingers of the pianist. He got up from his chair distractedly and walked over to the window.

His eyes wandered back to the order. The problem was that it was an order and was meant to be obeyed not negotiated, as negotiation was not a part of the culture of the Third Reich. He would have to follow the order, or? Or refuse. If he refused he would have his commission taken away, be assigned to the SS and sent to the eastern front, where at least he wouldn't live to see the consequences, or uncover the truth of the other letter.

He went back to his desk, sat down and resolutely pulled out the second paper. On it was a list of Norwegians who worked for the police force who were now under suspicion of being informers. Someone had leaked information on the transportation of the ration cards, information which was only at Victoria Terrasse and Mia was the only person on the list in front of him who worked at the Police Headquarters.

It was possible that the Government had also had the transport information, but they claimed not to. Mia was in the frame and he had to bust her.

He rose from his chair and paced back to the window. He knew what he was going to do, knew what he had to do, but which course of action required most courage, which course of action was the right one? He wished there was some grand gesture he could make, such as resigning his position in protest at the accusations made against Mia. He took a sharp breath and a pain and a doubt stabbed through his chest. Did he have the courage to turn over all the stones necessary to prove Mia's innocence? And if he turned over all those stones did he have the courage to face her betrayal? In either event how could he keep Mia's affection? How could she trust him after such a betrayal of his own trust in her?

***

Mia walked into the familiar little office which was still assigned to her although most of her work was now down in the cellars, either recording interviews with prisoners or typing up confessions. Friedrich had been busy with the official take-over of his new position and she hadn't seen him apart from the occasional meeting in a corridor. She felt bright, alert and had made the most of the last few nights to catch up on sleep. She checked her desk for assignments, there was some typing to do and then a confession scheduled for the afternoon. It promised to be another long working day, she thought, unless by some lucky fluke this poor prisoner was short and sweet and to the point.

She rattled through the typing which was surprisingly mundane and consisted mostly of duty lists changing because of the change in leadership. She was surprised that Friedrich hadn't popped in during the morning and wondered if he'd had to move rooms because of his promotion. It hadn't occurred to her that his promotion might make it harder for them to see each other.

She finished the typing and stretched out her back. She had an hour before she should report for duty in the cells below, which just gave her enough time to slip out for some fresh air and to eat her lunch in the park.

It was deliciously warm out in the open air. Mia sat on a bench and stretched out her legs enjoying the warmth of the sun filtering through her stockings. She chewed abstractedly on some of Astrid Maria's grey bread, which had got even greyer as the years went by, but it didn't matter so much any more, soon the war might end. Mia put her head back, closed her eyes, and let the sun stream down onto her face. News of an Allied invasion into France had finally reached them, yes, the war could end soon. What it would mean for her, or for Friedrich, were questions she didn't know how to contemplate, but that the war would end could, in itself, only be a good thing.

Glancing at her watch she reluctantly pulled in her legs and shook the crumbs off her dress. The war might end soon, but in the meantime she had to descend into some Nazi controlled prison and endure the confession of yet another of its victims. She picked up her things and headed back for Head Quarters. It would be unbearably hot and stuffy in the cells.

She went straight to reception where she was given a pass and an escort to lead her through a series of locked doors. So she would be with a high security prisoner this time, she surmised. What if it was someone she knew? She blanched at the thought. But it had never happened after that first, dreadful moment, not that that poor man lived to tell the tale even if he'd had a tale to tell. It was difficult not to get morbid in these warrens under the police head quarters, throbbing with heat and fear and long hidden from the light of day.

Mia was finally left in a room. It was a familiar scene: a barred window which was no more than an air vent, the iron hooks on the walls where the prisoner would be chained and a wooden table with a simple chair. The black typewriter gleamed dully in the artificial light and the usual paper and carbon copy paper were arranged neatly beside it. Mia sat at the desk and waited.

After about ten minutes guards came with the chained prisoner. The prisoner glanced at her and then withdrew into his misery while the guards chained him to the wall. No, it wasn't anyone she knew.

She fed the paper and carbon paper onto the carriage of the typewriter, aligned it, clamped it fast against the drum and then pressed the lever of the carriage return the statutory three times.

'When you're ready,' she said encouragingly to the prisoner.

He glanced at her again and licked his lips nervously. His story was a strange mixture of confused dates and names, followed by fluid accounts of actions, which sounded more like stories he'd learnt than experiences he'd endured. He licked his lips and glanced at her and Mia couldn't stop a feeling of dislike for him growing within her. Poor creature, she tried to convince herself, how could she be so quick to judge? How would she bear up to torture and the constant threat of death?

She typed, and the prisoner continued with his broken confession, licking his lips and glancing at her.

The names he listed were strangely normal, not the usual spattering of obviously made up names, like Arne Blaafager. It didn't seem to Mia that he had anything extraordinary to confess and she wondered why they were in a high security cell. Of course it might be all made up; she'd typed up quite a few of those over the past two years, even making the occasional alteration to make them sound more credible.

The confession moved on to a flesh wound he'd received. Mia couldn't help glancing over at his limbs as her fingers flew over the typewriter keys. There were no obvious signs of emaciation which may have followed such a wound, in fact he looked pretty well fed, and much healthier than the average prisoner she encountered.

He was talking about the doctor, yes he knew who the doctor was and he could take the police to him, and as Mia's eyes lifted from her veiled scrutiny of his sound limbs she caught the prisoner's eye. It was fixed on her with a brief, but piercing look. It was a look of fear, not fear of the guards, not even of his situation, but fear of her. And in that moment she knew not only who the doctor was, but that she was meant to know who the doctor was.

Christian! She thought, the panic rising in her throat. They'd all been rumbled and the prisoner was a stooge, set to lay a trap for her. Mia dragged her own eyes back to the type script in front of her, she felt her fingers stiffening with fear and she willed them to continue typing the sorry tale which poured out beside her.

Prisoners didn't look at her. They might glance at her, but their heads were bent, as it were, in shame. They didn't look at her. No, he was a stooge, there could be no doubt.

The confession came to an abrupt end and with a nervous glance in her direction the prisoner turned to the guards. Did he look at them with a question in his eyes? Mia tidied the papers and bent her head over her work. There were scarcely three pages, and she would be finished earlier than usual. And yet it also meant that she only had three pages to work out what was actually contained in this garbled confession. How much did they know? Who else was implicated in the veil of stories and how much of it did they suppose that she knew?

She translated it carefully, more carefully than usual, scanning the words, the names and the events. The prisoner rattled his chains impatiently, he'd done his bit and he wanted to get out, but the guards wouldn't risk any unorthodox course of action which might alert her. In fact, thought Mia, the guards might not know that there was anything unusual about the prisoner.

She forced her thoughts back to the document before her.

They obviously knew about Christian, they knew that he took calls and attended to patients, who he should have handed over to the authorities. They also assumed that Christian had a lot of inside knowledge of Resistance personnel and activities, which he didn't. They assumed that he had inside knowledge of the inner command of the Resistance, which he did. And what did they know, or think they knew about her? Not a lot it would seem. What would they suspect her of? Being an informer, of course, leaking names and places into a hidden network.

Christian was the bait. She would know it was him if she knew of his involvement with the Resistance, and, as on other occasions, she would pass that knowledge on to the network of which she was a part. Thus, as she triggered the usual train of action, the whole network would reveal itself like the flame which follows the wick leading to the dynamite.

Who had set this up? Friedrich? And a cold chill crept over her body, despite the heat. Friedrich, betrayed, would break, and in breaking would show no mercy.

She shook herself severely, pulling together her fragmenting thoughts. She gathered up the papers, smiled nervously, and stood up.

'All done,' she said with a forced brightness, 'ready for signing.'

The guards unlocked the prisoner and escorted him close enough to the desk to look over the papers and sign them. He glanced at them without reading anything and signed them. He was eager to escape, Mia thought grimly. She could feel his eyes on her again, but she turned to pick up her bag and concentrated her mind on the trivial things she would now normally do. The guards called from the cell door and requested a guard to escort Mia back to the sun. She wondered, for a moment, if they were going to arrest her there and then, but of course not. Now, if she took the bait, she would lead them to a whole network of resistance operatives.

She must concentrate on all her usual routines and not do anything which could arouse suspicion. She handed in her pass and went up the stairs to her office to check for messages. There was nothing. She took the light summer cardigan she'd left hanging on the back of the chair and went out. She paused in the corridor looking at the door opposite her office, which lead to Friedrich's rooms. Was he there? Was he avoiding her? That in itself should have been enough to arouse her suspicions.

She bade the duty officer standing by the main door her usual good evening and went round to the back of the building to retrieve her bicycle. A shadow lurked in a far doorway. She ignored it and pushed her bicycle out onto the road.

And then a new problem raced into her thoughts; Christian wasn't just bait to catch her, they were going to arrest him anyway, she had to get a warning message out. She slowed down by a row of shops and got off the bicycle, wheeling it along the pavement she browsed in the shop windows. She paused outside one of them as if to take a closer look, but not outside the one with one of her contacts. Pretending to have a stone in her shoe she leant the bicycle against a wall and took the shoe off to shake out the supposed stone. She hopped around on one leg as if struggling to keep balance and caught sight of it again, the shadow, her shadow, and there would be more than one of them; she knew too much about how the Gestapo made their arrests.

She took one of Friedrich's cigarettes out of her handbag, lit it and took her bicycle back from the wall and proceeded to push it up the street while drawing on the cigarette.

How could she get a message to Christian?

She could go to the Red Cross centre, or even the hospital. Her mother or aunt would willingly get a message sent to Christian, they could possibly just ring him up!

She pushed the bicycle over a loose paving stone and stopped to put her cigarette out. She dare not take any more action that might lead her shadows to think that she had either seen them or was looking out for them. She had to be just an innocent girl cycling home.

But if she went to the Centre or the hospital she would just spread the tale of guilt and involvement. The only thing she could do which would not implicate anyone else was to go home.

She arrived home all too soon, no message of warning sent and no clue as to how she was to send such a message.

She propped her bicycle up in the usual place and went round to the front of the building to let herself in the front door. There was someone on the far side of the square smoking a cigarette. They were watching her. How long would they stay? Would she be able to slip out later and ring Christian? But the surgery telephone would be tapped and the Gestapo would be on to both of them before they had chance to escape.

She went up the stairs and into the apartment. Astrid Maria wasn't at home, she was probably still at the Centre. She could go out, as if to do some shopping, or post a letter, and ring the Centre. Astrid Maria could then get word to Christian, but her call would be traced to the Centre and then the Centre would be watched as well.

She flung her things on a chair in the hall and walked through to the kitchen. She went straight to the window and looked out, something moved in the shadows of the backyard. The back was being watched as well. She turned away, trapped and helpless.

She had to keep calm. Was there any risk she could take herself that would still result in giving Christian a chance? Surely there must be something she could do? She went back out into the hall and paced up and down, it was the only place where she couldn't be seen and if she closed any curtains while it was still light it would arouse too much suspicion. Could she slip out under cover of dark? But it wouldn't be dark until ten or eleven o'clock, the weather was clear and the sun would stretch out its arm long after sunset.

She could go out now, trail round a few shops and cafés, slip down as many alleys as possible and then risk a telephone call to Christian. She could then try and vanish.

But any action that she took would bring down a whole fragile network of resistance activity. As far as Mia could understand it from the confession the Gestapo only had clear information on Christian; the rest was conjecture. Any action Mia took would only realise their worse suspicions and it wouldn't just be Mia they would arrest, even if Mia escaped they would arrest her family, and it was a very short hop from them to Siri's family, including Tom.

If she played the innocent they would only arrest Christian.

And if Christian talked? Mia sank to the floor, put her head on her knees and, wrapping her arms around her legs, wept hard and bitter tears.

Some time later a familiar rattling of keys in the door heralded the arrival of Astrid Maria.

'There's a nasty looking man on the corner by the Grobæk's

smoking, and it's not chicory he's smoking neither,' Astrid Maria said slamming the door shut, 'so if you're going out tonight I would give him a wide berth. Mia?' She shouted, having elicited no response. 'Oh, maybe she's already out,' she continued to herself and stepping forward nearly trod on Mia, who was still crouching on the floor in the gloom of the hall. 'Mia! What on earth...'

Mia looked up and rose slowly to her feet.

'You're not going out tonight?'

Mia shook her head.

'Anything wrong.'

Mia looked at her mother, a wry smile twisting her mouth.

'Oh. Does this mean it's all over then?' Astrid Maria questioned carefully, alluding to Mia's assignations with Friedrich, as she thought of them, and unaware of the painful irony in her words. Direct conversations with Mia about Friedrich were a taboo subject in Astrid Maria's world.

Mia looked at her mother steadily. 'What do you mean, it's all over?'

'Well, you know. That man.'

'Yes,' said Mia slowly, 'I suppose it must be.' She hadn't given any thought to Friedrich during the last hours, but, yes, whatever happened now, it was all over. She pressed a hand to her forehead wondering whether her heart or her head would break first.

She followed her mother into the kitchen. Astrid Maria put her hand out to flick on the electric light and Mia shot her own hand out and pulled Astrid Maria back. Her mother looked at her questioningly. Mia took her arm and lead her silently to the window. Astrid Maria looked out, stepped back from the window quickly and then, more cautiously this time, moved back to have another look out of the window. This time she stayed by the window craning her neck this way and that. She looked up sharply at her daughter and after a long silent exchange she said. 'So I wasn't imagining things then?'

Mia shook her head, still silent.

She took Astrid Maria's arm again and led her into the sitting room where they had a good view of the Square. A van was parked down a side street and the smoker was still at his post outside the Grobæk's house.

Mother and daughter shrank back into the room and stood there silently scrutinising one another, exchanging all the words they couldn't utter out loud.

Astrid Maria turned to go, grunting under her breath.

'Mother, don't go out tonight.'

Astrid Maria looked as though she was about to protest, then said stoutly. 'I wasn't going out anyway.'

She went out into the hall then turned back to Mia. 'Come and have some food.' She went on to the kitchen and with a grand gesture of defiance flicked on the electric light. She then dragged a chair over to the cupboard and standing up on the chair reached into the far depths to find one of the few remaining tins of sardines.

After a poor attempt at eating Mia did the rounds again to see if her shadows were still in position. They were. She went into her bedroom and flung herself on the bed. The strained silence was occasionally disturbed by Astrid Maria as she followed her usual routines around the house.

At some point Mia must have fallen asleep because she woke up in the early hours of the morning when the night was as black as it would be. She was still fully clothed and her limbs were stiff with a hanging tension which wouldn't leave them, even in sleep. She wondered what the time was. It was too dark to see her watch so she crept out of bed and went silently into the hall. There she took some matches from her bag and lit one. It was just two o'clock.

If Christian's arrest followed the usual pattern he would be arrested between four and five; in just two hours time. Mia went into the front room and stood quietly at the window for some minutes, waiting to see if she could see any signs of the men who watched her. She could no longer make out the grey shape of the car parked up the side street. She wondered for a moment if they had left their watch, which meant she could make a dash for it and ring Christian. Then she caught the veiled flash of a small flame flickering as the smoker lit another cigarette. Mia swung away from the window and leant against the wall by the curtains looking into the room. She moved to go back to her bedroom. Her foot caught on a table leg and she stumbled forward in the dark, blinded by defeat and impotence.

She lay sleepless on her bed, guessing the watches of the night. In her mind's eye she saw the shadows gathering outside the surgery. A grey van pulled up silently in the street and more shadows gathered at the back of the building surrounding the flat and surgery. Then the silence was broken by an eruption of knocking and shouting to open up.

Christian immediately alert, and wise to the significance, leapt out of bed and pulled on clothes, socks and shoes, Astrid became paralysed with fear and panic. Christian bundled her into Petter's room, closed the door on them and ran down the two sets of stairs before the door was broken in, giving himself up on the doorstep in the hope that his appearance would deflect attention from the house, his thoughts, for the moment, bent entirely on saving Astrid and Petter. Maybe a curtain twitched in a neighbouring house, but most people buried themselves deeper in their beds hoping the storm would pass and leave them alone.

Mia gazed up at her bedroom ceiling, her eyes dry and her face grey and hard as stone.

August, 1944
Seventeen

Astrid Maria woke up early. A quick glance out of the window revealed nothing worse than a thin gleam of sun catching the summer branches of the trees in the square. She presumed the building was still being watched but didn't wait to see any evidence of it. She went through to the kitchen and put the kettle on the stove. Her coffee mix was dwindling. If the allies didn't sort out Europe soon she would have to go on the scrounge again to get more supplies. The Centre was also woefully short of all essential first aid equipment. The hospital was now too short of medicines for Sophie to slip out extra supplies to her, so she'd sent off a request for help to the Red Cross in Sweden but, as yet, had had no reply.

She had a quick glance out of the kitchen window, but again didn't wait to get confirmation of her supposition that the watch continued. She put her coffee mixture into a pot and went to listen outside Mia's bedroom door. Although there was no sound she presumed that Mia was in there as Mia's bag and shoes were still in the hall. The kettle started to make the strangled whistling noises it always made when coming to the boil. Astrid Maria went back to the kitchen and poured the boiling water into the coffee pot, she got a cup and saucer out of the cupboard then went through to the front room while the coffee brewed. She watched out of the window and saw signs of the street coming to life. A couple of people were walking across the square and her neighbours had opened their curtains in the houses opposite. Astrid Maria glanced at her watch, it was just after seven o'clock. Another figure came into the square, its head was bent and it was hurrying. It crossed to the side of the street where the apartment was and Astrid Maria had to crane her neck to watch the rapid progress of the man. He paused outside the entrance to their building, as if checking the number, then advanced quickly to the door.

The silence was broken by the ringing of the doorbell in the hall. Astrid Maria left her post at the window, went quickly into the hall and rushed down the communal stairs to answer the door. The man ringing the bell was one of Christian and Astrid's neighbours. He stepped inside quickly, glanced nervously at Astrid Maria, then dropped his eyes.

'I'm just on my way to work,' he said, embarrassed.

Astrid Maria waited.

'There was a disturbance in the street last night, at about four o'clock.' He cleared his throat. 'We think they arrested the Doctor.'

There was a moment of silence between them.

'I tried knocking on the door, but the curtains were all still closed and no one answered. I hope I'm mistaken...' his voice trailed off, 'but I thought I should warn you.'

Astrid Maria roused herself. 'Thank you,' she said, 'yes, thank you.'

She ushered the man back out of the door.

'If there's anything we can do?'

'Yes, yes, that's very kind.'

'The Doctor was such a ...'

Astrid Maria shut the door. Her head was spinning and for a moment she thought she was going to faint. She muttered to herself crossly and forced herself back up the stairs, her breath was coming in gasps as if she'd been running.

Mia was standing in the hallway.

Astrid Maria looked at her, long and coolly. 'You knew didn't you?'

Mia said nothing, but she'd already put her shoes on and covered her summer dress with a light cardigan.

'I'll just find the spare key to the surgery,' continued Astrid Maria, fumbling in the chest of drawers, which stood in the hall. She found the key, took a light coat from the coat stand by the door and went out. Mia followed her.

'Are you coming?' Astrid Maria asked, surprised.

Mia nodded her answer. Her head ached and her limbs felt numb, but her thoughts were clear. The thought that nothing mattered anymore was drowned by the cold rationality of day. She had to do whatever one would do if one had just heard that one's brother-in-law had been arrested, and on hearing the news one would go straight to the house and try and find out if it was true and what had happened. She followed Astrid Maria silently out of the apartment. Assuming that the Gestapo had arrested Christian, but not yet searched the house, she also had this one opportunity to check for any incriminating evidence.

Astrid Maria and Mia walked side by side along the pavement, almost running in their haste. Mia's shadows followed them.

The surgery was still clothed in darkness. The door was locked and the curtains were shut. Astrid Maria opened the door and let them in to where the darkness was a welcome, if temporary shelter.

'Astrid!' Astrid Maria called up the stairs. 'It's only me,' she continued, 'and Mia's with me.' She went slowly up the stairs, surely they wouldn't have arrested her daughter as well?

Mia dived into the consulting room. She let her eyes adjust to the dark then made straight for the desk. She pulled open the drawers and put her hand in feeling for tell tale objects. She found pens, pencils, rulers, note pads, nothing untoward. Her fingers touched on the cold metal of a tin box, she pulled it out, opened it and peered into it in the gloom. It contained cough sweets, no wait a minute, a fragment of steel casing caught her attention. Mia didn't investigate further, she knew what it would be; a cyanide pill. She took out the pill in its casing and put the tin back in the drawer. She looked round the room quickly, wondering where on earth she could hide it, although hiding it wouldn't be good enough. She slipped down her stocking, pushed the pill in-between her toes, pulled up her stocking again, and put her shoe back on.

Astrid Maria found Astrid sitting on Petter's bed. The child was desolately playing with a wooden truck that Christian had made him for Christmas, looking helplessly at his mother. Astrid was pale and dry eyed, frozen with fear. Astrid Maria sat on the bed beside her daughter and put her arms around her. Mia came bounding up the stairs, where she found the desolate cameo all huddled miserably on Petter's bed.

Mia exchanged a look with her mother, and then turned to

Astrid. 'Astrid where do you keep photographs?' Astrid looked at her bemused. Mia tried to hold back her urgency. 'Astrid where do you have any photographs? Does Christian have any photographs anywhere?'

At the mention of his name Astrid stiffened. Mia's eyes bored into her willing her to speak.

'He has some in the bottom draw of the little desk in the sitting room,' Astrid said, the information coming out automatically, making no sense to her.

Mia sighed with relief and ran back down the stairs. As far as she could see she couldn't help obscure evidence connected with Christian's activities as a doctor, but the Gestapo suspected a close connection with Resistance leadership and all Mia could think of doing was minimising any link between Christian and Tom. She pulled out a wad of photos and started flipping through them quickly. There was just enough light to recognise the faces in the photographs. They were mostly of Astrid and Petter, but now and again she found one of Tom which she put on one side before continuing her search. There were four photographs in all. Mia shut the drawer. She could hear noises upstairs of drawers and cupboards opening, which suggested that Astrid Maria had persuaded Astrid to get dressed. Mia went over to the empty grate and put a match to the photos. She burned them slowly and carefully, hoping to finish before the others came down, but she was left with a rather telling mess of black ashes in the empty summer grate. She took the dust pan and brush which stood by the fire place and carefully swept up the mess, then she ground it down with her fingers, but it was poorly disguised to an expert. She looked around. She could hear steps on the stairs. She caught sight of Christian's pipe, she picked it up, it was half full of semi-burned out tobacco, or at least something which resembled tobacco. Mia emptied it into the dustpan and ground it into the ashes of the photographs just as the others came into the room.

'We're going back to the apartment,' Astrid Maria said.

'I'm just coming,' Mia answered. She slipped though into the kitchen and emptied the tobacco mess into the bin where she could smell the remains of other smoked pipes. She put the dust pan and brush back in their usual place and ran down the stairs after them.

***

Friedrich went down the last flight of steps leading to the high security cells. He stopped at the guard room to check the briefing.

'*Is everything ready?*' He asked the guard.

The guard scrambled to his feet and saluted. Friedrich responded impatiently with a cursory heil Hitler.

'*Yes, Herr Kriminalsekretaer.*'

'*Send for the latest reports as soon as they come in and bring them straight to me.*'

'*Yes, Herr Kriminalsekretaer.*'

Friedrich went past the guard room and on to one of the cells, a guard was standing to attention outside the cell.

'*Heil Hitler!*'

'*Heil Hitler!*'

The guard unlocked the cell and Friedrich went in. Another guard stood to attention inside the cell.

'*Heil Hitler!*'

'*Heil Hitler! Now leave us! You will not disturb us except to bring me all latest reports.*'

'*Yes, Herr Kriminalsekretaer!*'

Friedrich went over to the desk, which stood in the middle of the cell, and put his black briefcase on it. He pulled up the chair and sat down. One bare bulb lit up the small space into painful clarity, but Friedrich had yet to acknowledge the presence of the prisoner.

He took the papers out of the briefcase and fiddled with them as if sorting them. He then proceeded as if reading the reports, although he knew every word, every movement Mia had made since she left the Head Quarters at 1730 hours yesterday evening. He knew she had done some window shopping but not gone into any shops. He knew that she had smoked a cigarette then cycled home. She had been in her apartment alone until her mother came home when a light had gone on in the kitchen and the mother had closed the curtains. Lights had been seen in another room and those curtains had also been drawn. No other activity had been observed until someone opened the curtains just a little after six o'clock. A neighbour of the prisoner had been followed to the apartment. He had spoken to the mother and in less than five minutes mother and daughter had been followed to the prisoner's home. The prisoner's home still had all its heavy curtains closed, but within half an hour the women had left the building. The mother had taken the arm of the older daughter, who had walked slowly and uncertainly as if in deep shock. The younger daughter had followed behind her, nephew in one hand and a small case in the other. The suitcase was such as one would use as an overnight bag. The three women and the child had been followed back to the apartment.

That was all. The surgery had received no telephone calls that evening and Mia had not been observed to attempt to make contact with anyone apart from a natural contact with her family.

Once the women had left he had given orders to search the house, but as yet no other arrests were to be made.

Friedrich finally raised his eyes from the desk and slowly bent his gaze towards the prisoner. The prisoner, who, in ordinary times, Friedrich would have hoped to meet as a brother-in-law. The prisoner was tall, and feeling his eyes looking down on him Friedrich stood up. And there they stood, almost on a level, facing each other over the desk and under the cruel starkness of the electric light bulb.

Christian found himself looking straight into eyes which were so tormented that for a moment the pain smote him beyond his own fears and discomforts. Instinct raised his arm in comfort and his foot took a step forward, but the German stiffened and withdrew into a cold arrogance.

Christian sighed visibly in the still room, his tears may not be the only ones to be shed that day.

'You will talk. You will answer my questions, and if you do not I will use all in my power until you do talk,' Friedrich finally said coldly.

Christian hunched his shoulders slightly. He was under no

illusions as to what may be within the German's power to do, but his eyes remained steadfastly fixed on those of his interrogator. Friedrich returned the gaze, but his own eyes were now veiled.

'You are accused of aiding and abetting resistance activity. You have repeatedly attended criminals in your capacity as a doctor without bringing them to justice. You are also suspected, along with the whole of your family, of being part of a resistance organisation. You yourself are accused of having access to the highest authorities within the resistance organisation.'

Christian continued to gaze steadily at his accuser, but he had caught the word 'suspected', the others could yet be in the clear. Furthermore it occurred to Christian that it was neither in the interests of, nor desired by the man before him, to pursue suspicion of their family if such suspicion could not be founded. If Christian held out the damage could stop with him. It was a thin hope but enough to ease his worst fear that Astrid would be arrested and Petter put in a home. His motivation to protect Mia could not have had a greater incentive.

'I will tell you what I do of my own free will and you can be the judge of any culpability,' Christian said calmly. He wished he'd had time to attach a collar to his shirt and clean his glasses, it was not comfortable to feel dirty and inadequately dressed.

Friedrich continued to regard the prisoner inscrutably, but he indicated silently that, if he so wished, Christian could continue.

Perhaps it would have been better to answer questions as random talk could give far more away than direct answers to questions. Well, it was too late now, he would just have to keep it short and to the point.

'As you know I am a doctor. I have my own practice and where patients overlap I also do some work in the hospital. A large proportion of my work is home visits and I may make any thing between two and ten home visits in any one day, including weekends if the need is dire.'

'Your wife is also a doctor?'

'Yes.'

'And she continues to practice as a doctor?'

'Yes.'

'*She works in your practice and carries out the same work that you do.*'

'*No. She takes two or three morning surgeries a week. That is all.*'

'*It seems strange that she doesn't help you further with your work.*'

'*We have a small child and much of her time is spent taking care of him.*'

'*I would think that her family could help her.*'

'*Her mother works as a volunteer with a local Red Cross unit and her sister, as you know, works full time here, in your offices.*' Christian couldn't help a certain disdain in his tone as he mentioned Mia, but he had the satisfaction of detecting a slight flinch in Friedrich's cool stare, so perhaps the disdain had been just as well.

'*Your wife is intimate with all aspects of your work?*'

'*Indeed not. She is familiar only with surgery work. She tends to attract her own patients and will sometimes request that I make a home visit to some of her more severe cases. You will understand that we are bound by oath not to discuss anything which occurs during a consultation and even though we are husband and wife, in our professional life we adhere strictly to that code.*'

The ensuing silence between them was broken by the entrance of a guard. He gave more papers to Friedrich and then left. Friedrich read the report eagerly. The mother had been followed to a grocery store where she had queued for an hour for fish oil margarine and some oatmeal. The sisters had remained indoors and Mia had not reported in for work. Here was a new puzzle, if, if Mia was innocent she would be the one to feel hurt and betrayed. Friedrich had arrested Christian and he knew that Mia was very fond of the man. Perhaps she, too, felt disbelief and shock that Friedrich had been able to do such a thing; she may never want to see him again. He swallowed his despair, staring at the black print of the report. He would have to force the truth out of this man. The truth! There had been a time when Friedrich had believed in the truth, had believed that there was a correct interpretation of events and once this was forced out of people he could, at least, feel that he had arrived at the truth. But experience had taught him that this was not so, torture and force could distort the truth as much as cajoling and manipulation. Truth was whatever Friedrich decided was so.

He turned back to the prisoner. Christian had succumbed slightly to the discomfort of standing in the stuffy heat of the small cell. Good. Friedrich repeated the same line of questioning as before and listened carefully for deviations from the first answers. There were none and their own reports corroborated that it was unlikely that the wife was involved.

'*But you make home visits.*' Friedrich continued, suddenly switching the line of questioning.

'*Yes.*'

'*And you, of course, keep a record of all your home visits?*'

Christian caught his breath and took a moment before replying. '*I keep a record of all home visits made to my own patients.*'

'*I'm not sure I understand you. Do you, or do you not keep a record of all home visits?*'

Christian looked into the cold, grey light of the beautiful, brown eyes and made no reply.

'*So you will have recorded visits made to the following people and addresses?*' Friedrich referred to his notes and read out names and addresses from a list, names pouring out in rapid succession.

Christian remained silent.

'*Well it's no matter if you answer or not. We are at this moment checking through your files.*'

Christian's chin jerked up. '*What do you mean you're checking through my files? Those files are private records kept only for the eyes of patient and doctor. Who gave you...* '

'*You forget who you are speaking to,*' cut in the Kriminalsekretær.

They were searching the house. What had become of Astrid and Petter? Was it possible that Astrid Maria and Mia had heard of his arrest and removed them from the house before the police arrived?   Christian had forgotten about other possible incriminating evidence such as the cyanide pill, which Tom had given to him more than a year ago.

Christian slowly took off his glasses and began cleaning them with the handkerchief he kept in his trouser pocket.

'*I don't record visits to patients who are not on my books.*'

'*So you admit that you make irregular visits?*'

'*I make one-off visits, yes, but that is not irregular, it is, in fact, quite common practice. A duty doctor is bound to answer calls for assistance at any time of day or night.*'

'*A duty doctor will also keep a record of all such visits, and not to do so would be considered gross negligence on the part of the practitioner.*'

Christian made no reply.

'*If you had followed correct procedure you would have kept a record of suspicious wounds and bone fractures, even gun shot wounds, in many cases where hospitalisation would have been the only way of ensuring adequate recovery.*'

Christian said nothing, the trap was well laid and there was no way out of it.

'*In not recording these home visits you have not only risked the health of your patients but you have also violated the laws by not immediately handing over persons, under suspicion of violent and treasonable acts, to the police. You cannot claim that it was in the best interests of their health, as prisoners are given all necessary hospital treatment.*'

'*If I receive a call to treat someone I treat them, I'm not interested in the politics.*' Christian responded tiredly.

The questioning continued relentlessly. The cold eyes were fixed on him as the German sat at the desk, paced around the room or approached him from behind with a cold menace. Christian was either silent or repeated his last comment with dogged determination, hardly hearing what was being said to him. The effort of standing, the glare of the electric light bulb and the heat of the room made his head swim. He fixed his gaze on the desk in front of him and concentrated on keeping himself upright.

Occasionally their agony was disturbed by the delivery of reports, which Friedrich devoured with a greedy intensity, ignoring his prisoner for long periods of time.

'*It is known to us that you and your family have been involved with the so called Oslo Gang for some time.*'

Christian's head shot up. The question marked another sudden change of tack on the part of his interrogator. Christian had never heard of any such gang and his eyes shone fiercely with the indignant righteousness of innocence.

'*I have never heard of such a gang. Neither I nor my family have ever been part of any such groups or gang.*' For a moment the truth blazed between them and it was Friedrich who dropped his eyes first. Christian, concentrating his mind on his family, was not confused by thoughts of Mia or Tom.

The truth of his words had leapt like a flame around Friedrich's heart. It was a flame of hope. It was possible that Mia hadn't betrayed him. He should now torment the prisoner with a barrage of questions, pour scorn and doubt on Christian's claims of innocence, but he faltered and the words wouldn't come. He sat at the desk and looked at the reports. He tried to discipline his will into following the procedures he was so adept at. Instead a fraught silence grew in the room until both men felt faint with suffocation. Unable to bear it any longer Friedrich suddenly stood up, stuffed the papers in his briefcase, and left the cell.

The two men had endured their gruelling battle for over twelve hours.

Christian stood swaying in the empty room. His mouth was parched and a cold sweat made him feel feverish. He was too exhausted to realise the implications of Friedrich's sudden departure. He tried to concentrate his mind. He was in no doubt that he had incriminated himself and that he was to be sentenced to imprisonment, even deportation and death, but had he managed to save the others? Had he managed to hold out? What had he said? What questions had been asked? His mind went into panic and then a blankness spread through his whole body until he fell to the floor in a deathlike sleep.

***

Mia sat on a chair in the front room watching Astrid and Petter, who were sitting together on the sofa. Astrid was reading a book to Petter, but her voice was wooden and her face deathly pale. The child snuggled against his mother, confused and fearful.

Mia hadn't left the house since they had returned there with Astrid and Petter the previous morning. She had just sat waiting, her thoughts bent on Christian, wondering how long it would be before they came and arrested her. Astrid's thoughts were also bent on Christian, but with a dull dread, even an anger that he should be taken from her. It didn't occur to her that the circle of suspicion could soon tighten to include them all.

A ring on the doorbell shot through Mia like a bullet. Astrid Maria had gone to the Centre, her chin raised defiantly as she passed the shadows. Astrid carried on reading to Petter as if she hadn't heard the ringing. Mia got up and went down the communal stairs to answer the door, her hands trembling as she fumbled with the latch.

'Miss Gram?'

'Yes.'

'Telegram for you miss.'

Mia snatched the paper out of the youth's hands, slammed the door closed and ran back up the stairs. She tore open the seal and read the message.

'*Meetmeintheparkstop1600hrsstoponthebridgestop*'.

It was already three o'clock. She rushed to the bathroom and washed her face, she then changed her clothes. It was a colder day than yesterday so she took an old light coat of her mother's and ran back down the stairs and out of the house. Astrid continued to read as if oblivious to all else.

Interestingly the shadows didn't follow Mia as she slipped across the square, heading westwards towards Frogner Park. She didn't take her bicycle as she had plenty of time and she wanted to be quiet. It was a luxury to be suddenly on her own, unwatched and free from Astrid's stultifying pain.

She didn't go straight to the bridge but walked around an area with small shrubs, keeping in the shadows of tall trees and watching the area carefully. It might, after all, be a trap.

Friedrich was also early. Mia watched him as he walked up a broad avenue lined with mature lime trees. He was dressed in civvies, apparently on his own and unarmed, neither did he look to one side or another as he might have done if silently communicating with a hidden guard. Mia waited, watching him through her screen of bushes. He stopped on the bridge and leant heavily against the rail, as if burdened or extremely tired. The famous statue of the angry boy was at his back, but he was as if oblivious to all else apart from the torture of his own mind.

He looked quite broken. For a moment Mia forgot her own fears and was filled with an unlooked for compassion for this poor man. She stepped out from the shade of the trees and went quickly to him. She stood silently in front of him, one hand instinctively stretched towards him. He slowly raised his face to her, he was gaunt with lack of sleep and his eyes searched hers with both a question and an apology.

Christian hadn't talked.

Mia felt sudden tears well in her throat. She couldn't stop them and they ran down her cheeks unchecked. She put out her hand and taking Friedrich's between both of hers she leant against him. They stayed together in silence for a long, long time. The day took on the chill of early evening and in the distance they could hear the distant rumblings of trams taking people home from work. With one will they left the bridge and aimlessly wandered further into the park, following the lines of statues, the eternal symbols of love and procreation a stony witness to their pain.

Mia's tears were an agony to Friedrich. His own eyes were dry and aching, longing for release. He put his other hand over hers and held her tightly. She had loved him. Whether the discovery held more pain or joy he couldn't know, but either way it could only leave him with sorrow and loss.

Mia finally found the words to speak.

'*I can't come back,*' she said, '*I can't come back and work in the office, or, or...* '

Friedrich tried to speak, but his voice cracked, with an effort he took control of himself. '*I know.*'

They were both silent again. It was all over. They both stood there thinking it, knowing it, but unable to say it.

Mia wanted to ask him about Christian, but what was there to say? Was he all right? Were they going to release him? Of course not, they had too much evidence against him, just nothing on the real criminals. Her tears started again. Thinking of Christian should have hardened her heart against Friedrich, but Christian's involvement with illegal patients was hardly Friedrich's fault. It would feel better if she could blame someone, but who? Tom? Yes, she supposed Tom was to blame. But Christian hadn't blamed Tom, he must have protected them all through to the bitter end. She had to ask.

'*Is he, is he all right?*' Her voice was no more than a whisper.

Friedrich struggled to answer. He had spent one of the most gruelling twelve hours of his life with Christian. He owed to him the vindication of the girl he loved, but because of Christian he would have to renounce his love. If Christian had proved a lesser man, though unworthy of Mia's respect, a lesser man would have left Friedrich feeling a greater one.

'*He's okay.*' He said.

'*You'll, you'll leave Astrid alone? And the child?*'

'*Yes, no one will touch them.*'

Mia squeezed his hands in thanks and relief.

The streets were getting quieter again. A slash of red in the sky heralded the first of the sunset, Mia shivered suddenly in her light coat.

'*You're cold?*'

'*I'm all right. I should go.*'

She turned from the monuments of love and Friedrich followed, still holding her hand, then unable to bear it any longer he pulled her towards him and crushed her against him. She heard the tears welling in his chest and his shoulders heaving with the pain. She put her own arms around him and they stood together until a new silence descended on them. They finally drew apart and without looking at each other walked quickly away in opposite directions.

***

Siri was excitedly pinning a well used pattern to a large piece of white silk. Mia was holding the pin cushion and eyeing her fondly. The silk was a present from Tom, who was sitting in the Grobæk's drawing room drinking real coffee, apparently another present from Tom. How on earth did he manage it?

Mia smiled as Siri frowned over her sewing.

'You can't wear it to work, of course,' Mia said handing over another pin.

Siri ignored her, concentrating.

'And you'd better not wear it when you're out with what's his name.'

'Fred.'

'Fred.' Siri suddenly looked up. 'What do you mean I can't wear it?' she asked, dismayed.

'Well you know what it is don't you?'

'Of course I know what it is, it's white silk, it's a bit coarse but it's the best stuff I've seen in two years.'

'I mean you do know where it comes from?'

Siri shook her head.

'It's from a parachute silly.'

Siri suddenly looked uncertain and instinctively backed away from the cloth as if it might come to life and take on its former shape.

'Make something for your mother, I don't think she goes to so many dangerous places.'

Siri hardly knew whether to be relieved, cross or disappointed.

'I should get back.' Mia was serious again and a new frown furrowed her brow. She put out a hand to her friend and touched Siri on the arm. 'Can I come again soon?'

'Of course you can. Give my love to Astrid and your mother.'

'Thank you.'

Mia slipped out of the kitchen, while Siri stayed behind weighing up the risks of the white silk. Mia popped her head round the drawing room door and said her goodbyes quickly not wanting to get drawn into conversation. She was just putting on her coat when Tom came up quietly behind her and put a hand on her shoulder.

'I'll see you home.'

'No you won't.' Mia sounded irritated. She relented and turned to face him. 'They might still be keeping a watch on me, don't follow me and don't leave yet. You should even slip out the back way to be sure.'

Tom couldn't keep the admiration out of his look. 'You're a real pro,' he said.

Now she was irritated. Mia put her hand on the door handle, and then hesitated.

'Christian didn't talk,' Tom said.

Mia turned to him. 'No he didn't talk. You knew he wouldn't. You would never have exposed him to so much risk if you hadn't known he wouldn't talk.'

Tom withdrew from her slightly.

Mia put her hand back to the door, but her head was still turned towards Tom and her eyes fixed on him. 'I hope we're all worth it,' she said bitterly, 'I hope we're all worth one good man.'

October, 1944
Eighteen

Christian was in the hold of a transport ship. There were perhaps twenty other prisoners with him, but he hadn't befriended any of them. He was too empty, too numb to make contact with another human being. Armed guards were stationed by the ladder, which lead up to the deck. The ship smelled of oil and lurched and buffeted its way through the autumn sea. If the allies torpedoed them he would die, trapped in this stinking hole. He hardly knew if he wanted to die or not.

He ran his finger round his shirt collar. It was sticky with grime. His trousers hung limply off his hips and one of his shoe laces had broken. The toilet bucket in the corner slopped over with the lurching of the boat and Christian turned away his face in disgust. He tried to measure the hours, the days of their journey, but it seemed as a constant nightmare and he kept falling into fitful sleep so that it was hard to measure the time.

He knew when they finally docked because the boat made an awful shudder and the engines complained and whined. The slop bucket made one last glorious effort to move with the boat and rolled over onto its side spilling its putrid contents over the greasy boards. Expecting some temporary relief some of the prisoners stood up, but it was several hours before the guards rounded them up and they were hauled up the ladder and frogmarched off the boat, the guards' rifles levelled at them. They were then put into a temporary holding station. It was no more than nine feet square. There was an empty slops bucket in the corner, but not enough room to squat. A guard opened a small slatted window and miraculously they were all handed a cup of water and a small loaf of dark rye bread. They pressed against each other in the dark, trying not to spill the precious water and chewing on the bread. Not expecting many such miracles Christian ate sparingly of the bread, but the water he drank before it was spilt and wasted.

It was possibly the next day that guards came and opened the doors to the holding room. It now stank with sweat, fear and worse, the air was foul and thick with the fumes of human excrement. The prisoners almost fell out through the opening into the light of day. Christian felt, rather than knew, that somehow their numbers seemed reduced. He glanced back into the dark hole he had just escaped from and caught sight of the pallor of human flesh fallen to the floor, stiff as if dead for some hours. He put his hand to his mouth and breathed deeply to stem the wave of nausea that threatened to overtake him.

'*Get in line,*' barked one of the guards.

Guns were levelled at them again and they forced their stiff limbs into a quick march through an industrial area of a small town. Christian attempted to distract his misery by trying to work out where they were, but his thoughts were too fragmented and he couldn't concentrate. They arrived at a railway station, or was it a railway siding? There were two trains pulled up on opposite tracks, they pulled two carriages and the rest were transport wagons. The guards marched the prisoners down the length of a train to an assigned wagon, unlocked a door and thrust the prisoners in.

'*Not you!*'

Christian swung round in bewilderment. The words were directed at him. The door was banged shut and the other prisoners were locked in the transport wagon. A rifle prodded him in the back and he was marched over the rail tracks to the other train. Another wagon door was opened and he was thrust into the dark once more. There were other people in the wagon and someone shuffled over to make room for him. Someone spoke in a language he couldn't immediately identify, and then they were all silent again, but at least there was room to sit down.

Christian heard the low rumble of an engine starting, but the slow clanking sound of departing train must have been the other one, as the one they were in remained still and silent.

Later, roused by the lurching of wheels and the bracing of couplings, Christian awoke to the final stage of his journey.

After several hours the train ground to a halt, and, assuming they had come to the end of their journey, Christian roused himself and sat up expectantly, but nothing happened. They sat in the dark and waited. Then the silence was broken by a familiar sound; the drone of heavy bombers. A watchful silence descended over the wagon. Those of the prisoners who were alert enough picked out the persistent staccato of anti-aircraft guns followed by a dull boom as the heavy bombers emptied their loads. After a prolonged silence the train slowly groaned into life again and they lurched forward. This time the journey can't have been much more than half an hour. The wagon door was flung open and Christian found himself falling out of the train into a cold dawn. The light hurt his eyes, he fumbled for his glasses and his legs buckled with the stiffness of inaction.

'*Get into line,*' came the familiar command and the prisoners tried to stumble into some semblance of order.

Christian risked a quick glance at his surroundings. This time they were in an actual station. Christian caught the name before turning his head rigidly before him. Oranienburg? Oranienburg? If he remembered aright it was somewhere near Berlin, to the North, he thought. So it had been the allies bombing Berlin that had disturbed their night.

It was cold. The surroundings were flat, and an icy wind blew across desolate autumn fields, picking up dust and fallen leaves along the straight road they were marched down. After a while, perhaps they had walked three or four kilometres, it couldn't have been further, they drew along side a compound wall. It was built of brick, and rendered with concrete, which was flaking and cracked, the top was crenulated and fixed with rolls of barbed wire and it was about three metres high. The prisoners now turned to the left and marched along the outside of the wall. On their right Christian thought he could make out brick built residences, perhaps military barracks, which neatly backed onto the track, but he dare not turn his head and before he got a better look the prisoners were turned to the left and marched through a gate in the compound wall. They entered an open space. There were, perhaps, offices on their right and a substantial brick built dwelling on their left.

The prisoners were marched on, a further gate was opened up to greet them and they passed under the unforgettable insignia, '*Arbeit macht frei*', Labour Brings Freedom. The iron gate clanged shut behind them and they had entered Sachsenhausen concentration camp.

Christian found himself standing to attention on a broad concrete path, which lead on down the centre of the camp. They were standing in the middle of a large open space surfaced with black cinder. At the far end of the open space the path ran through the centre of row upon row of barracks, or huts, constructed in a semi-circle round the open space. Straight ahead of them he could see the unmistakable outline of a gallows.

Despite the buildings and the high compound wall the open space was not at all protected from the prevailing wind, which swirled dust from the cinder compound along the road and into their eyes. Christian's summer clothes were also grossly inadequate in the bitter autumn temperature.

The new inmates stood in frozen stillness and a guard with a loaded weapon stood watch over them. They were aware of other prisoners running round the outer semi-circle around where they stood. At first Christian had assumed that it was prisoners running errands, they were undoubtedly prisoners as they were all wearing an ugly striped uniform. They were also emaciated, some beyond cure. Then he noticed a mad routine to their running. They were running, as it were, around a track and on their heels were guards with whips, which occasionally spewed up dust from the cinder surface or licked at the heels of the runners. And the runners seemed so poorly shod! Some ran on their toes as if the shoes were much too tight and others shuffled and struggled to keep on shoes, which flapped up and down against their heels. What new nightmare was this?

Attempting to keep his gaze forward Christian couldn't help his eyes wandering trying to make sense of the madness before him. One of the runners finally fell out of line, rolled himself into a ball and lay quite still. A guard was upon him in no time, he was kicked off the track and with one swift movement the guard levelled his revolver at him and shot him in the head.

The shock was like a blow to the stomach. Christian took an involuntary step forward, but a fellow new inmate risked a sideways glance of warning and Christian stood back to attention. Luckily the shooting had distracted their own guard and Christian's deflection had gone undetected.

At last they were told to move again. They were marched off to the right and into one of the huts, where they were registered. They gave their names and dates of birth and in return were given a scrap of paper with a large number on, this number they had to memorise, as it was now their identity.

They were then moved into another room where they were made to strip. Their unwashed clothes were put in a bag identified by their number. They were all allowed to keep their shoes and Christian his glasses. Clutching these and his bit of paper Christian followed the others into yet another room, where they were herded into a central tiled area and made to stand under showers of cold water, which periodically suddenly spewed out brief jets of scalding, hot water. Unable to take more grief Christian abandoned himself to the physical relief of washing in clean water, even the choking smell of carbolic was a relief after days of sweat, fear and excrement.

One by one they were then ordered out of the showers. A guard took Christian's shoes and glasses, and, unable to focus, he stumbled on the tiled step as he tried to follow the guard into another room.

There were no words spoken, one guard with a rifle gestured that Christian should stand in the middle of the room and stretch out his arms. Cold water dripped onto the concrete floor and Christian tried to control his convulsive shivering from the cold. Still unable to focus on his surroundings he was aware of a man in a white coat approaching him, but he didn't see the glint of the razor in the man's hands until he started to shave Christian of all his body hair.

Christian waited motionless, the feverish heat of fear keeping him still. His arms stretched out and his head drooped as he stood there, naked and unseeing, while the prison authorities prepared him for hell.

November, 1944
Nineteen

Mia had been sent out by Astrid Maria to a grocer, who reputedly had onions. Mia had become a professional queuer during the last months and had become adept at successfully scouring the city following rumours of supplies, both legal and black. It was even harder in the winter to find fresh food. She hadn't found the onions, but cutting down Industri Gata from Bogstadveien to get home, she had gone past a small fishmongers, who were selling fishcakes. They didn't smell very fishy but the potato would be a treat. They hadn't got their usual supply of potatoes from the farm this year as Astrid had forbidden use of the car.

Mia hurried home with her gleanings, not that home was much of a haven. Astrid had hardly spoken to her since Christian's arrest. Astrid Maria had tried to bully Astrid into going back to her own home and opening up the surgery again, but Astrid had turned her face to the wall and spent her days in the apartment in dogged misery compounded by fear. Frustrated, Astrid Maria spent more time than ever at the Centre. Mia was reconciled to, almost thankful for, the quiet months which slipped by. She hardly knew what she wished for anymore and was so confused by the conflicting loyalties she felt towards the war, Tom's group and Friedrich that she had allowed herself to drift emotionally, decisions would come soon enough as the last phases of the war finally unfurled. Instead she thought of Christian. In fact the whole apartment seemed to brood on Christian, although scarcely mentioned amongst the mother and her two daughters, they all of them thought of little else. Desire for him hung heavy in the closed atmosphere of the still apartment. Mia thought of Christian because the end of the war and his safe return were the only things she could look forward to without confusion or regret.

Mia crossed the square. Her shadows were long gone and she was now a forgotten pawn in a bigger war game. She turned the key in the door and went into the communal lobby. There was a letter in their post box, hand written, it was from Christian at last. It was addressed to Astrid. There was a German postmark and the authorisation stamp on the back stated that it had come from K. Z. Sachsenhausen. Mia's heart sank, she had hoped beyond hope that they would keep him in Grini[5], but a concentration camp in Germany meant that his chances of survival were much lower. If only the war would end soon.

She took the letter upstairs and found Astrid in her usual place on the sofa. Petter was driving his wooden truck round and round the front room, restless with inactivity. Mia handed the letter to Astrid. She watched her sister's face flush with fear and joy, and then, feeling Mia's eyes on her, hide the letter from sight waiting for Mia to turn away before she opened it. Mia sighed. She turned to Petter.

'Look!' She said, 'it's started to snow. Shall we run to the park and chase the snowflakes?'

'Yes!' Petter leapt up in delight.

Astrid was too taken up with her letter to resist and Mia took Petter out of the room, squeezed him into last year's snow suit and hurried off outside with him. Petter danced with delight as they skipped down the street towards the park.

Astrid sat for some time clutching her letter. They hadn't had news of Christian since September when he had got a message to them from Grini reassuring them that all was well. It was now already November. Astrid had been sitting waiting every day for news of his death, but he wasn't dead, he had written to her. She finally roused herself and tore open the envelope. For some moments she gazed at the opening address in confusion. It didn't say 'Dear Astrid', it said 'Liebe Astrid'. The whole letter was written in German![6] Why on earth would he write to her in German, he knew that she didn't speak German? She re-examined the envelope and then realised the significance of the German stamp. Christian had been sent to Germany. Rumours of conditions in German concentration camps were common knowledge. She set up a low murmuring

---

[5] Prison in the Oslo area used by the Gestapo for political prisoners during the occupation.

[6] All letters from concentration camps had to be written in German to pass the censors.

of pain. She was going to lose him. Why? Why had he done this to her?

***

Astrid Maria and Mia were in the kitchen drinking a very watery version of Astrid Maria's coffee mix. Astrid had gone to bed early. She and Petter were sharing the guest room. Astrid Maria indicated that Mia should be quiet and they both listened for a few minutes.

'Good, she seems to have settled for the night.' Astrid Maria gave Mia a conspiratorial look and then produced the brown envelope of Christian's letter out of her pocket.

'How on earth did you get hold of it?'

'I said I would like to peruse it later in the evening when I had more time to make it out.'

'I offered to read it for her,' said Mia.

'Well, she won't let you anywhere near it.'

'I know that, it's so ridiculous.'

'Anyway she thinks you're out with Siri, or at least planning to go out with Siri.'

'Mother!'

'I know, but it'll take me all night to translate this letter. It's ridiculous not to read it. What if there's some urgent message?'

'Mother!'

'All right. I know that's not likely, but it is very likely that he's written a list of things he'd like us to try and get for him.'

'Why should he do that?'

Astrid Maria looked at her daughter. 'You don't know everything about the German system you know. We've been getting requests from prisoners and families throughout the war and Red Cross parcels have been getting through for the past year.'

'To Sachsenhausen?'

'One of the most reliable destinations.'

Mia held out her hand. 'Hand it over then.'

December, 1944

It was Christmas Eve. Mia would have to go home at some point. She took yet another detour wondering how she could further delay sitting at the Christmas dinner table facing Astrid. Unwittingly she had walked into the neighbourhood of the café where she used to meet Frank. Bored and restless, wondering if it still existed, she turned down the street where it used to be and walked towards it. There was a sign outside, yes it was still there, more surprisingly it was open and without pausing for thought she pulled open the door and walked in. For a confused minute, as in a time warp, she stood just inside the doorway looking at Frank, Frank sitting just as he had been when she had left him 1942. She stood frozen with shock. Frank recovered more quickly and taking her arm lead her quickly back out into the street.

'Mia!'

'Frank.'

She could see the questions racing through his mind. He had had no news of her since they had last met at this same café nearly three years ago.

Holding her arm he led her at a rapid walk down the street.

'You should be somewhere. At home,' he said at last.

'I know. I'm on my way there now, but it's not, er, very festive at home these days.'

'We can't... God, I've missed you.'

Mia didn't say anything. Her mouth twitched and her eyes were fixed on the pavement.

'I shouldn't have... come here.' She looked up briefly.

'Well you've just made my Christmas. God bless you. Hang on in there Mia, it can't be much longer now.' And he turned and left her, making rapid strides back down the street.

Mia watched him fading into the night, then turned back home. She'd almost forgotten the fragmented pieces of her former life, pieces just waiting to be put back into place.

If Christian came back, she thought, everything would be all right, everything would be as it should be. She longed for another letter, the German he had to write giving her a strange feeling of comradeship and easing her loneliness.

March, 1945
Twenty

A hint of spring was in the air. Astrid Maria had just received word that the Swedish Red Cross, the so called white buses, were now in Germany. There must be every hope that they would get Christian home safely. Astrid Maria was hurrying home with the news when she met Mia in the doorway of the apartment building on her way out.

At the sight of Mia her brow suddenly clouded. 'Where are you going?' She asked sharply.

Mia sighed. 'If you must know I'm going to see Siri.'

'Oh.'

'You're home early?' Mia, in turn, questioned her mother.

The smile returned to Astrid Maria's face. 'The Swedish Red Cross are in Germany. He might be home soon.'

Mia looked at her mother steadily, taking in the import of the words. Astrid Maria turned to go into the apartment house, but on a sudden impulse Mia stepped forward and held her mother back.

'Wait. What if. What if he doesn't come back?'

'Why shouldn't he come back?'

'Mother, we haven't heard anything since Christmas!'

'Communications have been difficult ever since the allied advances.'

'Mother, what if you tell her and he doesn't come back?'

'We can't keep everything from her,' said Astrid Maria, suddenly irritated and frustrated.

'We know that prisoners are being rescued,' said Mia quietly, 'but we don't know who yet.' She bit her lip and Astrid Maria was surprised to see that she was crying. The tears moved her more than any words could.

'We can't suddenly stop protecting her, mother,' continued Mia, the tears now dry. 'We've been doing it all her life after all,' she added quietly.

Astrid Maria ignored the last remark, but doubt had now stayed her hand.

'We'll just have to wait,' finished Mia.

'Oh.' Now she was no longer the bearer of good news Astrid Maria was not so keen to return to her eldest daughter. Astrid's gloom defeated and depressed her.

'Actually,' she said changing tack, 'I might just pop over to the Grobæk's with you.'

Mia smiled wryly at her mother. 'You do know that Mrs Grobæk's out of town, staying with some cousins in Kongsberg?' She asked her mother.

'Oh? No. Why would she do that?'

'I think Tom must have frightened them with stories of capitulation and invasion. Mrs Grobæk sometimes gets confused about who the enemies really are and she thinks that the Allies are going to bomb Oslo.'

'Don't be ridiculous!'

'Ridiculous or not she's not home. Actually, mother, I thought I might stay with Siri for a bit, just while her mother's away.'

Astrid Maria looked up at her daughter with suspicion. 'Has she asked you?' She questioned sharply.

'Yes, sort of.'

'Well you'll do what you like anyway.'

Mia was about to respond but Astrid Maria cut in with a sigh. 'Perhaps after all it's best, but you'll come home again, won't you? When Astrid goes back to the surgery?'

Mia suddenly smiled at her mother and bent over and kissed her on the cheek.

'Well, well, I'd better get back then.'

'Yes you had.'

Astrid Maria turned back and Mia went on to Siri's house. She wondered, with a smile, if her mother was 'getting back' to Astrid or slipping off back to the Centre.

It took ages for anyone to answer the door at the Grobæk's. Mia was about to give up when finally Mr Grobæk came and let her in. He looked rather worn and worried.

'Oh Mia, good to see you, my dear, come in. She's, er, in the kitchen.' His voice was laden with embarrassment and Mia wondered what was up. She ran down the small flight of stairs which lead to the back of the house and into the kitchen.

Siri was sitting at the kitchen table in a miserable heap. A large wet handkerchief was in her hands and her face was all red and blotchy with crying.

Mia went towards her uncertainly. They couldn't have arrested Tom! It wasn't possible, not so near the end. If they had they would just shoot him. Friedrich would shoot him. Friedrich would understand, would see the whole sordid business for what it had been. Mia felt the panic rising in her throat, it hurt too much to think about Friedrich. Mia put her arm around Siri. It mustn't be Tom. Tom is all we have left, she then thought irrelevantly, sadly.

'Fred's gone.'

For a moment Mia's relief was so great that she couldn't remember who Fred was.

'He's gone. He said that I,' Siri broke out into sobs again. She dabbed at her eyes with the handkerchief then blew her nose noisily. 'He said, well he said lots of unpleasant things, about me, and then he went.'

'The blighter! What a skunk. The miserable coward's gone into hiding. You're well shot of him Siri!'

Siri dissolved into more sobs.

'Look Siri, in maybe as little as a month's time Oslo's going to be full of real Norwegians in Kaki uniforms all desperate to find the girl of their dreams and settle down at last.'

Siri couldn't resist a tearful smile. She took her friend's hand.

'What's his name, Fred, is a worm!'

'A worm,' repeated Siri.

'Mia you'll come and stay with us won't you?'

Mia sat down next to Siri and took both her hands in her own. 'Gladly,' she said.

***

No one else was home. Astrid walked wearily from the sitting room to the kitchen, where Petter was sitting at the table drawing careful outlines of animals with a pencil stub. She should feed the child, but she was so tired, she just wanted to sleep. She wondered how long she could go on longing, longing that none of it had happened; that it would all soon be over didn't interest her. She had nursed a dull hatred for the Germans, for Tom, for Mia, but really, in her heart of hearts, she blamed Christian and the blame was a poison which slowed her heart, slowed her thoughts and paralysed her ability to act, to reason, to do anything.

May, 1945
Twenty-One

There was a hammering on the back door of the Grobæk's house. What, in happier times, one might have called the tradesman's entrance. Siri and Mia were sitting in the kitchen playing cards.

'I'll get it.' Mia put the cards down. She went first to the window which looked out onto the back garden, but whoever was knocking on the door was keeping well within the shade of the frame. It was rather late in the evening for either visitors or deliveries, although the days were lengthening now and it was still light.

'I can't see anything,' Mia said to the curious Siri.

She went out of the kitchen and down the passage to the back door. She opened it cautiously.

'Frank!'

'Your mother said you were here.'

'My mother? When did you meet my mother?'

'Just now.'

'What do you mean just now?'

'I called at your home.'

'Frank!'

'Mia,' he tried to take her in his arms. 'Mia, it's all over. Hitler's killed himself. The war's over.'

'Are you sure?'

'Well all over bar the shouting. Helge reckons it's just a matter of days.'

'Oh. You'd better come in.' Mia lead him up the stairs and into the kitchen. Her legs were trembling and she sat down on a chair.

'Frank Olsen, Siri Grobæk,' she said, introducing her two friends.

'Does Tom know you're here?' Mia asked, avoiding Frank's intense gaze.

'Tom?'

Mia looked up at him suddenly remembering. 'I mean Helge.'

'No. What's it got to do with Helge?' He paused. 'So

Helge's real name is Tom?'

'Tom Grobæk.'

Frank took a sharp breath and looked at Mia open-mouthed. 'Did you know who he was all along?'

Mia nodded. 'He's Siri's cousin.'

'Tom?' Questioned Siri in bewilderment, trying to follow the conversation.

'But if you knew who he was?' Frank continued ignoring Siri.

'I know. He risked everything on me.'

'Wow. I mean I never thought about it. I just assumed...'

'Well there's nothing to think about. It's over now,' said Mia sharply. 'But Frank you shouldn't be here, not yet, surely, now, you understand the risk. Until the Allies...'

'The Homefront,' broke in Frank proudly.

'Whoever. Until power is transferred and the police are Norwegian again.'

'Mia it's a matter of days.'

She smiled. 'In a matter of days then. Come I'll show you out.'

She led him back down the passage. He put his arms round her, but when he tried to kiss her she turned her face away.

Mia went back to the kitchen.

'Mia what's all this about Tom? And who's Helge?' Siri accosted her as soon as she entered the room.

'Helge is Tom. Helge is just a code name, in fact one of his many code names. Tom is going to be the hero of the hour.'

Siri still looked confused.

'Tom has played one of the key roles in the resistance movement throughout the war.'

'You're kidding!' Siri's mouth was gaping with astonishment.

Mia smiled wryly; it had probably been no bad thing that Tom's relatives were rather slow on the up-take.

'And who's this Frank?' Siri went on to demand.

'One of Tom's agents.'

'I don't mean that. I mean who is he? You know!'

Mia smiled rather flatly. 'He's my fiancé. I suppose.'

It was chaos in the streets. Norwegian flags were everywhere. Mia didn't believe it possible that so many people owned Norwegian flags. It seemed that everyone was in the streets. Shop attendants were all out on the pavement and people stopped and shook her hand. Homefront workers, now dressed in makeshift kaki uniforms wandered in happy gangs, smoking provender and wolf-whistling at the pretty girls.

Mia smiled tiredly at a group of them and cut off down a side street where it was quieter. Frank was driving another victory convoy full of dignitaries and officers and she'd sort of promised to meet him. She had let the time slip past and she was going to be late.

She turned the corner into another narrow lane where a group of youths were blocking the entrance onto the main road. She was just pushing her way through them when she noticed a familiar face leering at her. She was trying to put a name to it when she heard it hiss to the others in the group.

'She's one of them, German whore,' and he spat in her face.

It was what's his name, Fred, the worm.

The others, blood up, grabbed her from behind. She started kicking and shouting. 'Let me go you creeps. You viscous, lousy creeps.'

Someone twisted her arm. 'She probably likes a bit of beating, leather whips,' another one laughed nastily.

'Help, help,' Mia let out an ear splitting scream. She hadn't gone through agony and torment to be mishandled by a bunch of good for nothings. 'Help!'

Someone shoved a handkerchief into her mouth and someone else grabbed her hair and pulled her down. She saw the glint of a blade and then felt the hair being wrenched from her head. They were sitting on her legs and arms. Laughing. Laughing.

Having hacked off her hair in short angry tufts they released their hold on her. She staggered to her feet and blindly turning went back the way she had come. The shouts of, 'Whore!' and mock cat calls, followed her down the lane.

After the first waves of shock had subsided Mia slowed her

pace. She had borrowed a light coat from Siri and stuffing her hand in the pocket found a beret neatly folded inside. Typical Siri, she thought, to be so organised. The normality steadied her a little, and, wincing at the pain as she touched her head, she carefully put the beret on.

Her first instinct was to go home and before she'd thought out the consequences she found herself ringing the bell to the apartment. It took ages for anyone to answer. Her mother must be out. Astrid opened the door reluctantly and Mia pushed it open and forced her way in past Astrid. Astrid held the door looking coldly at her sister. Mia pulled off the beret in a gesture of defiance and Astrid flinched visibly. Her hatred for Mia filled the vestibule and taking in Mia's shame Astrid felt a new strength empowering her disdain. With a quiet triumph she held the door open for Mia and simply waited for Mia to leave. If Astrid spoke Mia didn't take in her words. The hatred was enough.

Angry with herself for feeling strangely ashamed and frightened she turned away from the square and, remembering over the vistas of the past years, she headed towards Frank's old flat. Frank wouldn't be ashamed of her.

It was much later when she finally woke up in Frank's bedroom. Someone had switched the lamp off and Mia could see the faint residue of light hanging in the May sky through the window. Her head ached and her eyes felt heavy with unshed tears.

She heard Frank moving around in the other room and getting up from the bed she went softly through to him. He was beside her in a moment and his arms were around her. She leant against him willing herself to abandon herself to his affection. When she finally pulled away from him a few unbidden tears clogged in her throat. She looked up at him briefly then lowered her eyes.

'Mia,' he began.

'I'm sorry Frank. I shouldn't have come here.'

'Of course you should have. This is where you should be. I want you to be here, with me.'

'There's too much hatred, Frank,' she said inconsequentially.

'Not any more. It's all over Mia.' He tried to take her in his arms again, but this time she stepped back from him.

Yes, it was all over.

'I didn't know where else to go, but I shouldn't have come here. I'm sorry Frank.'

He caught a finality in her tone and hesitated.

'Mia, I know about the letter. It doesn't matter, that's all in the past now.'

She smiled sadly and put out a hand to him. 'I can't go on betraying people, Frank. We all have to learn how to distinguish the truth again, otherwise it will have all been for nothing.'

The silence between them grew and the dusk turned into its brief midnight black before the first shimmer of dawn crept across the sky.

'You don't love me any more do you Mia?'

She shook her head.

Frank's frustration and disappointment bubbled into anger and Mia turned away from him. 'You didn't have to have the affair you know Mia, you didn't have to sleep with him.'

Friedrich was just a 'him' to them all, a faceless enemy. How they must hate him, or perhaps they just hated all Germans!

'I know,' she said sadly.

'I don't know what Tom was thinking of, I still don't. Do you think he could have been jealous of us?'

Poor Frank still needed reasons, reasons to excuse her.

'It doesn't matter. It doesn't matter about Tom,' she said wearily. 'I didn't have an affair with Friedrich because of Tom, but because I ...' The words came out in a rush, then she paused suddenly and turning away from him walked across the small room and stood by the window. The thin light of the early May dawn was already spreading a pink haze over the sky. Mia watched the eternal miracle for some minutes before turning back to Frank.

'I had an affair with Friedrich because I wanted to,' she finished.

The disdain of the rejected lover passed over Frank's features. Mia shrugged and remained silent and an awkward tension spread through the space between them.

'Did you ever? Did you ever love me' He wished he didn't have to ask the question.

He deserved an answer. She looked up at him. 'Do you remember that summer we spent together? Perhaps I loved you then.' She looked down again. 'I feel rather ashamed of myself,' she whispered into the room, 'I hope there's enough forgiveness to go round.'

Frank coughed awkwardly. 'Where will you go?'

'Where I should have gone to start with.'

Frank looked unenlightened.

'I'll go Siri's. She won't understand, but she won't judge me either,' she said. What she actually thought was, Tom, she would go to Tom.

***

Tom sat at the plush desk in his office in Victoria Terrasse. He had got used to having his own way over the past years and didn't like to feel his authority was being questioned.

Mia repeated her request. 'I want a security pass, I need to talk to him.' She looked at Tom unflinchingly. 'I need to see Friedrich.'

At the mention of his name Tom let out a strangled sound of disdain, his face hard with anger. Mia eyed him coolly from the other side of the desk. She was wearing a close fitting hat and a fresh scar could still be seen running down her forehead. Her face was pale and she wore no make-up. She was still beautiful though, more beautiful than ever, Tom thought with a familiar little twist of pain.

'Mia what are you playing at?' He questioned, giving himself time, trying to hide his pain and suppress his anger.

'It's all over Tom and I don't want to play anymore.' She put a little ironic emphasis on the word 'play'.

'But don't you want to nail the bastard!' Tom exclaimed frustrated.

'No.'

'What about Frank?'

'What about Frank? As I said Tom, it's all over.' She shifted uncomfortably in her chair and her eyes dropped from his, so she missed the sudden flash of light which escaped them at her last words.

'Let me see him, Tom.'

'You'll get him to talk?' Tom asked eagerly, even hopefully.

'I didn't say that, I said I wanted to see him.'

'I don't understand what you're about!'

'You don't need to understand. You just need to...' she stopped and the frustration slipped from her. 'Please, Tom.'

Tom continued to scrutinise Mia with a veiled menace.

'I suppose you think that you're in love with him,' he said nastily.

'Love!' Mia spat the word back at him. 'What do you, or I for that matter, know about love? You have to be good to love, Tom.'

He reached in his pocket for a cigarette packet, Mia's presence was too uncomfortably close.

'But he loved me,' Mia continued relentlessly.

Tom tore the packet open with an angry gesture and Mia tossed her battered head back and held his eyes.

'How do you think your plan worked so well?' She challenged. 'Why do you think we all survived?'

'That was Christian!' Tom shouted.

Tom's sudden mention of Christian unsettled them both. Mia gritted her teeth to stop the pain and Tom's frustration bubbled out of control. He put out impotent arms and cleared his desk in a single, angry sweep. Papers and pencils fluttered to the floor and the black telephone crashed amongst them, the bell ringing confusedly as the casing cracked. Tom put his head in his hands and hid his face from Mia.

'Don't you think that Friedrich could have got whatever he wanted to out of Christian if he'd really tried?' Mia continued remorselessly. She wasn't intimidated by Tom's anger, she never had been, his razor like and destructive intellect may be, but not his anger, at least his anger demonstrated that he was human, that he suffered.

Tom made no movement.

'I know Christian loved us all, Christian loved, loves

humanity,' her voice faded and she bit her lips to stop her tears, she mustn't start thinking about Christian now, it would overwhelm her, overwhelm them both. She had to concentrate on Friedrich. 'Christian loved us all,' she repeated quietly, 'but Friedrich loved me.' Loves me, she thought sadly. 'You know that's why we're all still here and you know we'll have to live with that love for the rest of our lives.'

A heavy silence followed Mia's words. Tom raised his head and without looking at her bent down over the scattered papers around his desk. Finding a stamp and a pass he signed the document and pushed it across the empty desk towards Mia. What he felt beyond anger Mia didn't want to know. She stood up, took the authorisation and walked quickly to the door, but something made her pause and she turned back, briefly to face Tom.

'Christian may still come back,' he said, the steady menace returning.

'And you think that'll make everything all right do you?' Mia flung at him.

She opened the door and shut it sharply behind her. She tried to move forwards but her head was spinning and for a moment she paused, her hand still on the door handle, before she made her one last trip down into the high security cells underneath Victoria Terrasse.

She knew where Friedrich was and was waiting outside his cell by the time her escort had caught up with her.

'Wait outside,' she said imperiously. The poor youth sent to escort her didn't know what to do, but she was known to be a personal friend of the boss. He hesitated too long and Mia had slipped into the cell and closed the door behind her before he had decided what the correct procedure should be.

Friedrich stared at her, amazement and confusion rendering him speechless. Then he noticed the hat and the scar.

'*Mia, what happened?*'

She shrugged, indifferent. '*A lot of things are falling apart. I suppose it will start to get better again for some of us.*' She moved towards him awkwardly.

'*Friedrich.*' She didn't know what to say. His uniform was dirty and his shirt hadn't been changed. Lack of care and uncleanliness perhaps was a fitting punishment she supposed, but she'd seen enough of deprivation.

'*Friedrich,*' she repeated. It was hot in the small cell and she felt the heat rush to her head. She swayed, uncertain, a faintness blacking out her eyes. Friedrich stepped towards her and took her in his arms.

'*Mia, what have they done to you?*' He exclaimed, his own misery momentarily forgotten.

She shook her head against his chest. The feel of his arms was so familiar that she felt strangely comforted, as if time stood still and held them in a safe eternity.

'*It doesn't matter,*' she tried to say. She moved away from him and smiled, but there were tears in her eyes.

'*Come!*' He took her hand and they sat on the narrow bed together, remembering.

'*I'm glad not all memories are bad,*' Mia said softly.

'*Nor all tears,*' said Friedrich. The frustrated pain and loss had gone from his face and his beautiful eyes shone with happiness. '*It should have been otherwise,*' he said sadly.

'*Yes, yes it should have been otherwise.*' Mia almost laughed through her tears, it sounded so simple. '*I won't forget,*' she said, she wished she could tell him that she loved him.

'*I love you,*' said Friedrich.

'*I know.*'

'*They can take everything else away from me, but not that. I shall die loving you, Mia.*' He was so grateful to be able to tell her, it was as if a burden was lifted from him.

Mia turned to him and cupping her hands around his face she kissed him tenderly, then she stood up.

'*We don't have long,*' she said awkwardly.

She started rummaging in her bag until she felt the hard stab of metal against her nail. She put her fingers round the small metal casing and took it out of her bag; Christian's cyanide pill. She held it up so that the light caught on the polished metal, then she put it on the palm of her hand and held it out to Friedrich.

His eyes never left her face. He stood up and they faced each other, trapped in the tiny cell with the cyanide pill between them. The eternity between life and death encompassed them. Friedrich took the pill from her open palm and sank back down on the bed.

Mia backed towards the door and banged on it with the side of her fist, it opened and she slipped out. Her escort was still hovering in the corridor and Mia indicated that he should take her back up to the main offices. Relentless and romantic strains of Schubert, the songs which Friedrich had taught her, kept distracting her thoughts.

'Und wenn sich die liebe dem Schmerz entringt,
ein Sternlein, ein neues, am Himmel erblinkt.'[7]

She sang softly.

'What was that, miss?' asked the youth still leading her up the stairs.

Mia shook herself harshly. 'Nothing,' she said, 'nothing. Take me back to the boss.'

She had intended to go straight back to Siri's, but her steps were leading her, yet again, to Tom's office. He was on the telephone and indicated, rather irritably, that she should sit down and wait. The telephone had a large piece of ugly brown tape holding it together and Tom's papers were still scattered all over the floor.

He put the telephone down and a familiar sneer curled his lip. 'Finished already, then.'

'Don't you start,' Mia said sharply. 'I want you to give me his things. When. When he's dead.'

She marched out of his office and this time did go on home.

Tom stared after her, and then he realised what she'd done. He ran to the door and yelling for assistance, carried on running down the corridors, by the time he reached the cell three other soldiers had joined him.

'Open the door,' he yelled at the bewildered guard behind him. The guard opened the door and Tom pushed his way through.

The prisoner was already dead.

---

[7] And when love tears itself free of sorrow, a new star twinkles in the sky.

August, 1945
Twenty-Two

Astrid ushered the last patient out. 'The arm's healing really well,' she said. 'I wouldn't think there's any need to go back to the hospital. If you come back here next week I can take out the stitches for you.'

'Thank you, Doctor, you're very kind.'

'Not at all, just doing my job. Be careful you don't over do it though, good bye.'

'Good bye.'

Astrid had found it surprisingly easy to become a doctor again, it was rewarding and she was good at it. Petter had started at a kindergarten attached to the local school and for the first time since he was born she had long, clear days.

She locked the door behind her patient and turned back to the consulting room. She took off her white jacket, put away a couple of files and walked to the foot of the stairs. There was a small parcel, addressed in a strange hand and postmarked from Germany, waiting for her upstairs. It had been waiting, unopened now, for two days. She knew what it would be. It would be confirmation that Christian was gone, that he was dead.

She walked slowly up the stairs. She took the package off the small desk in the sitting room and sat down in Christian's chair by the empty summer grate. She opened the parcel and a few small objects fell out on her lap; a dog eared photograph of herself and Petter, the familiar metal rimmed glasses and Christian's pipe, which they'd sent in a Red Cross parcel.

There was also a letter. It was written in German and was not from Christian. Astrid looked at the German words, which danced and merged senselessly in front of her, then she carefully folded the papers together again and put them back in the envelope. It was all gone, all lost. She fingered Christian's glasses, cupped her fingers round the bowl of the pipe and looked, as it were, with Christian's eyes at the photograph of herself and Petter. What had he seen through those same glasses, in that same picture? Yes, he had loved her, but had he loved her any more than he had loved the rest of them? His life had become such a mystery to her and his death another loss, another betrayal amongst many episodes of bitterness. There was a little hard canker of hatred in Astrid's heart and no room for forgiveness.

A few hours later Astrid Maria let herself into the surgery.

'We're home,' she called up. She had collected Petter from the school.

'Astrid? Oh, perhaps mummy's out,' she said to Petter. Petter ran up the stairs ahead of her clutching a drawing he'd done of a bicycle, and Astrid Maria followed close on his heels.

Astrid was still sitting in Christian's chair.

'Are you all right?' Her mother said peering at her.

Astrid looked up, for a moment not registering, and then she roused herself. 'You should get your eyes tested, mother.'

'There's nothing wrong with my eyes.'

'It's a letter from Germany. It's Christian's things.' Astrid held out the letter to her mother.

Astrid Maria continued to peer for a moment, and then took the letter from Astrid. Petter was crashing around in the kitchen shouting. 'I'm hungry!'

Astrid Maria handed the letter back to Astrid, but Astrid didn't take it. Astrid Maria hesitated. 'Can I, can I ask Mia to read it?'

Astrid didn't say anything. Her chest felt tight, and she was a little light headed from not eating any lunch after surgery closed. She put Christian's things into the little desk which contained other forgotten mementos and went into the kitchen.

'What shall we have for tea?' She asked Petter. 'Shall we have some eggs?'

Astrid Maria stood in the middle of the room holding the letter, her mouth a question. Then blinking away her confusion she turned and hurried out of the house, clutching the letter, before Astrid changed her mind.

***

Mia was waiting outside Tom's office again. She walked to the window and looked out into the late summer sunshine. She heard the door open from the corridor behind her and turned round. It was Frank with some papers for Tom.

Mia nodded her head towards the door. 'He's in with the General.'

'Oh.' Frank shuffled, embarrassed, and Mia tried to think of something to say.

She cleared her throat. 'We heard from Christian,' she said. 'Well not from Christian, but we had a letter from someone who was, well, with him at the end.' Mia dropped her gaze and took a deep breath to control the emotion. 'I wanted to show the letter to Tom.'

Frank looked confused.

'They were very close you know.'

'No, I didn't know.' Frank felt rather foolish. There was a lot he hadn't known.

Mia shrugged and turned back to the window.

Frank hesitated outside Tom's door, and then turned tail. 'I'll come back later,' he said, hating the peevish tone he had failed to keep out of his voice.

Tom looked up at Mia suspiciously as she entered, but there was no antagonism or defiance in Mia's eyes. She took the letter out of her bag and handed it to Tom. Tom turned the envelope over in his hands, taking in the address and the postmark. He looked up at her with a question.

She nodded her head. 'He's not coming back, Tom.'

He continued to look at her, his blue eyes shadowed and brooding.

'Read it, read the letter,' Mia urged, 'it sort of helps.'

His eyes still on her Tom took the pages out of the envelope and spread them carefully on the desk in front of him.

'Liebe Frau Dr Krogvold,' he read, 'ich...' he couldn't form the German words, he paused, then translating the words into Norwegian he continued.

'I am sure that you have long since been informed by the authorities of the sad news of your husband's death.' He stopped. 'When was this written?'

'About two weeks ago.'

'Have you checked?' His voice sounded hard.

'Yes, mother checked. He's not coming back, Tom. Read on.'

He turned back to the letter.

'I would myself have written sooner, but I didn't want to be the first bearer of such sad tidings. Also things have been hectic and chaotic here since the Russians arrived and until now I have been working all hours in the hospital. Now I have a few days leave and I am determined to get my letter to you finished. You must forgive my officiousness in taking it upon myself to keep your husband's things, but if I hadn't they would have long since been lost or destroyed. I'm afraid there is very little to remember him by, but these small tokens will be familiar to you and I know that if I was in your case I would treasure any small remembrance that remained of such a husband.'

Tom paused. He pushed the papers over to Mia. 'You read it,' he said. There was a slight crack in his voice.

Mia continued.

'Such as they are I will enclose them in a small parcel and send them with this letter.

'My dear Frau Doktor your husband was a remarkable man and I will try and find the words to convey to you something of the last few weeks of his life. I am sure all such remembrance is still very painful for you, but I hope there will come a time when you can read my letter and take comfort from the good that your husband has done in the world, and, God knows, there has been little enough of goodness amongst us for the past six years.

'I first met your husband just before Christmas as of last year. There had been an out break of scarlet fever amongst some women and children, who were new inmates in the prison camp. The camp had not had any woman or children before this time. Your husband had been assigned the task of isolation doctor and had sole charge of these poor patients. I am a nurse and had been called in from my job at the local hospital to help him, as it was known by the authorities that I had previously recovered from a bout of scarlet fever and was therefore most unlikely to succumb again.

'The Herr Doktor had been given an isolation room but little else, and he spent the first few days of his new assignment working without ceasing until he had procured beds, linen, and even some medication. As you can imagine the women and children in his care received every attention, including his own extra Christmas allowance of sausage.

'By the end of March we had nearly cleared the outbreak. The Herr Doktor was worn to nothing and I begged him to take some rest as I could easily cover for him. It then came to my notice that the Scandinavian prisoners were being released and sent back home with Swedish Red Cross transport. I exhorted the Herr Doktor to leave with his compatriots, but he wasn't to be persuaded. I am sure you know only too well how stubborn he could be over matters of principle and his patients' health!

'As I say the Herr Doktor was not to be persuaded, which at the time did puzzle me a little as the outbreak of infection was sufficiently under control at this time for me to have dealt with the remaining patients quite adequately. At first I took his decision to be the action of a stubborn man, but later I uncovered the real reason for his reluctance to travel. Given the now low incidence of infection our isolation room was still packed with mothers and children to whom the Herr Doktor carefully administered each day and about a week after the last Swedish Red Cross transport left Sachenhausen I discovered that these woman and children were perfectly healthy. At first I felt almost angry and immediately challenged the Herr Doktor for occupying beds, which might be needed by others. He took me to one side and carefully explained his reasoning, and with hindsight his reasoning was frighteningly close to what actually happened. He explained that the war was obviously in its final stages and that camps such as ours were going to be the first places to suffer. People may be suddenly moved, left without proper care and mothers separated from children. He felt that if he could keep as many of these poor suffering people as possible under his care he might be able to protect them until some kind of proper authority was able to take charge of them, and there was no risk of the present authorities discovering the Herr

Doktor's secret as the camp doctors kept well away from our isolation ward. I must admit that at the time I thought he was wrong and that these women and children would be just as well off back in their barracks. However, I was wrong, for just a few weeks later, the camp authorities started a mass removal of all prisoners. The orders were hurried and unclear and all we knew was that everyone was being moved out. I tried to find out more from the camp doctors but apart from one, who was also a prisoner like your husband, they had all fled. Our two hospital barracks had been forgotten and in the course of a few days we found ourselves suddenly completely alone in the camp. We discovered later that many of the poor prisoners who left the camp died on the journey and it was then I realised the full extent of your husband's goodness for he had indeed saved the lives of those women and children whom he had hidden in the isolation ward.

'However I am getting ahead of myself. It was now the end of April and although about to fall, Germany had yet to surrender. We, your husband and I, plus the other doctor I mentioned above and two more nurses, like myself drafted in from the local hospital, found ourselves in sole charge of our two hospital barracks full of all manner of disease and suffering.

'The Herr Doktor immediately took charge. He had us give basic training to some of his healthy patients and others of them he assigned to the kitchens. He himself took the worst cases and the Herr Doktor saved many, many lives. Sometimes I try to count them, but then I stop myself because the Herr Doktor would have acted in the same way if only one life was to be saved.

'I am sorry, but I have had to take a little pause here, as when I recall the Herr Doktor's bravery the memory is still a little too fresh for me, but now I will try and continue my story. Just a day after the last prisoners were force marched out of the camp Russian and Polish troops finally took our small town to the North of Berlin and were able to relieve our poor camp hospital. I had expected that, now it was all over, the Herr Doktor would be sent home. Alas the war still raged on around us for its last few days and the Herr Doktor would not leave his patients. I myself returned to my work in the hospital and it was not until a month later that I had chance to return to the camp hospital. Many of the inmates had now been transferred or sent home, and only the most critical cases remained. It was with much fear, although by now with little surprise, that I found the Herr Doktor, although no longer a prisoner and as free to go as any man, still working in the hospital. He had spent the last two weeks working with an outbreak of diphtheria and for the first time I gave way to fears about the Herr Doktor's own health. I exhorted him to take care and said I would visit him again as soon as I was able.

'It was about a week later that I made another visit to the camp hospital, but I couldn't find the Herr Doktor, and things generally seemed more disorganised again. At first I believed that he had finally left Germany and was on his way home. However it was not to be. One of the patients approached me and asked if I was the nurse who was friendly with the Norwegian Doctor and I said that yes that was me. The Herr Doktor, he said, was very sick and told me where I could find him. As soon as I saw the Herr Doktor I knew it was too late and that he had only a few more hours to live. He had contracted diphtheria himself and was so run down and undernourished that it had soon infected him to the point of death. I took a chair and sat by his bedside. He was feverish and sleeping fitfully. I determined to stay with him until the end, the least we all owed him was that he should not die alone. I found a cloth and some cool water and offered what comfort I could by bathing his forehead. After some time he seemed to rally a little and his eyes tried to focus on me. I explained who I was and took his hand. He lay back in the pillows and smiled a quite beautiful smile. I wondered what thoughts had come to him in this his moment of dying. Did he think of the women and children he had both united and saved from certain death, did he think of his own home, or had our Lord sent him some vision of the glories to come? For surely such a man has been given a place amongst the saints in Heaven.

'My dear Frau Doktor your husband departed this life on 29th May at four o'clock in the afternoon. His last hours were peaceful and he did not suffer. I offer you my deepest sympathies and regret that the world has had to lose such a man as he was.

'I send my best wishes to you and your son,

in friendship,

Frauline nurse Grete Baumann'

Mia folded the pages carefully together again and put them back in the envelope, which lay on the desk between them. Tom looked down at it, unseeing and expressionless. He was silent for a long time, and then he turned with a bitter look to Mia.

'Does it matter?' He asked.

'What do you mean?'

'Does it matter how he died?'

'It matters to him,' she said quietly and taking the letter back off Tom turned to go.

'Mia?'

She stopped, but didn't turn around.

'Mia, about this other business.'

She still didn't turn. 'I got clearance to travel and I'm leaving by boat on the 29th of this month.' She turned to face him. 'Is that all?'

No it wasn't all! But she'd gone out and shut the door behind her. Tom brought a fist crashing down on his desk and the receiver fell off his telephone.

Remorse, guilt and loss threatened to overcome him. He clung onto his anger as the only safe place to hide. What did she want from him? He wasn't afraid of accepting responsibility for what had happened but neither was he going to accept that he'd done anything wrong. He'd done what he'd had to do, and if the Soviet army had suddenly steamed up Karl Johan in the wake of the German withdrawal from Norway he would have done it all again.

But nonetheless something had happened to Tom and as he continued to gaze blindly at the desk in front of him he became painfully aware of the friend he had lost. This last reminder of

Christian slowly calmed his thoughts and the remorse which now filtered through his mind did not turn to easy anger and frustration but to the realisation of regret. If he could do it all again he could not, again, sacrifice Christian so wantonly.

For the first time in his life he was touched by love rather than the impossibility of it.

***

Astrid Maria and Siri walked all the way to the docks with Mia. She had a small suitcase and another travelling bag, which contained Friedrich's things. She had a permit to travel to Hanover and her visa was valid for ten days. Siri was helping to carry the bags and Astrid Maria was muttering along beside them.

'Couldn't you just send the wretched things,' she said crossly, trying to keep up.

'That's not enough mother. Imagine if he was your son?'

'Well, he's not my son.'

Mia sighed, and exchanged a look with Siri, not that Siri understood either.

'Don't be obtuse, mother.'

'And how do you know that his parents are still alive?'

'I've checked.' She hardly understood herself why she had decided to go all the way to Germany, as it was, torn in two and reeling with the shock and guilt of war, just to hand over some random objects to Friedrich's parents, who would be desolate at losing their only son. But it was something she had to do for herself. She hated all the accusation and blame around her; she wanted to forgive and in return find forgiveness.

The dock was busy with the turmoil of travellers and sailors and officials all getting in each other's way. Siri was eyeing up the officers and suddenly let out a little squeak. She pulled Mia's arm. 'Look, it's Tom,' she pointed, 'over there. I think he's looking for someone.' She jumped up and down shouting. 'Tom! Hi Tom!'

Tom heard her, and to Mia's surprise came rushing over, pushing aside the crowds.

'I was looking for you.' He was looking directly at Mia as he spoke the words. 'I'll take these and help you find a berth.' He took the bags from Mia and Siri.

Mia raised her eyebrows in a big question, and a knowing look suddenly sprang into Siri's eyes.

'Come on Mrs Gram, I don't think we're allowed up there,' and taking a hasty leave of Mia she led Astrid Maria away to the edge of the quay, where they could stand and wave at passengers.

Mia followed Tom up the gangplank. His uniform certainly cut an easy swathe through the crowd.

'Glad to see it has its uses, that Kaki,' Mia said ironically.

'Actually I'm hanging it up for good next week.'

'Oh?'

'I've been appointed director of the new University Hospital.'

'What new University Hospital?'

'The one that comes into being next week.'

Mia smiled, Tom hadn't been able to keep a certain smugness out of his voice. They squeezed past some more passengers and finally landed on the boat.

Tom had stopped smiling and stood and faced her awkwardly. 'Look I'm sorry. I can't help feeling I've behaved rather badly.'

'Couldn't have been worse,' said Mia lightly.

'I mean I think I understand.'

'No, you don't understand.'

'Okay, then I'd like to understand,' and his eyes looked straight into hers. 'Mia I think I've had enough too. I want it all to be over. I want to get back to normal, start over again, whatever, because we can, those of us who are left, we can get back to normal.'

Mia was silent, but her eyes rested on his. The last passengers were coming on board.

'I think you'd better go before you end up coming to Germany too,' she said gently.

He put a restraining hand on her arm. 'I want to believe in a happy ending Mia,' he said, suddenly desperate.

'A happy ending?'

'I want… I want you.'

Mia looked shocked and her eyes opened wide in astonishment. 'Me?' She stared at him in disbelief and then she started to laugh. The sound bubbled in her chest and burst out of her like a dam bursting.

Tom smiled, but his eyes looked hurt. 'I was being serious,' he said.

Mia caught her breath and pulled back the gushing flow. 'I know,' she said.

'Mia I...'

'I'm coming back Tom,' she said lightly. Reaching to take her bags from him she stood on tiptoes and planted a kiss on his cheek, but Tom let the bags fall and taking her in his arms he kissed her.

'I'll be waiting,' he said, 'I'll be waiting when you do come back.'

Mia took her bags and walked slowly onto the deck of the boat. She put the bags down and joining the other passengers pushed her way to the port side to wave to the bystanders on the quay.

She soon picked out her mother and Siri, and then she saw Tom join them. She waved and smiled at them, her future.